I0736468

APOSTASY RISING

END TIMES CHRONICLES SEASON 1
EPISODE 4

J. A. BOUMA

EmmausWay
P R E S S

CHAPTER 1

NICAEA, ARABIA-PERSIA. AD 2123.

Thunder rumbled in the near distance as John Mark Ford raced along the magnapavement back to HQ, his fingers twitching for an apple, or a banana, or something—anything to take his mind off the worry pulsing between his eyes.

Dark clouds loomed over the horizon as a cloudless sunset vanished behind a curtain hiding ill intent while the agents were taking care of Ministerium business. The blanket marched in force with threatening menace, promising a wicked storm ahead. And Ford didn't like it one bit.

It had advanced while he and Luciana Jane were occupied in a nondescript building of gleaming glass and titanium identified by Ministerium drones as the final destination for the thief who had stolen Ichthus's precious relic. Cardinal James Ferraro had dispatched them to retrieve it. Not only given its significance for advancing and preserving the faith, but also for the clandestine message it was rumored to hold that could save the Church.

Surprisingly, the mission went swimmingly. Banging a few Enforcers' heads together was sorta fun, and meeting that Colonel Sanders look-alike was sorta weird. But he was as happy as he could be as director of operations for the Ministerium, given they had retrieved the relic and, well, they were still alive.

Purplish-white lightning brightened the sky like a nuclear bomb, its electric tendrils coursing across the sky above and reaching from one cloud to the next like rivulets of water through a barren desert. Ford startled at the sight then waited for—

A booming reply sent his heart strumming faster against his ribs than it already had been from their mission.

Boy, did he hate storms. Hated weather period, especially on mission. Experience taught him bad things accompanied bad weather. Whether it was nighttime raids that failed to factor in the variables that Mother Nature threw at them, and the Unfits used to their advantage to evade capture from his team of Purifiers. Or it was Pops flying into a drunken rage when nothing occupied him but a twelve pack of Bud Lite during the helluva crazy storms that ravaged Noramericana during his childhood.

Ford took in a breath and shook his head to get it back on straight, a silent curse slipping his lips at the turn.

Bad weather, bad things. Never one without—

Another flash of lightning bolted across the sky, followed quickly by another booming, thunderous reply.

—the other.

This was going to be a bad storm.

And his stomach clenched with dread at the bad it portended.

It was bad enough that one of their own had stolen the Holy Shroud—the ancient relic of Ichthus thought lost to history that had been Jesus Christ's burial linen, bearing his resurrection image and offering the Church the kind of proof and inspiration it needed during these dark and dastardly times. To keep believing even and keep holding steady while the steeple came crashing through the high altar straight through to the bottom floor.

That bad act, and all it threatened, had made him rethink what the heck he had signed up for when Father Benedict introduced him to Father Jim. Thought he was jumping into a cushy gig after all those years doing Solterra's bidding. Would bide his time and lie low under the Republic's radar, given what he had now become.

A Defector. A traitor to the Republic. Fodder for the reprogramming camps.

The fact the Ministerium had been infiltrated by the resurrected enemy of the Church stretching back to its founding—some crazy-ass outfit called Nous was enough to send him seriously regretting his choice of vocational shift. Then to find out that one of their own Ministerium agents was also an operative of the Republic and said crazy outfit...that was enough to turn tail and get the heck out of Dodge. Pronto.

Drops the size of hornets started smacking into the windshield, making the same popping sound those buggers made back home riding through the countryside in one of Pop's vintage F-150s. Right on cue, the magnacar's auto wipers kicked in.

Then there was the cockamamy fact said crazy-ass outfit called Nous and the Republic were seemingly in cahoots, and with Ichthus's latest enemy: Panligo World Assembly, the second crazy-ass outfit that was serving as a spiritual-but-not-religious religious answer to the Church, dismantling it in one fell swoop and now acting as the official religious arm of Solterra—a true imperial cult system to rival the Roman Empire's from days of yore.

So now three fronts threatened Ichthus's ongoing fight for survival.

Three for the price of one. How'd he get so lucky?

How'd he get so foolish, more like it.

'The damn fool couldn't tie his laceless boots!'

Ford's stomach clenched at the voice of Pops rising from that shallow Civil War II grave at the border between Noramericana and Americana. So much so that he missed more of those purplish-white electric tendrils racing to catch him, followed by a boom that shook the vehicle so that even Lucy jumped.

He gripped the steering wheel as the magnacar continued trundling along toward HQ, the rain picking up its assault in unrelenting watery sheets.

But John Mark Ford was no fool. He knew a magnavan of Enforcers in a neighboring town a few klicks from HQ could mean major trouble for the Ministerium.

Strike that. *Did* mean major trouble for the Ministerium. Because that outfit and those Augers, with all of their sophisticated AI-somatic augmentation to the musclehead humans that reminded him of home, looked mighty close to the sort of outfit he'd run back in the day.

Which, again, meant major trouble for the Ministerium.

So that far he'd gotten in his head since jumping back into the saddle and leaving a trail of dust. How to break it to Lucy and Father Jim and the others was what he was working on. And that wasn't even touching the contingency plans—or rather, the lack of anything smacking of a contingency plan if things went south the way he thought they might, given his experience with the Republic Legion.

But time was up. And it was time for the Ministerium to saddle up for what was to come.

"Slow down, would ya?" Lucy said, clutching the relic that looked like a rolled-up carpet.

Ford wiped a line of sweat beading at his brow. "Now why

the heck would I do that? You want those Enforcers to come up and drag our butts to a reprogramming camp?"

"No, but they'll do it anyway if we get caught speeding!"

Ford scoffed. "We're not gonna get caught speed—"

Blue and white lights suddenly flashed behind them in prismatic splinters through the watery rear windshield. A rapid whirl of the sirens that screamed *'Pull over polis scum!'* sealed the deal.

An Enforcer cruiser.

"Son of a monkey's uncle..."

"That's one way of putting it," Lucy said, twisting in her seat for a look.

"What do we do?" Ford said in a panicked rush.

"Act normal."

"I am acting normal!"

"Then pull the cotton pickin' magnacar to the side of the road. Maybe he'll pass by."

"Or maybe he'll pull our butts over and bust 'em wide open with his Neutralizer!"

Ford twisted around for a look himself, letting the magnacar's auto drive take over for a while. The blues-and-whites strobed in his eyes with wicked intent, but his mind was a jumble of indecision with no way out.

If he pulled over, the man or woman or humanoid could give him a ticket, then they'd be on their merry way.

Or maybe they'd just zoom on by, then off they'd go into the wild blue yonder.

Or there was door number three: said man or woman or humanoid would recognize him in some Republic DiviNet database as a Defector.

Or, God forbid, they'd both be recognized as the yahoos who had just assaulted agents of the Republic and absconded with property that belonged to them anyhow. They'd both end up on the raw end of a Neutralizer and sent packing for a camp that would scramble their brains like an omelet something fierce.

Either way, no way in hot Hades was he gonna get sent back to no reprogramming camp.

Been there. Done that. Bought the beer koozie.

"I'm gonna run for it," he said with determination, his blood now flooding with the coolness of adrenaline-fueled resolve.

"No! Don't do it, Ford," Lucy pleaded.

"We'll be fine."

"My aunt's petunias we will! He'll auto-lock our vehicle faster than you can say Noramericana!"

Ford shook his head. "Naw, you see this here magnacraft is off the DiviNet grid."

"Even more reason to pull over and let it play out!"

The siren wailed in a livid burst of irritation, and the numbskull behind the wheel bellowed for them to pull over.

What to do, what to do...

Run, or pull over?

Flee through the countryside back to HQ, or freeze on the side of the road?

Or fight like hot Hades?

Then all at once, a peace that surpassed understanding washed over him. And he knew what to do. As crazy as it seemed.

Ford returned to the steering wheel and eased the craft to the side of the road, putting on its hazards and girding his loins for the follow through.

Which amounted to the Enforcer cruiser following them to the side of the road.

Ford closed his eyes and sighed.

Lord, throw us a bone here!

"Alright, now don't panic," Lucy said with a hint of tremble and holding the rolled up Shroud tightly to her chest.

Ford said nothing. He simply stared out ahead as the late-night traffic zoomed on while the county mounty took his sweet time doing whatever.

He heard the soft clicking of a door unlocking and swinging up. Then the *one-two* crunch of gravel as the county mounty sturdied his feet before the sauntering crunch of someone with all the time in the world to make his two victims sweat like pigs in a bacon farm.

The weapon buried at his back throbbed with a mixture of worrisome dread and anxious activation. If they were searched, then their identities would be the least of their problems. An armed citizenry had been promptly banned by the goons in the Capitolium post-Reckoning. All in the interest of peace and prosperity and progress. *'For Humanity!'* of course. Boy, were his teeth set on edge every time he heard the polis bleat that Fifth Avenue-crafted slogan—or, what's left of Fifth Avenue after the Armageddon climate catastrophe buried it under—

His jumbled thoughts were interrupted by a beast of a man rapping on his window and the muffled sound of his command to lower it and present themselves for a status check.

Just their luck, they got a real live human this time around.

Ford lowered his window and flashed the man his pearly whites. "Howdy, officer. What seems to be the problem?"

"Eyes and fingers. The both of you."

"Were we speeding?"

The man hesitated, staring them down with the vacant eyes he knew all too well during his service with the Republic. Then he said, "A hundred in a seventy."

Ford scoffed. "A hundred kilos an hour in a seventy!" He turned to Lucy, mouth agape with feigned surprise. "Why, honey, I quite reckon I haven't driven that fast since we left for our weddin' night."

Her eyes widened slightly with obvious shock before returning to rest, a slight grin playing across her face.

He turned back to the Enforcer. "There must be some mis—"

"Out. Now. The both of you."

A worried breath seeped through his nose. He nodded and opened the door, followed by Lucy.

It lifted, and he stepped out, taking care to keep his backside bearing the contraband angled away from the county mounty that could definitely stand to lose a kilo or two. The rain had eased to a drizzle now, so at least they had that going for them.

Lucy sidled up next to him. He threw her a worried look before snapping back to his senses.

No room for fear. Fear leads to error. And error will get you either cancelled or reprogrammed. Didn't know which was worse. All he knew was he'd be tar and feathered before he let Lucy fall victim to any of those options.

"Eyes and fingers," the man grunted, holding up a retinal scanner and palm reader.

Ford's heart dropped to the magnapavement and bowels went with it.

But he knew he couldn't oblige.

Lucy was the first to step up to the plate, dutifully craning her neck forward and sticking out her finger.

Giving him precious seconds to think.

And land on the only option he had.

A distant siren wailed like a needy child. Up the road from where they'd come.

Then the man's radio crackled to life, just as Lucy's status check threw up an undecided answer.

And then he heard it. The call letters to end all call letters.

'*... a 10-60 responding to 10-35, copy. Hold until further notice.*'

An Enforcer Squad in the vicinity. Responding to a crime of terroristic proportions.

Then it all happened in slow-mo chaos.

Ford saw the whites of the Enforcer's eyes flitter from Lucy to Ford and back again.

Before his left hand slipped to his hip.

Where Ford knew a Blastgun was hibernating until activation.

Lucky for him, he was on the county mounty's left side. Which would give him a teeny window to act.

And act he did.

Pivoting left while whipping out his piece and cold cocking the bugger in his left temple.

Just like that. Wam. Bam. Thank you, Mr. Enforcer man.

He slumped to the floor like a well-used bathrobe.

But not before getting off a tasing shot that danced across the wet pavement with sparking interest.

Lucy shrieked and threw her hands on her head.

"I understand the sentiments, sassafras, but we best get out of Dodge before the po-po drop in like its 2099 again."

"What the hey-ho day did you do?" Lucy yelled.

Ford wrenched open the up door as Lucy shuffled around to the passenger's side.

"Saved our backsides, that's what I did."

"But—"

"No buts about it, little missy." He roared the magnacar to life and sped out.

Just as those blasted lights splintered through the water-streaked rear windshield again in faint strokes of blue and white.

"I'm a Defector, remember?" he went on, flooring the vehicle and praying to the good Lord for both forgiveness and protection. "No way I was gettin' out of that status check in one piece. And besides, Enforcer command dropped the 411 on our extracurricular activity."

"Well, then what now?"

"We scram like it's nobody's business."

And scram he did, weaving in and out of side streets as they made their way back to HQ. All the while those blasted Enforcer sirens screamed bloody murder in a stereophonic rage. They couldn't escape it, and it sounded like they were getting boxed in.

But he continued driving, taking it slow and methodical like until they had reached the outskirts of the city. Nearly an hour later, but at least their time hadn't run out. Yet.

Ford eased a breath out then crossed himself as they slipped onto a tertiary highway that looked like it hadn't received an upgrade since the Reckoning, then beelined it for HQ.

"That was some mighty fancy footwork you did there, getting us out of that city," Lucy said, leaning against her window and taking a breath of her own.

Ford scoffed. "That one wasn't on me. That was all the good Lord's doin', I can tell you that."

"I guess so. But we best hustle back to Ministerium headquarters. Don't want to exhaust the Lord's favor."

Ford nodded and eased the magnacar behind a granny craft that would check his speed this time.

Half an hour later, they reached the Church of the Dormition, headquarters to the Ministerium. Ford circled around a few blocks before coming in for a landing, giving it a wide berth in case Enforcers decided to show their mugs—or worse.

Satisfied they were in the clear, he brought their magnacar around to the entrance that led beneath the ancient basilica.

When he did, his mobile rang.

Cardinal James Ferraro, Master of the Ministerium and his boss.

Ford eased the vehicle to a stop and answered. "Hey there, Padre, we—"

"Where are you?" the cardinal said in an interruptive rush.

"Literally on the doorstep of the Ministerium."

"Well, what are you waiting for? Get in here. The Republic has let slip the dogs of war!"

Now what…

CHAPTER 2

LED lights led Ford and Lucy down through a winding cavern, first through layers of packed bricks that bespoke the ancient world before transitioning into the cold, sterile concrete of the future one. Several important Church councils had taken place in the soil up top through the centuries, not least of which was the most famous that handed Ichthus its defining creed, the Nicene Creed, from the First Council of Nicaea in AD 325.

As they wound their way to the bottom, his heart strumming a mean beat at the latest from the Republic, his mind snapped to the Church's central creed, considering it and contemplating its continued relevance—especially in the face of Father Jim's warning.

He'd memorized it as a young boy back in Noramericana. Never paid it much mind. Only really made sense of it when he finally turned the reins of his life over to Jesus thanks to that kind monk before he nearly cancelled him.

But after the past few weeks' events—with those bozos establishing Panligo and defecting from Christianity, the Church's enemy rearing its ugly head again, the Republic taking an interest in the new upstart faith, the freakin' Enforcers zipping around their HQ with Trackers and setting up camp a stone's throw away, and now with whatever crazy was cooking Father Jim's gander—with all of it his brain started spooling out snippets of the Creed he had given his life to:

'*I believe in one God, the Father almighty, maker of heaven and earth, of all things visible and invisible*' it began. Simple, to the point. Might as well start at the top.

And then on to believing in '*one Lord Jesus Christ, the Only Begotten Son of God, born of the Father before all ages. God from God, Light from Light, true God from true God, begotten, not made, consubstantial with the Father; through him all things were made. For us men and for our salvation he came down from heaven...*'

Never understood the gravity of that *begettin'* and *comin' down* and *savin'* until he understood the depths of his own rebellious, depraved heart as an agent of the Republic. The things he saw others do, the things he himself did...

They were almost to the bottom now, and the Creed went on:

> *by the Holy Spirit was incarnate of the Virgin*
> *Mary, and became man.*
> *For our sake he was crucified under Pontius*
> *Pilate, he suffered death and was buried, and*
> *rose again on the third day in accordance*
> *with the Scriptures.*
> *He ascended into heaven and is seated at the*
> *right hand of the Father.*
> *He will come again in glory to judge the living*
> *and the dead and his kingdom will have*
> *no end.*

Lord Jesus Christ, come quickly and rescue us from this hellhole...

They reached the bottom of the ramp to an expansive car park below. Just as he reached the Creed's end, with its declaration of belief in '*the Holy Spirit, the Lord, the giver of life,*' and '*one, holy, catholic and apostolic Church,*' and its confession in '*one Baptism for the forgiveness of sin.*'

And then the part where the rubber meets the magnapavement that kept him going during those dark days in that blasted reprogramming camp: '*I look forward to the resurrection of the dead and the life of the world to come.*'

Jesus, you have no idea...

"Amen," Ford mumbled as he parked at the threshold of Ministerium headquarters.

"What's that?" asked Lucy.

He shook his head and slid out of the magnacar. "Nothin' to worry your pretty little head over, sassafras. Come on. Let's deliver this rug—err, this holy relic of ours to Padre."

She replied, "And let's pray we've escaped the worst of it."

"Amen to that," he said, hustling through the doors as they *whooshed* open.

Hustling toward them on the other side was the cardinal himself.

Face fallen and grim.

Ford had had enough fun for one night. But that face told him the fun was just beginning.

He sighed. *No rest for the weary, I guess.*

"Praise God from whom all blessings flow!" Father Jim said on their approach.

"Agree," Ford said, "but why the sour face? And what's this about the Republic? Someone get cancelled or reprogrammed?"

"In a manner of speaking...But first things first," Father Jim went on, eyes wide with greedy inquiry. "Did you retrieve it, the Holy Shroud?"

Lucy held out the rolled-up burial cloth of Christ with pride. "That we did."

"Thank you, Jesus!" the cardinal said, throwing his head back with a grin and pumping a fist into the air. Then he closed his eyes and sighed. "There is still hope..."

Ford furrowed his brow and threw a glance at Lucy, who frowned and shook her head.

"Hope the recovery wasn't too much of a bother."

He gave Lucy a sideways glance. "Yeah, well, let's just say I'd soon enough not lose this relic of yours again, Padre. If it's alright with you."

"Not to worry. We've got special plans for it, and I imagine Alexander won't let it out of his sight again."

Ford smirked and mumbled, "Better not. Or I'll beat his butt until next Tuesday."

"Now, John Mark. If you're to give Alexander a hard time, I suppose you ought to give yourself an equal dose of scorn."

"Believe me, I have been. Speaking of which, have Alexander and Rebekah returned back to the future?"

Father Jim shook his head. "Not yet. I imagine it should be any hour now given how long they've been gone since making the jump. Apparently, it takes time to travel through time. But enough dilly dallying."

He turned to leave when Ford grabbed his arm.

"Hold up. You offered some dire-sounding words when you rang. Not that I'm one to drink from a spigot spoiled of bad news...but what's happened?"

Father Jim sighed. "Our operatives around the Republic are reporting curious activity around our major Ichthus centers of power."

Ford stepped closer and folded his arms. "Activity? What kind?"

"Trackers. Enforcers. Some have even said Purifiers are lurking about, but nothing confirmed."

Ford's heart sank and his bowels went cold. The Republic had long tolerated Christianity even after its unification efforts post-Reckoning to harmonize every aspect of the global community, their *'Harmony Above Distinction!'* mantra as eye-rolling as their *'For Humanity!'* one. But with the recent Edict of Cooperation and the evidence that Nous was somehow partnering with the Republic—he feared Padre was right: the gears were turning into place to open a can of whoop-ass on the Church. And soon.

"Damn—" he said before snapping upright at the slip. Knew how much Padre didn't care for such Legion language.

Father Jim frowned. "Just this once, I'll say I agree with the sentiment."

"Sorry, sir...but, what do you think it all means?"

He shook his head. "I dare not say just yet. But we best get to it. The Shroud is our best hope girding Ichthus for what may lie ahead—both the proof of our central belief, the resurrection of Jesus embedded in the memory-marker containing Christ's image, as well as whatever hidden message the Order of Thaddeus may have secreted away on its backside. Sasha is all set up to get the party started, as he has been pestering me for the past few hours. So I dare hope that your recovery efforts were worth it."

"Me too. For Ichthus's sake."

"And the sake of every one of the Church's precious souls. Come along."

The cardinal led them through the familiar hallways of ancient brown misshapen bricks stacked in awkward rows before stopping short at the main door that led into the Ministerium headquarters. He offered his biometric data to the unit standing guard, which Ford noticed seemed to be an upgrade from when they left last.

He said, "I see the Ministerium is already jumping on security improvements in my absence."

"Indeed, we have," Father Jim said. "We're taking no more chances given the infiltration we suffered. And apparently at both the hands of our sworn enemy and the Republic. The last thing we need is a legion of Enforcers storming the gates and gaining entrance."

Ford snorted. "Nice one. The day I spot an actual Solterra agent storming the gates is the day genetically engineered pigs fly. Although..."

The door clicked unlock with an echo. Father Jim shoved through. "Don't count your chickens before they've hatched, John Mark. Genetically engineered, or not."

He followed him into the hallway, mumbling, "I think you've mixed your metaphors there, chief."

"I heard that. This way..."

Ford followed the man through the winding hallways, Lucy coming up to his side bearing the rolled-up Shroud.

"Where we headed, anyhow?" he asked.

"Professor Pavlovich's laboratory," replied Father Jim.

Ford scoffed. "If you ask me, the man's overstayed his welcome a tad too long. And with all the demands he's made to retrofit our last remaining conference rooms, I'd just as soon he found a new abode, give us back our elbow room."

Lucy gently slapped his arm. "Be nice. The man nearly died, didn't he?"

"And at the hands of the Church's nemesis stretching back two millennia," Father Jim added. "If I were you, John Mark, I would listen to the young lady. I do believe she's liable to snatch you out from the clutches of a sticky wicket or two in the coming months."

Ford frowned but nodded. He murmured, "Yes, sir."

"Ahh, here we are."

The cardinal went through the familiar security measures at the door before it unlocked. He led them into an office glowing bright yellow and far too stuffy for Ford's liking.

"Jeez Louise, bro, it's hot as Hades in here!"

Sasha spun around from a grouping of three tripod lamps throwing light and heat against an easel contraption. The size of the Holy Shroud they had just rescued, if Ford were to guess.

"You are bringing me the prize, then?" the man said smiling, his mop of curly blond hair bouncing as he walked over while rubbing his hands together.

"Indeed, Sasha, my boy. Here it is." Father Jim retrieved the rolled-up burial linen of Christ from Lucy and eased it into Sasha's awaiting hands.

Taking it with ginger care, he whispered, "Excellent..." before bringing it over to a large frame resting on the long work bench of polished steel. He set it in the middle and motioned for Ford to join him.

"Now we are going to be needing to work together to unroll the burial linen so that it is not breaking and crumbling. Got it?"

"Looks simple enough."

Sasha raised a finger and wagged it. "*Nyet*. It is not being simple."

"Let's just get to it. After all, the future of Ichthus is hanging in the balance and all that jazz."

The two each took an end and began carefully unrolling the ancient cloth, its fibers offering a surprising degree of flexibility and strength that caused not a single incident. Soon, the brown negative image of Jesus in repose, mirrored from head to toe on two sides, was evident.

When they were finished, the room held its breath, the four

of them taking in the sight of obvious marks of crucifixion—the rivulets of blood running up and down the man's legs and arms, the lacerations on his back, the blood above the brow from the crown, the nail-scarred hands and feet.

"'*After his suffering, he presented himself to them and gave many convincing proofs that he was alive...*'" Father Jim murmured.

"What's that, chief?" asked Lucy.

He startled. "What? Oh, just a bit of Scripture from the Book of Acts. About how our Lord Jesus continued to offer his disciples proof that he was in fact alive, raised from the dead through the resurrecting power of God the Father. Whether or not the Shroud was one of those proofs, we do not know for sure. But I pray this relic does for Ichthus, and all of Solterra really, what it has done for the Church across two millennia."

"And what is that being?" asked Sasha.

"Provoke, confirm, nourish, and sustain faith, my boy."

The man nodded, then grinned and rubbed his hands together. "Enough talk. Time to work some magic."

Ford nodded. "Agree. Help me lift this frame to that heated contraption of yours."

All four took part in lifting the massive frame containing the Shroud over to the series of easels, exposing the backside to the lights Sasha had set up. He then brought them closer, the lamplight making the linen pulse with an almost holy glow.

When he was satisfied, the professor stepped back and folded his arms. "Now we wait to see if there is being a second image on the linen."

The seconds ticked by as the heat radiated across the underside of the Holy Shroud, the impatience of the Minis terium agents palpable.

Then all at once, the room gasped as a collective one.

There it was, an image coming into view just as the late Master Theophilus had voiced.

Dark brown lines wove their way across the aged linen and similarly darkened spots dotted it along various routes combined with stars and tiny notations in a foreign hand. Other lines like swollen veins revealed themselves as well, winding their way and splitting off in various directions. Confirming what Ford had suspected: The Order had used lemon juice to transcribe a secret message visible only to heat.

He folded his arms and lifted his head with pride. "Told you so."

Father Jim approached the linen, arms outstretched and palms reaching for it with a reverent grasp.

"You certainly did, my boy," he said, "though we could do without the histrionics."

Ford frowned and joined the man at his side. Furrowing his brow and bringing a hand to his mouth, he said, "What do you make of it?"

"Don't know, my boy," Father Jim mumbled, standing back with arms folded and stroking his beard. "Don't know…"

"Perhaps it's a message," Lucy said, coming up to Ford's side.

"Like what, old school Morse code?" asked Ford.

"Perhaps, but definitely not Morse code. Something more ancient. Who knows how long this hidden message has been sitting there waiting for a revealing."

The three fell silent as they stood studying the revelation.

"It's easy."

The cardinal and pair of Ministerium agents turned toward the voice.

Sasha nodded toward the linen and pointed. "It's a map. Of the Mediterranean."

The trio spun back around, squinting and taking a step back to take in the mystery at a better angle.

Tilting his head, Father Jim said, "Ahh, I see…"

"Bravo, comrade," Ford said. He added with a mumble, "I would have gotten there, eventually."

"See, there," the cardinal said, pointing, "that's the coast of the Great Sea, tracing along the bottom and curling up along the coast of Judea and around Asia Minor. Those lines forking at the bottom and coming together must be the Nile Delta, with that star there signifying Alexandria."

"What do you suppose the star means?" asked Lucy.

Father Jim shrugged. "Not entirely sure. During the early period of the Church, Alexandria was a major power center competing with… Ahh, yes! Antioch, there it is up above Judea."

"And signified with another star," said Ford.

"Now, wait just a minute…" Father Jim muttered.

More of the map began to reveal itself toward the left, extending the line along Alkebulana and revealing the boot of Roma that now mostly lay beneath the Mediterranean.

The cardinal approached one end of the former African continent reaching up toward the tip of former Italy, another star showing itself as strongly as Alexandria.

"That there must be Carthage, another epicenter of early Christianity. And then there is another star on Malta, which is interesting…" Father Jim trailed off, furrowing his brow with contemplation.

"But what about Jerusalem?" asked Lucy.

"What do you mean?"

"Doesn't right look like what you'd expect, now does it?"

"Whatcha mean?" asked Ford.

She pointed at the map. "Look. It's just a plain old smudge.

Wouldn't you expect it to be a star, along with the other power centers of early Christianity?"

"Perhaps..." Father Jim said, stroking his beard. "But surprisingly, after the first century of the apostolic movement, Jerusalem pretty well fell out of favor as a hub for the Church's activity."

Ford stared at the smudge and cocked his head. "*But you will receive power when the Holy Spirit comes on you; and you will be my witnesses in Jerusalem, and in all Judea and Samaria, and to the ends of the earth.'*"

Lucy looked at him and offered a congratulatory smile. "Acts 1:8. Impressive. For a Noramericana boy, of course."

"Oh, I got plenty more where that came from, sister."

"Alright, let's leave the adolescent banter for another time," Father Jim complained. "But yes, point taken. Jesus Christ instructed his disciples to remain in Jerusalem where they would receive power from the Holy Spirit to bear witness to the gospel—the good news of the forgiveness of sins and eternal life through Jesus' life, death, resurrection, and exaltation; the reparation of the breach in the relationship between God and humanity through Jesus' incarnation and sacrifice on the cross. But Jerusalem wasn't the end goal. The entire world was to receive the good news of God's grace in Christ, which would have meant the entire Roman Empire—"

"Ringing the Great Sea..." Lucy interrupted.

"Precisely."

"But hold the mobile," Ford said. "Master Theo said the Shroud bore two images—the Holy Image of Christ, and presumably this one—right after he told Alexander about there being a remnant of the lost Order of Thaddeus."

"What are you playing on about?" asked Father Jim.

"What I'm playing on about is," Ford said, turning to the linen map, "what if those stars represent the remnant? What if those locations, the stars at Alexandria and Antioch and Carthage and wherever else, what if they mark gathering spots or hideouts for the last members of the lost Order?"

Father Jim's eyes went wide with recognition; his mouth curled upward in hope. "That could very well be—"

A muffled rumble interrupted him, its bassy timbre barely audible but clearly there. More felt than heard.

Ford looked to the ceiling. "What the—"

Suddenly the lights gave out, plunging the room into a menacing darkness.

Lucy screamed; Sasha gave a start.

Then emergency lighting clicked on a second later, dousing the room in a bloody red that felt nearly as horrific as the black of darkness.

"John Mark..." Father Jim said, turning to Ford for guidance.

His mouth opened to offer a reply, but none came.

He froze with the truth of what he knew his bone-deep Enforcer experience had taught him was happening.

The Ministerium was under attack.

And with Alexander and Rebekah still back in time.

CHAPTER 3

THE ECHOING blast of a thousand klaxon electric horns sounded a frantic warning as more booming reverberations tremored through the laboratory.

Ford knew exactly what they meant. Not only the meaning of the alarms themselves and tremors, but the dimming darkness beforehand.

A C-Class Queller. Packing the right amount of *ka-pow* for civilian use.

They'd been a stock measure in his Purifier arsenal rooting out Unfits for the Republic—the men and women whom Solterra deemed either a burden or menace on society. All in the interest of peace and prosperity and progress, 'For Humanity!'

Part electromagnetic pulse bomb to knock out electrical devices, part actual bomb to destroy escape routes and cause general chaotic mayhem.

The work of the Devil himself is what it was. A work he'd had a hand in triggering more times than he'd care to remember. Nearly triggered it on Father Benedict and his clan of monks had it not been for the intervention of the Holy Spirit up in the Blue Ridge Mountains those many months ago.

Which would have led to a whole ball of ugly he'd rather not remember in that moment. A ball of ugly he would have led once those Quellers finished having their way.

Knowing what came next kept Ford rooted to the floor with indecision, his legs frozen like massive Yukonian glaciers—planted, numbing, immovable. His mouth was drier than the Yazoo-Mississippi Delta, tasting of chalk and those old-world pennies.

It was back. The Grip.

Boy, did he hate how he got when the pressure mounted, pressing in and tightening around his chest like a vice grip and flaring without warning. Had stretched back to boyhood, having a rough time of keeping it together under pressure. And Pops had smacked him around plenty for it. Basic training with the Legion helped some, and he eventually managed to get it under control. Mostly thanks to bottles of moonshine his grand-pappy had taught him to brew.

No moonshine was in reach now. And it was up to him to make damn sure that what hadn't happened to Benedict and his kindly monks sure as hot Hades didn't happen to Father Jim and Lucy and Sasha and the rest of the guardians of Ichthus.

Sweet Jesus, help...

About as spiritually unsophisticated as one could get. But given his immaturity in the faith and under the conditions, the three-word prayer was about as much as he could muster.

Suddenly, as fast as it had descended on him, the Grip lifted.

His mind sharpened into focused clarity and heart rate slowed with a calming peace that surpassed understanding.

And no more Mr. Freeze.

It's go time, Ford.

And go he did.

"Pack up the relic and meet me in the command center,"

Ford commanded. "Lucy, you're with me. Sasha, stay with Father Jim and the Shroud. The Bishops—Father Kojo, Mama Mara, Sister Kayo. Are they safe, Padre?"

The cardinal, face drawn and gaunt, swallowed and nodded. "I assume so. Left during the night on Ministerium business, just after you and Lucy went on mission."

Ford nodded with relief and bolted for the door to leave.

"But what is it that is going on in this crazy place of yours?" the Ukrainski professor questioned in a rush, adding a string of panicked Muscovia for good measure.

Ford grasped the polished chrome handle and stopped short.

Spinning around, he said, "The sun has set on Pax Solterra, I'm afraid. That's the bald-faced truth of it."

The others stood still, his words not registering.

He huffed, then added: "Those Trackers and Enforcers and..." His throat caught with fear, but he pushed through. "And those Purifiers you said were congregatin' around the world, Padre—well, they're congregatin' no more. We spied a similar outfit when we absconded with that there burial linen. Not like the hordes that are circling the wagon up top, but..."

He paused to take a breath, then said it plainly: "We're under attack. And by the Republic, no less."

"Attack?" Father Jim said, staggering back on uncertain legs. He added with a rushed whisper, "As in, the Republic? As in, Solterra?"

Ford mumbled, "Any other Republic outfit we should know about, Padre?"

The cardinal ignored him, glancing around the room as another shuddering tremor took hold. "But...but why? The Church has long enjoyed protections and special tolerations. How do you know this is them?"

"Because those reverberations we heard and felt are

Quellers. Used 'em myself a time or—doesn't matter. They're meant to knock out the power and do a right amount of damage. But I'm guessing our county mounties didn't figure us having backup generators, and probably didn't have the full lay of the subterranean land. So kudos to whoever put those backups in place and decided to secure the Ministerium—"

"Ford!" It was Lucy, her face stricken with panic. "What is the Republic thinking?"

He snapped out of his babbling and shook his head. "What else? It's the Republic. And they've partnered with the Church's enemy. So you can kiss those protections and tolerations goodbye because—"

A blast above seized the room in quaking tremors, sending cracks lancing through the concrete and debris falling without discrimination.

Those Enforcers weren't messing around!

Father Jim cried out, his head having been struck by a piece of concrete.

He staggered to the floor, Lucy offering her arm with reflexive help along with Sasha.

Ford rushed to their side as the cardinal dropped from their grip, blood trickling freely from his wound.

But he was conscious, thank the Lord.

"Padre..."

"I'm alright. Just a bit of a head scratch." He touched his wound and winced; his eyes went wide when he pulled his wet hand away with the truth of it.

Lucy laid him on his back and shot Ford a fright-filled glance, the red emergency lights and frantic warnings a reminder of the pressing danger.

"Go, my boy," Father Jim said on a shaky breath. "Secure the Ministerium. Secure Ichthus. For Christ and his Church."

Ford clenched his jaw and nodded. "For Christ..."

"May the Lord be with you."

He stood and motioned for Lucy to join him, instructing Sasha to pack up the Shroud and stay with the cardinal until he sent help.

Ford led the pair hustling through the winding hallways leading to the command center, dodging chunks of debris and Ministerium personnel confused and injured in the chaos.

Another rumble tore through the ceiling above, sending sparks shooting from a gaping hole up ahead, a wire snaking out to the tune of Solterra's assault.

"I didn't sign up for this," Lucy complained behind Ford. "I'm a *researcher* for cotton pickin' sake."

Which sent his blood boiling with a shot of irritation.

Ford stopped and spun around, nearly colliding with the woman whose eyes were wide and forehead creased with fright.

"None of us did, sassafras," he hissed with more vinegar than he intended.

She recoiled and stiffened, glancing around at the chaos and looking like she wanted a quick escape.

Ford took Lucy by the shoulders, gently but firmly. "Look, I had the same reaction the first time I saw combat. Nearly shat myself, too. And I better never catch you sayin' a word about that to no one."

She shook her head and offered a weak smile, her body relaxing at Ford's self-confession.

Another tremor shook the hallway, and the two glanced around before locking eyes again.

"Like it or lump it," he went on, "it's the hand we've been dealt. And I need you on your best California game, sister, alright? You got my back?"

She swallowed hard and nodded, straightening with resolve and clearly getting back in the game.

Ford flashed a grin. "Then saddle up, partner. Because this rodeo's about to get real. And the bucking bronco is about ready to bust through the ceiling. Now come on!"

He spun around and rushed back toward the command center, finding the door securely closed and a brand-new security device standing guard. He slapped his hand against it. Within seconds, it flashed an all-clear green and opened the door.

Revealing a room in chaos.

Gray-clad personnel darted from workstation to workstation in jumbled bursts, waving their arms and pointing at tablets and monitors with frantic effort. At one end, a crack the size of what was left of the Mississippi River reached down the floor and kept going clear across the length of the room. Large sapphire displays on the far end—usually calm, cool, and collected with information boredom—flashed red with warnings and indicated threatening danger. But the worst of it was the supersize display at the center.

Last time Ford had relied on it to secure the Ministerium, three dots had pulsed lazily across the screen with roaming disinterest, as if they were just getting the lay of the land. Trackers, they were, the Republic's eyes-and-ears drones that flared up on the display thanks to the extra security measures Ford had sprung for when he got the gig.

Boy, what he wouldn't give for those three lazy dots again.

Now the map was awash in livid crimson, as if someone slit the neck of a goat and let its blood pulse across the screen. Shifting blobs undulated in waves like ants swarming a discarded apple core. Ministerium security measures were tracking a whole mess of something encircling the property of the Church of the Dormition, picking it apart for scraps and no doubt trying to gain entrance.

Ford took a breath then plunged into the deep end, crossing himself for good measure.

He was going to need all the providential protection he could get for this fight.

"Alright, talk to me, Jin," he said, sidling up to his operational support, a thin man from the lunar nation-state Lunattica, his thick black glasses barely perched at the end of his nose.

Jin pushed them back up to his round face, eyes bulging in a panic, and pointed dead-center screen. "It's gone..."

Ford leaned in for a look. "What's gone?"

"The basilica above. When the Enforcers rained down their Queller payload—it, well..." He couldn't voice the truth of it.

But Ford understood. "So they're presiding over our funeral, is that it? Trying to bury us alive down here by bombing us to kingdom come?"

Jin leaned back and shook his head. "Dunno."

He huffed and folded his arms. "That's a fine kettle of fish we've got—"

He stopped short when he glanced at the largest of the broadcasters and saw the blob had shifted dramatically from encircling the now-dead basilica to oozing down and congregatin' around a single point.

Eyes squinting, he walked over to figure it all out—

When it hit him.

Not a funeral.

An invasion!

Ford shuffled back over to Jin, breath hot and heavy in his mouth gone dry from fight-or-flight adrenaline shooting through his veins.

"Please, tell me you dropped the blast doors to the entrance when you got wind of Solterra's crazy-ass plot."

"Done. And still activated."

Ford sighed with relief. Then he broke into a smile and pumped his fist in the air with a cheer. "That's my boy, Jin. Good work!"

The Lunattican grinned as he clacked away at his keyboard. "And look…"

He followed Jin's finger to a new window he had brought up on his screen, a picture of an outside perimeter camera showing exactly what he suspected.

Droves and droves of Enforcers. An entire division, all clad in the familiar charcoal he himself wore for a time and brandishing menacing weapons that sent his skin crawling with memory.

Good news was that the Queller blasts had buried the entrance. Doubt they didn't anticipate that oopsie. So score one for the Ministerium.

Or perhaps the Holy Spirit in answering his prayer for—

Another rumble sounded above, deep and guttural and menacing.

Help…

All heads tilted toward the ceiling as the aural intruder continued roiling through the subterranean structure for second after agonizing second. Far longer than the previous iterations.

What the…

And then he saw it. Smoke and debris and ash pluming on the screen from the camera angled at the entrance.

Ford's heart seized in his chest; his bowels went weak.

The cloud hovered over the world above, hiding any indication of what was happening beyond the camera's eye.

Another rumble sounded. But this one was not like the other.

Different timbre, different tone.

Less a bassy rumble and more a trebley rattle. And none of that crazy quaking that shook his fillings loose.

There it was again.

A muffled rattle that threw a thumping pulse through the concrete walls of the command center.

Ford twisted around and craned his neck, intuiting and discerning what it was—dreading what it meant.

Lucy slid to his side. "What is—"

"Shh!" he twisted in reply, spreading his arms to tell the world to shut up and stand still.

More rumbling disturbance in the distance.

No. Not rumbling. Not even rattling.

Chew-chew-chewing.

From a Republic-issued Neutralizer.

The weapon of choice for an all-out assault.

On the Ministerium.

CHAPTER 4

Ford raked a hand over his close-cropped blond hair and heaved stabilizing breaths, legs firmly planted to the floor and mind spinning its wheels trying to extract itself from the Grip.

To say this day turned out to be a terribly rotten, no good, very bad day was the understatement of the century.

More *chew-chew-chews* beyond the wall; more rumbling vibrations above.

Alright, maybe the millennium.

Faint, tingey *pop-pop-pops* sounded a reply, no doubt Ministerium-issued contraband now being put to good use by the guards at the doors to the subterranean facility.

But no match for the Enforcers storming Ichthus's gates.

Not even close.

But it was enough to snap him out of it, riding on the thin wave of hope brought on by the sweet sound of back up and plucky heroics.

"Evacuate..." Ford whispered on a shaky breath that sounded more like an uncertain question.

"Come again, commander?" Jim asked.

"I said—" he swallowed hard, his words tripping over his dry tongue. "I said, evacuate."

He spun around toward the back of the room, eyeing the other personnel who had frozen at the sound of the Neutralizers. Had expected to see Father Jim standing at the back with Sasha, Holy Shroud and all.

But no cigar.

Shucky ducky...

How long had it been since he and Lucy had left them to pack up and ship out? No clue. And now who knew where they were. Could be caught up in the melee on the—

Another *chew-chew-chew* and accompanying quixotic *pop-pop-pop* reply snapped him back to the moment and sent him into a frenzy.

"*EVACUATE!*" he shouted, spinning back to Jin. "Give the order. Sound the alarm. Whatever the heck y'all do to get people's backsides in gear and—"

"*Evacuate. Evacuate,*" a female Britannia voice boomed overhead, commanding yet calm. Exactly what the situation called for.

"That'll work," Ford mumbled before withdrawing his trusty Sig Sauer P365 and checking his clip.

Ready, willing, and able with a full mouth of teeth to bare.

He grinned and slid it back inside, chambering a round. "That'll work, too."

The Britannian announcer repeated the phrase in another language, before moving on to another, urging the global Ministerium agents to flee.

And for their lives. Because the alternative was a reprogramming camp.

And Ford would be damned if he went back there again...

"Come on, sassafras," he said, rushing for the exit. He stopped short and spun around. "You ready for this?"

Lucy chambered her own round and nodded with grim determination. "Locked and loaded, chief."

He flashed a grin and nodded back.

My kind of lady.

"Then let's get to it."

He hustled up to the door and waited, pressing his ear against its cold, hard steel.

Listening, he continued, "Father Jim and Sasha and that bedshe—err, burial linen...they're our only hope to staying alive in this mess. And by *our*, I mean the Church. Ichthus. Because the Ministerium as we know it has sung its last tune."

"And we're its understudies?" Lucy said.

"Mixing metaphors a bit there, but I get your drift. And, yeah, whoever makes it out of here is what's left to carry on the tune. Or the production, as you say. That and the remnant Order of Thaddeus marked out on the Shroud."

"Then I'd say we should get this party started and go get our boys. What do you say?"

He flashed her a grin and nodded.

Again, my kind of lady.

More *chew-chew-chews* and *pop-pop-pop* replies seeped through the door. Could be just on the other side for all he knew.

They say you should prepare for the worst but hope for the best. Bollocks.

Prepare for the worst and hope to God that's all you get. Because in his line of work, there's no bottom to worst's well

Regardless, no more dilly dallying. It was go time.

"On three," Ford said.

Lucy nodded and grabbed the handle, readying their entrance.

"One...Two... Three..."

Lucy pulled back the door.

Ford snapped his arm to attention with outstretched weapon, come what may.

And was met by a beast wrapped in the familiar charcoal, face concealed by a flat-faced black visor, arms bulging with hubs concealing microprocessors that augmented his body with AI-algorithmic enhancements—and brandishing a menacing Neutralizer with a barrel the size of Ford's arm.

Ford went to offer the man a howdy-do when a *pop-pop-pop* sounded from behind, and he was smacked in the face by a burst of slippery, slimy something.

He gave a cry and stumbled back, looking down to find pinkish-grey globs clinging to his chest. The body slumped through the doorway, the top of his skull blown to hot Hades.

Glancing back with wide eyes and open mouth, Ford found Jin planted to the floor and brandishing his own Ministerium-issued contraband.

A Heckler & Koch, but it would do.

"I didn't know you could hold your own at the OK-Corral!" he said on a shaken breath.

Jin shrugged. "You didn't ask."

"Well, join the party! The more the merrier, as far as I'm concerned."

He jolted at another *chew-chew-chew* volley, fiercer and closer than ever. Just outside the threshold into the Ministerium command center and gaining a head of steam.

"Seriously, partner, climb on board the crazy train. You and Lucy can get my six."

In one motion, Ford wiped himself clean of the brain matter, doing little more than smearing it down his charcoal jumpsuit.

"At least it was one of the other guys," he mumbled "So score one for the Ministerium on that front."

Leaping over the downed Enforcer, he scooped up the man's Neutralizer and pumped it to life. Oddly, it felt good to be holding one again. Like he'd regained use of a missing limb with how much he had relied on his own piece working as a Purifier.

A beat later, Ford put it to good use, spotting another crimson-clad figure darting through the smoke-filled corridor pulsing orange.

He squeezed the trigger without a thought.

Three bluish-white electric blobs burst from the barrel and landed squarely in his back, sending shocking tendrils skipping across the man until he slumped to the ground like a bathrobe.

Two Ministerium personnel rushed through in his place, thanking him for saving their lives.

"The Republic has breached the Ministerium!" one of the men said with a frantic squeak.

Ford frowned. "You think?"

Another firefight echoed toward them down the hallway from the car park, sending the men in a sputtering frenzy into the command center.

The few, the proud...

But he had to give them some slack. Most hadn't signed up for that sort of combat and weren't at all cut out for what he knew the Republic could dish out when it put its mind to it.

He pulled the door behind them with a slam, locking it again.

The firefight was coming on hot and heavy now, with far more Republic *chew-chew-chews* than Ministerium *pop pop pops*.

Which meant they were losing. And, by the sound of it, big time.

"Come on!" Ford commanded.

Without waiting for his companions, he eased around the corner shrouded in smoke, his heart keeping pace with the continued reverberations of the assault.

A part of him wanted to dart into the smoky void and push

back those Enforcer whack jobs. Not only to lead his men into the charge, but lay the smackdown on the Republic.

But he knew he had bigger fish to fry.

He stepped into the corridor that took them back toward the Ukrainski professor's laboratory.

When *one-two-three* blue blobs smacked into the wall above his head.

Then another four rounds, their electric cores doing damage to the concrete and spidering out across the surface with menacing intent.

"Stay back!" Ford yelled, holding out his hand.

He scrunched up his face as he sent his own *one-two-three-four* rejoinder into the void.

But Lucy and Jin were having none of it.

Crouching, they pinched off their own *one-two-three* reply, then another set.

Which seemed to keep the encroaching enemy on their toes long enough to offer a window of escape.

Ford popped off another few Neutralizer rounds for good measure while Lucy and Jin slipped behind him. Then he backed up and spun after them, making his way to Father Jim and Sasha.

Praying to the good Lord above they were still alive.

Coast was clear so far as the trio padded forward on swift feet, the smoke thinning a bit the farther they got away from the source of the firefight and beelining it before the Enforcers advanced. Soon, they came up to the lab.

Ford slammed his hand against the security keypad standing guard. Within seconds it gave the green go-ahead. He pushed through.

Only to find it empty.

He rushed inside, circling the space twice over as if it would help.

It didn't.

"Where the heck did they run off to?" Lucy asked.

"I told them to stay put until help arrived!" Ford said on a panicked breath.

"You don't think they were captured, do you?"

Truth be told, the thought hadn't entered his mind until she voiced it.

My God...

A thudding sound snapped him back to the moment.

He held his breath and glanced around; the other two joined the search.

There it was again. Somewhere from behind.

"There," Lucy said, rushing over to a closet next to Sasha's cluttered desk.

She grabbed the handle to open it.

It didn't turn. Totally locked tight.

"John Mark, my boy?" a muffled Father Jim sounded through the door.

Relief flooded Ford. "Yeah, it's us, Padre. Feel free to come out now. Coast is clear. At least in here."

"Would love to, but it appears we've locked ourselves inside."

Of course you did...

A volley of *chew-chew-chews* sounded inside from outside the door, the fight drawing closer and the window of escape closing.

Ford eyed the lock protruding from the face of the closet and readied the only remedy he could come up with on short notice.

"Stand back. I'm gonna blow the lock off, and you may want to flatten yourself like Wonder Bread."

A muffled protest tinged by a frantic Ukrainski tongue sought a hearing, but Ford ignored the man.

He shoved aside on the desk a laptop and scraps of paper with foreign notations and a plate of stale food. The guy lived like a pig. Then he climbed up on top and whipped out his handgun.

He eased around the side of the closet on crouched feet, pressing his back against the wall and taking aim so that the bullet would spit out into the lab.

At least, that was the idea.

Ford nodded toward Lucy and Jin to step aside. "You may want to back up. No telling where this thing could land."

They promptly complied, shuffling out of the way against Sasha's messy desk and waiting for Ford to make his move.

Ford waited a beat, then one more for good measure. Then he angled his gun so that he'd blow the lock clear off.

And he did.

Two short *pop-pops* sent the internal mechanism sailing a meter or two and clanging to the floor, and the door popping open.

Sasha shrieked a muffled cry in his native tongue. Padre gave a startled *'Hallelujah'* once it was over and done with.

Ford hopped off from the desk and he helped the cardinal step out, followed quickly by Sasha.

"You could have been blowing us to bits!" the professor complained, his brow beading with sweat and Father Jim looking about as flushed.

Ford frowned. "You're welcome. Besides, that's the least of your worries given what—"

More livid *chew-chew-chews* interrupted with alarm.

"—is coming at us hot and heavy outside that door. Come on..."

He shoved the handgun at his back and swung the Neutralizer around for its second act.

"Whoa, whoa, whoa!" Sasha said, throwing his hands up

and stumbling backwards into his couch. "Where did you be getting that?"

He held it up and shrugged. "Had a run in with an Enforcer. We won, he lost, and I collected the spoils."

Father Jim groaned. "So they've breached the ramparts, then, the Republic?"

"Oh, it's more than the city walls, Padre. They're about to have the run of the place! Which means we best get going. No time like the present to save our necks while the ship is going down."

"Going?" Sasha exclaimed. "But what about all of my equipment, the workstations and servers?"

"Sorry, partner. We'll rustle up some new doodads on DiviNet once we're in the clear."

"Then I am going to be needing to shut it all down and secure the cloud before Solterra is getting their grubby little hands on it all."

Without waiting, Ford hustled to the door while Sasha started clacking away on the laptop at his desk.

Father Jim said, "What does this mean for Alexander and Rebekah?"

Good question. And one more wrinkle.

Ford turned back toward the Ukrainski professor. "Yeah, what does it mean for our fearless time travelers?"

Sasha shrugged, continuing to type command lines. "They should be fine. I think..."

"Should—You think?" he exclaimed.

"Yes, I *think*."

"But you said those time travel doohickeys would just auto matically zip peeps back across phases through your time travel wormhole thingy!"

Sasha threw his hands up in the air and stood. "What is it you are wanting from me? I am not knowing for certain because

I was not anticipating losing all of my equipment to a Republic invasion! Never mind having to jump peeps phases through time without my equipment."

The man plopped back down in a huff and continued clacking away, muttering in his Ukrainski tongue.

Ford raked a hand across his close-cropped hair.

Always one more wrinkle...

He paced as the Ukrainski prof continued working, the sounds of continued battle keeping time with irritating dread.

A muffled *boom* seemed to underline his fear.

Which didn't bode well for the pair back in time.

CHAPTER 5

SMYRNA. AD 107.

A CLEAR SKY, dappled by thousands upon thousands, millions even, of stars strewn across the darkened night sky, covered Alexander Zarruq and Rebekah Kony like a diamond canopy as they weaved their way through the cramped, muddy Smyrnean streets on their way back to the olive grove that stood on the edge of town.

Alexander chanced a look above as squat buildings of stone and wood pressed in against them and the nighttime crowd made their movement difficult. His breath was stolen at the sight completely foreign in his future world, with all the city lights of ultramodernity in their perpetual brightness drowning out the majesty of God's created order. Not in the past. A sea of shimmering blue-and-white lights set against indigo, with the Milky Way cutting a path through the center, edged by purples and yellows, was their sendoff back to the future.

This is what the past looked like. And it was marvelous.

But then the past's smell snapped him out of his enamored trance, turning his stomach with the miasmic stench of boiled cabbage oozing from the homes' pores, and raw sewage piled in clumps along the street, and animal dung hanging heavy in the humid air left behind from the late-afternoon rainstorm.

On the plus side, he was racing through the muddy streets now caking his sandals with a woman whose beauty was only outmatched by her cleverness and wit and intelligence and—

Alex...rein it in!

He took a stabilizing breath as they weaved past a group of evening revelers and down an alley that continued on toward the olive farm. He was getting way ahead of himself. He'd hardly known Rebekah. Or, now that they had jumped phases back two millennia, did that mean he didn't know her at all? Or that he'd know her umpteen lifetimes?

He shook his head from the mind-numbing science of it all, fixing his shawl around his head protecting the neural sensory receptor. Didn't matter. What did matter was that he had been partnered with this amazing woman whose story he wanted to plumb the depths in all of its mystery and intrigue.

"You sure you know where we're going?" Alexander asked Rebekah. "No offense or anything. It's all running together for me, but you're like a Republic Tracker drone, homing in with ease."

Rebekah flashed him that million-*merca* smile, with gleaming white teeth set against her dark skin behind parted full, dark lips that sent his heart rate soaring.

"I had a little practice after Daddy sold me off as a child soldier back home. Tracking was my specialty."

His grinning face fell at the mention of her past, remembering that she was the daughter of Mbutu Kony, the Minister of Peace with Solterra Republic. The man who had been responsible for wresting a peace out from Alkebulana with a vengeance, a land of three billion people that had been consumed by relentless, terrifying wars stretching from ultra-modernity back to the imperial age of old Europe.

Never did get the full story behind that one, how her own father could have sold her off into slavery—as a child soldier no less. He wasn't sure he wanted it, given what might lay behind the details.

A silence fell between the pair as they continued weaving through the town.

Alexander's mind leaped to what he had just witnessed from Ignatius, reconsidering all that the man had spoken to them—all that the neural sensory receptor had recorded that the future Church needed to survive the burgeoning assaults from inside and out.

The early Church father's exhortation about martyrdom and sacrifice as the measure of true discipleship. About false teaching and false teachers, and guarding against their poisonous ruin. His advice about the unity of the Church in the face of schismatics, those who would seek to divide Ichthus. And about the commingling of Christian teaching with other religions—all of it was a blessed word.

And he wondered what it would mean for his people back home. For those who he had left behind in Tripolitania to fulfill his crazy calling as Order of Thaddeus Master, the ones who had survived the persecuting violence that had torn his church apart. What it would mean for the apostatizing heretics Apollos Nicolai and Dominic Weiss, even his recently apostatized friend Josiah Abasi. For all who had jettisoned the once-for-all faith in favor of a pluralistic, pantheistic abomination now under the control of the Republic.

"There it is," Rebekah said lowly, snapping Alexander back to the moment.

At the end of the road stood the modest well-constructed home of mud and timber, roof thatched with straw and pitch. A chimney jutted from the center and tendrils of spicy smoke chased by a tinge of char continued rising high into the starry night.

The scent of the grilled meat they had smelled when they

had made the jump from the future still hung heavy in the air riding on a cool breeze from the sea beyond, sending Alexander's mouth lusting for Tripolitanian kabobs and drawing him toward the home like a tractor beam.

Until a side door suddenly thudded open, and a man built like a Solterran Destroyer sauntered out of the house on unsteady legs, whistling to his heart's content and waving his arms around in sync.

Alexander stopped short, a ping of adrenaline seizing his chest. He grabbed for Rebekah's arm and dragged her behind a pack of slender cypress trees edging the property in a surprisingly tidy row, waiting to see what transpired and holding their breath that they hadn't been seen.

He motioned toward the man and held his finger up to his lips.

Lord Jesus Christ, Son of God, please shield us from his eyes and send him quickly away!

The Lord must have been busy with other things.

For instead, the man turned toward them, continuing his merry whistle and unsteady gait, adding a few slurred complaints about the weather and the missus Alexander assumed was still inside. Apparently, she had burned his precious lamb to a bloody crisp.

Which would explain the charred smell they caught whiff of on their arrival.

Rebekah tugged at Alexander's arm as the man approached, and guided him back along the tree line, the man coming mercilessly close for comfort.

Alexander's mouth started watering with anxious dread for his pack of narcowafers with every unsteady step the man took toward them, his heart strumming a mean beat against his chest and head feeling like it would explode with indecision.

What should they do? Run? Hide? Keep going and playing it cool, or—

The sound of water trickling into a streaming gush down into the already muddy ground interrupted his panicked plotting.

Is he seriously taking a leak? And a few meters from our hiding spot!

Yep, there he was. Tunic hiked over a generous gut up to his chest, still whistling to his heart's content, one hand keeping his stream steady while the other continued waving instructions at a phantom orchestra.

Rebekah bowed her head to avert her gaze from the immodesty of it all; Alexander joined her.

"What black magic has befallen this world..." the man muttered, making no sense as the stream continued. "What does it mean..."

There they stood, huddling in first-century foliage while a bloke took care of the oldest business in the book.

And kept taking care of business, so that Alexander wondered whether he held his own personal font inside his bowels.

Rebekah stifled a giggle just as the streaming stopped.

"Oy! Who be going thar?!" the man slurred, his tunic now back in place.

She gasped with squeaking alarm and turned to Alexander, face screaming an apology as much as anxiety at being caught.

Alexander put his hands out to steady her as much as himself as the man came creeping over, bent with quizzical intrigue and muttering words of alarm to himself in a way that made him think the man wasn't right in his head.

Suddenly, the man jumped out from behind the line-leading cypress with a menacing *"Ha'ya!"* His legs were positioned one behind the other and hands raised for a fight.

Rebekah shrieked with surprise and leaped into Alexander.

He gave a cry of his own at the sudden move and wrapped his arms around her with protection as much as welcome.

And then the man toppled to the ground, wobbling on those unsteady feet clearly lubricated by first-century spirits. The stench from the man confirmed it. A salty, sour mixture of body odor and the sort of moonshine he had tried as a teenager rebelling against his overbearing bishop father.

"Oof," the man said from the ground before uttering a string of garbled Aramaic Alexander swore were slurred curses that would make Father Jim blush.

He didn't know what to do, whether he should run or help the man.

"Aww, would ye look'e thar," he said from the ground, his mouth as wide as a Cheshire Cat, missing teeth and hiccuping with such force Alexander thought he might topple over sitting on the ground.

He held his breath and looked down at Rebekah, who looked up at him for guidance.

"Lubbers," the man slurred before another hiccup escaped. Then he clutched his chest and grinned, letting a giggle slip while sitting up with legs crossed under him like a pretzel. "Out fer a nighttime stroll, are ye? Makin' out like it's nobody's bizzniss, are ye?"

Alexander stifled a giggle at the sight, but went along with it. The perfect excuse as far as he was concerned.

"Why yes, sir," he said, taking a step towards the man and extending a helping hand.

The man took it, faltering at first and nearly taking them both to the ground. But he recovered, and Alexander helped him to his feet.

Alexander looked at Rebekah and laughed nervously

before offering a why-not shoulder shrug. For this little ruse, they were lovers.

She grinned and raked a hand across her short-cropped hair, letting a nervous giggle of her own slip.

"Thank ye kindly," the man said, taking a step once righted and stumbling into Alexander.

"Whoa, there. You alright?"

"I be dandy and fine. Fine and dandy. Oh, bover. I mean, bother..."

The man stood straight and dusted off his tunic before smoothing down his salt-and-pepper hair that ran down to his ears.

"Ahh, lubbers," the man went on, grinning and staring off into the night sky. "I was in lub once. Long time ago, I was. Yesh, indeed. And the missus was as well. That is, until the kids came along, and then the farm and then—"

The man hiccuped and threw a hand to his mouth, eyes wide and cheeks puffing out as if he were about to retch.

He didn't, recovering with a belch and smiling. "Now, how long ye been togever?"

Alexander looked at Rebekah, who seemed to be blushing. She brought a hand up to her ear and started playing with it.

He fished for words when the man hiccuped again and then suddenly stood straight.

The bloke's eyes grew big, and he heaved a breath before lunging for the trees and letting it rip with doubled-over heaves.

Alexander stepped to Rebekah's side and scrunched up his face with revulsion while the man continued retching.

"He's a ripe one, ain't he," she whispered.

"I guess so. At least it seems we're in the clear. Can't imagine he'll be too interested in interrogating us when—"

More bending over, more retching followed by another loud belch that seemed to finish the job.

"Oy," the man moaned, wiping his mouth and looking way past the proverbial three sheets to the wind. He was likely to borrow one of those sheets and sleep off the booze then and there.

"Fergive me," he continued, "but I must be retiring."

He spun around, his back to the pair from the future and nearly taking another tumble. But he recovered and sauntered back to the door that still stood open, whistling and waving those arms again like a conductor until the sound of a slamming door told them they were safe.

Alexander finally sighed his held breath once the coast was clear. He wiped his brow, brimming with perspiration. "That was a close one."

"I reckon we best get to it," Rebekah said, shuffling to the line-leading cypress tree and craning her neck around with observation.

He came up to her side. Close, in fact, so that he felt he could feel her heat in the coolness of the night, her skin smelling of salt and lavender as they stood still—intuiting, discerning, deciding if all was safe to proceed.

Seconds later, Rebekah eased her head around and gave Alexander a wry glance. "I suppose our little date is over with, and we'll have to hang up our 'lubbers' costumes for the night."

Alexander took a step back and flashed her a grin. "I suppose so."

Although, perhaps if we can't change the past, we could always change the future...

She nodded toward the house. "Come on."

Without waiting for Alexander, she padded forward on cautious feet.

He glanced around the area, searching for signs of life and others who might have been eavesdropping on them. Satisfied, he took off after her, gravel crunching underneath his sandals as they came around the backside of the home.

A window glowed with firelight inside, the fireplace still burning with intent and the smell of spicy wood and charred lamb that much stronger at the source.

They ducked underneath it as they scurried past the house on toward the olive grove beyond, neither of them chancing a glance and satisfied the man had dozed off from drunkenness.

Clearing the home, they picked up their pace, hustling past overturned wood barrels and ducking underneath squat trees burdened by olives filling the grounds with a pungent aroma that paired nicely with the fish and salt breezing in from the distant sea.

Alexander's mouth watered with the memory of home, and the dish of pupfish pasta with kalamata olives and crushed grape tomatoes his father had specialized in making them as a teenager. With a dash of crushed pink sea salt and ground pepper, garnished with shaved parmesan cheese. His stomach literally rumbled thinking about it.

Those were the days, when he and Papa were getting along, when Papa was blissfully content with his parish duties and paying no mind to the compromised Christian teachings roiling other parts of the world in an effort to accommodate and placate culture. Before he was tried as a heretic. Before he threw himself from that bridge.

Alexander's heart sank thinking about all that had transpired in those years between teenager and thirtysomething, when his father began drifting from the faith, when he began innovating in a way that led to his excommunication from the Ministerium and eventual suicide.

He shook his head as they padded across soft earth smelling of life and the dull tang of rot, trying to stay focused on the task at hand. Why his father popped into his head as they raced through the grove, he didn't understand. Perhaps it was the smells, or the way the man had spoken of his wife, in all of his drunken disgruntlement—which surely reminded him of Papa, given his own troubles with alcohol and the pains of marriage with a woman who had a psychotic breakdown.

Either way, he needed to get his head back into the game. They were at the finish line, with several more steps to go.

The overturned wooden cart where he had stashed their time travel gear suddenly came into view, almost illuminated by a spot of moonlight inside the grove, as if heaven itself were shining down upon them with a beacon guiding them to safe harbor.

Almost there...

Alexander rushed to the cart, his heart pounding from anticipation and mind readying itself for the jump back to the future.

He crouched down and grasped the handles resting on the soft earth, the wood rough and weathered grey and of a craftsmanship he wouldn't have believed existed in the first century had he not seen it for himself.

He chanced a glance around the grove and cocked his head with discernment to ensure all was clear. Waves crashing against the coast were the only sound to be heard; olive trees swaying in the breeze, casting undulating shadows underneath the moonlight the only sight to behold.

Satisfied, he overturned the cart to retrieve their time travel devices.

And found nothing but air and dirt, a waft of sour soil and musty wood as his only reply.

His heart stopped, his breath held itself inside his chest. The moment slowed to nothing and all sound wound down to zero decibels chased by a rising, heady tuning-fork ting at the realization the only gateway back home was not where they left it.

Missing. Gone.

A cracking stick jolted his heart forward and sparked his lungs to heave a desperate breath under a surge of fight-or-flight adrenaline.

And then a voice sliced through the night.

"Looking for these?"

Alexander bolted to his feet and spun around, leaving the cart to crash to the ground and finding the last thing he wanted to see.

The drunken fool from earlier standing on uncertain feet, hands clutching two charcoal belts at his generous belly. Looking very much like their time travel devices.

They were officially screwed.

CHAPTER 6

ALEXANDER FROZE, his entire being paralyzed with indecision and freighted fright.

Rebekah did the same, holding her position with back to the man and glancing at Alexander with wide eyes.

Not good...

The man himself swallowed, then adjusted his grip on the belts with one hand before stuffing them under one arm. Then he slid something out from the side of his tunic set snug against his leg through a piece of rope tied around his waist as a belt.

A sword.

Pockmarked with plenty of use, but the moonlight glinted off the edge in a way that told him it was sharpened to kill.

The man thrust it toward them with the flick of his wrist, telling them he meant business.

Big business.

Worst. Case. Scenario. Ever...

Alexander swallowed hard, his throat dry and coarse from the sudden shock of the night's turn. He cursed himself for not verifying they were in the clear. Thought the man was passed out back at the farmhouse, sleeping off the hangover and snoring to beat the band.

He thought dead wrong.

Especially since it was Rebekah who was standing between him and the blade. And would bear the brunt of any sudden movements.

His heart started strumming a mean beat against his ribcage now. His breaths grew shallow and his mind was filling with cold dread that could only be ameliorated by those bloody narcowafers he had come to rely upon in times like these. Those wretched ribbons of relief filled with synthetic narcotics that had come to define him and help him navigate life—in many ways more than the Spirit of God himself.

And there they were, staring down the blade of a drunkard probably freaking out of his inebriated mind at the dark magical talismans from the future he was holding at the crook of his armpit.

Suppose it was remarkable something like this hadn't happened already, with all of their clandestine dealings across phases and subterfuge from Patmos to Beirut and now to Smyrna. They'd rolled the dice each time they had jumped phases, relying on the good Lord's providence and a dose of luck to get them through the ordeal.

He prayed the power of Christ's Spirit would fill in the gaps where Lady Luck had left them high and dry.

"Saw ye 'merge from that thar plot of land, earlier in the ev'ning, I did," the man said, words rolling off a thick tongue with deliberation. "Saw ye run yer legs faster thana jackal in heat, me did. Creeped up and 'round me house, ye did. Off into town, ye wint. Din't git a good look atcha, but I came up 'ere right fast to 'nspectigate whatchye was doin'. Couldn't make no sense of it. Till I saw yer tracks in that thar dirt 'round that thar wheelbara and took me a look 'nside."

The arm bearing the time travel belts suddenly thrust out from underneath his armpit toward the pair, the devices shaking from his outstretched arm like rattlesnakes, their tails wagging with livid intent and startling the pair from the future.

Alexander faltered from the sudden movement, but caught his step. Almost had sense enough to use the moment to turn it all back on the man, but the bloke held that bloody sword steady, its point looking even deadlier than he had noticed the first time.

Stuffing the belts back under his armpit but holding the sword aloft, the man went on, voice low and growly now: "Had Iya known ye bein' the pair at me pissin' spot, Ida 'rested ye meself!"

He paused his travelogue and muttered something to himself, hiccuping before belching and sending a hot breath blooming across the pair chased by the sour smell of that moonshine.

Keeping his body still, feet firmly rooted in the ground, body bent slightly, and arms at his side but taut, Alexander chanced a glance at Rebekah, whose eyes were closed and herself muttering. Probably a prayer, which was a good idea.

Psalm 23 came to mind, and he prayed part of it silently to himself: '*Even though I walk through the darkest valley, I will fear no evil, for you are with me; your rod and your staff, they comfort me.*'

Alexander snorted to himself. What good was a rod and staff when a bloody sword was staring you in the face?! And wielded by a drunkard who thought he'd been visited by aliens or the Devil himself?

While Rebekah continued lifting up her soul heavenward, his was a jumbled mess of thoughts with no way to put the pieces together, leaving him crashing and burning there on Earth.

Should they make a run for it? They surely would leave the

drunk in their dust. But then he would still have their time travel devices, and they'd still be screwed.

They could just grab the devices and then make a run for it. Seemed likely they'd win with their decent two-to-one odds. But the man looked like he had a tight grip on them, his biceps bulging thicker than his neck with the way that arm was clenching them against his side again. And while Alexander matched the man's size, though without the generous gut, the man was twice as large as Rebekah and packing far more hard-labor hardened muscle. Than either of them, really.

What about trying to reason with the man or explain the situation as vaguely as possible using complicated lingo and confusing terms, given he was three sheets to the wind and all? Definitely an option, but what would that do to the time-space continuum—or the space-time continuum as Sasha would have surely corrected?

Then there was the nuclear option: put up a fight. Again, two against one was pretty good odds. But again, the man was a beast. And then there was the whole space-time continuum issue again.

Although, they probably just blew whatever law that governed the Universe to smithereens with the drunkard's discovery and their lovely conversation at the cypress trees before their current lot in life.

Alexander's tongue tingled for narco relief as his mind continued swimming under the weight of indecision.

What to do, what to do, what to—

"So who are ye being, anyhow?" the man snapped with interruption. "And don't ye be thinkin' 'bout no funny bizzniss neither."

On instinct, Alexander opened his mouth to offer a word.

But was intercepted by Rebekah, who offered a sudden, enthusiastic shout as she spun around to face the man. A sort of

'*Ha'ya!*' battle cry that changed the dynamics before either Alexander or the poor man knew what hit them.

Raising a knee and pivoting her left foot, she sent her right leg sailing high into the air.

She planted her foot with a roundhouse kick squarely against the man's wrist and the sword's hilt with a thud.

Sending it sailing with blessed escape through a nearby olive tree with slicing abandon, leaves fluttering to the ground with violation.

The man was too stunned to understand what had hit him, the wheels of his still-lubricious brain trying its darnedest to work out an explanation, much less a solution, and coming up dry.

In one motion, she pivoted her body so that it angled the other direction before she ran through the wickedly cool routine once again in rapid-fire release.

Knee raised. Right foot pivoted. Left leg sailing high into the air and planting her foot with a roundhouse kick squarely against the man's head with a loud *smack!*

Sending the poor guy crumpling to the ground like a sack of potatoes.

Alexander was too stunned for words to do anything. He just dropped his jaw with dumbfounded disbelief at the magical woman who was his partner before a marveling giggle slipped through lips widening into a smile.

"Where did you learn to do that?" he said with a breathless whisper, as if he would wake the man who was lying prone in the dirt and clearly unconscious.

Rebekah stooped down and wrenched his hands open, retrieving the belts.

She stood then handed one to Alexander and shrugged. "I don't know what they teach you growing up in Tripolitania, but down south, a girl learns early how to hold her own. Especially against drunk oxen."

"I guess so..."

"We best get to it. Who knows how long our resident drunkard will be out. And our little party could have drawn attention elsewhere. Something we should probably avoid given the test we've already given the Lord's providential care."

Alexander nodded and wrapped his belt around his waist, securing it in place. Rebekah did the same.

"Right," he said, putting his hands on his hips and scanning the surrounding grove. "I believe we jumped phases a few paces this way..."

He walked through a row of trees, carefully tracing his steps from the cart under the clear-sky moonlight, the shadows from waving olive branches making it difficult but his memory now clicking into gear.

"That looks about right," he said.

"But what happens if it isn't?" Rebekah asked, a slight quiver in her tone betraying fear. A far cry from the fearless one he had just witnessed. What a contradiction this woman was. One he wanted to explore once they jumped back home.

He shrugged. "Not sure, exactly. Sasha never made mention of that aspect of time travel. But I have to imagine if we escaped being impaled by olive trees, then we ought to be alright."

Rebekah took in a breath and bit her lip, then started playing with her ear. A nervous tell that seemed to betray fear with jumping back to the future.

Alexander smiled and took her hand. He said gently, "It'll be alright. The Lord is with us."

She managed a fleeting grin and nodded.

He nodded back and let her hand drop. "Shall we?"

She swallowed hard then grabbed his hand again and held on tight. "Yes. Now I am ready."

His breath caught in his chest at her touch. He noticed how small her hand was in his large palm. And soft. As soft as he imagined a newborn's skin.

He cleared his throat and nodded.

"Alright, let's do this thing. All that is necessary is to press—"

Alexander went to point at the now-familiar green button flashing the Ukrainski word for 'GO.'

But it wasn't flashing. It wasn't even green.

"Wait a minute..."

Alexander bent over and craned his neck to inspect his own belt.

Same blank screen, same bad result.

No Ukrainski word for 'GO'!

Alexander furrowed his brow, the panic rising to a wicked throb in his ears.

He hesitated, but decided to punch the button. Pretty sure what would happen, but he held his breath and prepared himself for the jump just in case.

Nothing.

A cold panic flooded him now, radiating out from just above his kidneys until his entire body from head to toe was filled with dread.

"What's the matter?" Rebekah said on a shaky breath.

He ignored her, jamming the button again but getting no time-travel love as his head filled with dizzying panic and heart felt like it would explode from the freighted weight of the truth of the matter.

"Why isn't it flashing? Why isn't it even green?" he mumbled to himself as he jammed the belt like there was no tomorrow.

Because they had no tomorrow if something had happened to their devices.

With shaking arms now, Alexander unclipped his belt to inspect it.

Maybe it was damaged on the jump over somehow. Or from that drunk who was still blessedly passed out when he retrieved them from the wheelbarrow, or inspected them in that house of his back toward town. Or from low power or from some other malfunction he was neither capable nor equipped to fix.

He stretched his belt flat between his hands, going over every inch of it with his eyes until he came up empty. Which was a good thing, because it seemed undamaged.

"Alexander," Rebekah said as he continued his inspection.

Then he held the face of it up. The unit was surely powered and turned on, a digital battery indicator in the upper right corner telling him all he needed to know on that front. He remembered Sasha saying that the unit was programmed to never need the user to turn it on and off. And it was supposed to have been all set to go, receiving a feed from Sasha in the future through DiviNet or whatever and wherever.

But that end of the equation was missing a few crucial lines of code.

And that's when Alexander saw it.

Next to the battery indicator light was another: a blinking red light in the shape of a signal with the Cyrillic *'Nyet'* blinking next to it in sync.

Which Alexander knew from countless conversations with his good friend Sasha Pavlovich, stretching all the way back to dorm room and barroom and every other room chit-chats, meant a big fat *'No!'*

In other words: No go.

"Alexander..." Rebekah said again, her voice a mixture of irritation and alarm.

He replied, "The time travel device is not receiving a signal."

Her face fell. "What does that mean?"

Alexander turned to Rebekah, face straining to keep it together and not reveal how utterly fearful he was for what it did in fact mean.

Then, with all the matter-of-factness of announcing the weather, he said, "It means the devices are not activated."

He paused, grinning and letting a drunken-like giggle slip on par with the bloke still passed out on the ground while Rebekah penetrated him with wide, questioning eyes. Couldn't help it. It all seemed positively unbelievably hilarious that a pair of travelers from the future had found themselves stuck—in the past of all places!

Another giggle slipped before he put it even more plainly: "It means we're stuck in time."

But what he wondered, and what he didn't voice, was a question as frightful:

What the heck was happening back in the future?

CHAPTER 7

NICAEA, ARABIA-PERSIA. AD 2123.

Ford paced the length of Sasha's makeshift laboratory as the prof continued clacking away on his laptop while the Ministerium crashed and burned outside their doors.

As far as he was concerned, using way too many precious minutes the Ministerium five didn't have. Wasn't this guy supposed to be some Solterra-renowned scientist? Who discovered time travel, of all things? And the guy can't type and shut down his work any faster?

When he couldn't take it anymore, he stopped in a huff and asked, "You finished ye—"

"*Nyet,*" was the only interrupting reply from across the room.

Ford huffed again and resumed his pacing, waiting as the sands of time slipped to empty while Sasha backed up his redundancy systems on the masked Ministerium node floating out somewhere on DiviNet. None of which he understood, except for something about an advanced AI algorithm responsible for jumping phases through the wormhole opened up by the time travel devices strapped to Alexander and Rebekah. All he cared about was making sure they could come back in one piece and then turning tail before the Purifiers came to cancel their butts and throw 'em in a reprogramming camp.

Finally, Sasha announced with a flourish: "*Zakonchennyy.*"

Which Ford took as the man having gotten off the pony and stowed it safely inside its stall.

"So it's done, then?" Father Jim said as he and Lucy carefully rolled the Shroud relic for extraction, sounding as relieved to get the show on the road as Ford.

He stood with a grin. "*Da.* The phasement kernel," he paused and turned toward his companions, "the AI algorithm that is being responsible for bringing our friends back across the phases of time, it is now being safely stowed in a hidden node within Divi—"

"Great," Ford interrupted. "Let's saddle up and move on out."

"Let me just disconnect my workstation laptop from the trunk of the network..."

"Laptop?" Ford said, eying the man's hardware. "We're going old-school twenty-first-century tech now, ehh?"

"It is not being old school," Sasha said as he disconnected the device from the Ministerium's main network trunk. "This *laptop* as you call it is the equivalent of an entire mainframe workstation from a century ago!"

"I don't remember this from your last university laboratory."

He shrugged. "I upgraded."

With a final yank, he disconnected the device from a cable snaking from the wall to the workstation laptop device.

Picking up the device and holding it on one palm while working some further configurations on the screen, Sasha went on, "I am being able to control the entire jump through phases of time through this powerful little puppy through a connection with—"

He stopped short; his face fell.

Then he gave a sharp gasp, a squeaking intake of air that sounded like the end of a balloon being cinched.

"Uh, oh..." he said, setting his laptop down on the desk with a sudden thud and mumbling something in his Ukrainski mother dialect of Muscovia.

Ford clenched his jaw and hustled to his side. "Never say *'uh, oh'* when the Republic is storming the gates, partner. What the hot Hades is going on?"

Now Father Jim was alert, as was Lucy. They left the rolled up Holy Shroud on the table and came to the other side of Sasha as he inspected a series of readouts.

And an alert box flashing yellow dead-center screen.

Sasha said nothing, merely pointing at the cautious warning. Which, of course, was in Cyrillic, so it did them no good while the Ukrainski professor contemplated the gravity of said cautious warning in silence.

"Sasha, my boy," Father Jim said, "I dare say the enemy is climbing the ramparts as we speak. Or, rather, as you don't speak."

"Translation into Solterrish, partner," Ford said. "Speak!"

Sasha took a breath. "It is looking that our friends are being—how are you saying it..."

He went silent again, shaking his head and returning to clacking away on the device in search of answers.

"How are you saying what, my boy?" Father Jim said.

Ford huffed. "I swear to the good Lord above, if you don't spill it—"

"They are being trapped," Sasha said. He spun around and put his hands on his head, looking toward the ceiling with wide eyes and a fallen face. Then he shot to one of the cabinets and started rummaging around for something.

"Trapped?" Ford exclaimed, spinning around toward the man who continued his search for Lord knew what.

He pulled out a large glass bottle filled with clear liquid.

Ukrainski candy. Vodka.

Heat flashed across Ford's face, and his muscles tensed with irritation. "Oh, no you don't, homefry."

He walked over to the man and snatched the bottle. Prompting an immediate outcry from the professor with a string of curses in his native tongue.

Ford held the bottle up and away from the man as he tried grabbing for it.

He said, "Now just hold your horses! What the heck do you mean, trapped?"

Sasha threw his hands up in the air and huffed before raking them through his unkempt hair and slouching on his couch.

"I am meaning trapped trapped."

Ford slammed the bottle on a worktable commanding the center of the room and slid next to Sasha on the couch.

"As in, they can't come back to the future? Can't jump...phases or phasements or whatever the heck it is they do with those belts strapped to their waists?"

Sasha leaned forward, unblinking and unmoving. His eyes filling with emotion, he simply said, "*Da...*"

A stunned, contemplative silence spread across the room. More booming and Neutralizer *chew-chew-chews*, followed by diminishing rounds of handgun *pop-pop-pops* was the only soundtrack as the seconds ticked by.

Finally, Ford stood and spoke. "I don't understand how this is possible. But we've got to go. Sasha, grab that laptop of yours, and pray to the good Lord above there's still a way to bring them back."

Sasha went to protest, but Ford kept going. Turning to Father Jim, he said, "Padre, I'm afraid I'm plumb out of options for us escaping, given my newness to y'alls operation here. So I'm hoping you can shed some light on our predicament. Any escape routes we can use to hustle out of here right quick?"

Father Jim's face was gaunt, having been too stunned for words at the revelation about Alexander and Rebekah. But then it began to lighten with resolution. There was still fight in the man.

"The Archives, at the farthest end of the Ministerium headquarters. We had the foresight to build into the designs such a route of escape should we require it in the event of extreme entanglements."

"I'd say this is one of those events of extreme entanglements."

The ceiling shuddered with agreement, dust and a few loose chunks falling to the floor.

"Time's up. Move 'em on out." Turning to Lucy, Ford said, "We're not out of Kansas yet, sassafras, so let's arm up and prepare for the worst."

"Kansas?" she said, withdrawing her sidearm and joining Sasha at his side, who had already gathered up the laptop under his arm.

Ford padded to the exit, Neutralizer in hand, the stout, black barrel looking more than ready for action

"Yeah, Kansas," he said, pressing his ear against the door. "A play off that old-school black and white movie of Dorothy and Auntie Ann, Toto and that Wicked Witch of the West."

Blank stares from the group was his only reply. As were a series of unrelenting *chew-chew-chew* Neutralizer blasts sounding forth unabated now. Distant, but closing in. The tide seemed to be turning.

And not in the Ministerium's favor.

Satisfied with what he heard closer their way, Ford pushed off from the door and shook his head. "So uncultured..."

"Are we in the clear, my boy?" Father Jim said with a surprisingly stable breath given the circumstances.

Ford laughed. "In the clear? Not in the slightest. Sounds like the fighting is still several doors down. But it's coming in hot and heavy. And if we don't scram soon, we're liable to be goners. Can you manhandle the Shroud on your own, Padre?"

Father Jim nodded and went to the table, carefully placing the holy relic in his arms.

Coming up to the door, Lucy grabbed the handle and nodded at Ford. "On three."

He nodded back and brought the Neutralizer up to his chest.

It was go time on all cylinders.

She counted, "Three...two...one." Then opened the door.

He lunged into the hallway, finding it darkened but for faint crimson emergency lighting struggling through smoke and debris. It smelled like static-charge and the sour scent of death. And he heard the groans of the dying and injured combined with the continued battle beyond.

No matter. The sights and sounds and smells were no match for his Solterra-trained sense of mission.

Ford whipped the Neutralizer right toward the still-unrelenting sounds of all-out war echoing toward them.

Clear, as far as Enforcers were concerned.

Then he whipped it left, seeing not a soul.

He edged forward, training the weapon back toward the mayhemic noise through the smoldering corridor, the smoke flashing whitish-blue, and instructed the others to move it down to the Archives.

Lucy padded to the front with Father Jim on toward their escape route. Sasha was close behind with Jin at his side. Ford picked up the rear, putting himself between the Republic and his friends for the Ministerium's last stand.

"I don't understand," Ford said, coming up to Sasha's side. "How is it possible that Alexander and Rebekah are trapped? I thought the time travel belt contraption thingy was on some sort of autopilot."

Sasha frowned and shook his head. "That is not exactly being right. The algorithmic signal from across DiviNet cloud canopy is traveling through the wormhole opened up by the electromagnetic force field created by the belts."

"It can do that?" Ford whispered with wonder.

Sasha glanced at him. "*Da.* The atmosphere in past phases is allowing for the same electromagnetic frequency transmissions as being in our future world. But with having to disconnect from the Ministerium's main trunk into the node I created on DiviNet, we lost the connection."

Another round of *chew-chew-chews* broke out back from where they came. Blessedly distant but sounding alarmingly closer than the last time.

Sasha jumped, but swallowed hard and kept going.

Ford continued, "Why can't you still transmit wirelessly," Ford went on, "like all the rest of humanity across Solterra with all their devices and such?"

Sasha replied, "Because the Ministerium's own network was offering a series of masking algorithms that was allowing me to piggyback off from DiviNet to transmit from the node. It is being most impressive, actually. More than I thought Ichthus was capable of doing."

"That was my doing," Father Jim said with a touch of pride from the front.

"*Khorosho*, Padre."

"Please tell me we—"

The cardinal was cut off by *one-two-three-four* rounds slugging it out with menacing intent.

Startled, Ford spun around and aimed with protective intent.

No one, no how.

Lucy!

He spun back to find Father Jim crouched against the threshold of an office door and Lucy standing over a body.

An Enforcer, charcoal helmet cracked in the face and oozing blood. Must have caught him flatfooted.

Good girl!

She was wrenching the man's Neutralizer off from around his shoulder.

More weapons the merrier.

Jin continued padding forward several more meters beyond with weapon raised. Which was a good idea, scoping out the rest of the way to make sure no more Enforcers surprised them.

"I didn't think they had made it this far," Ford said with a concerned breath, hustling to her side. "Must have gotten lost."

"Or scoping things out for the next wave. And look..." She pointed at his wrist, sleeve pulled up and bearing the markings they had groan to loath.

Two intersecting lines bent at the ends.

Ford clenched his jaw and shook his head. "Nous..."

"So there you have it," Lucy said. "The Church's nemesis in official cahoots with the Republic's military policing arm."

Which didn't bode well for the group.

Jin came back and gave a thumbs up. "Looks like he was the only one."

At least they had that going for them.

"Let's keep moving," he said. "The Archives are just up ahead. Any minute now."

Father Jim stood and started forward with Sasha, with Lucy on point again out front joined by Jin with Ford making up the rear.

No more surprises this time.

Crimson light, unhindered by the fallout of battle, guided them onward. Within a minute, the familiar door to the Ministerium's research arm came into view.

And then all at once the *chew-chew-chewing* that had been mercilessly familiar the past hour ceased.

No more booming. No more Neutralizer blasts. No more *pop-pop-pops* from replying handguns.

No more nothing.

The group stopped, the threshold to the Archives a few meters away. No one moved, no one said a word.

An eerie silence enveloped them like a cold fog as they waited, intuited, discerned what was happening farther back in the bowels of the Ministerium headquarters.

Ford's heart was strumming a mean beat now at the obvious shift. His chest tightened with searching breath, his bowels grew cold with the dread he had been anticipating from the start but dismissed as the hauntings of his past.

Father Jim finally broke it, saying lowly: "Ford, what is—"

Ford put out a quieting hand, his face scrunched up with concentration to discern whether what he thought was about to go down, was about to go down.

Waiting for the moment when he was certain he and his friends were about to get a taste of his old medicine.

And then he knew.

Smelled it before he saw its gaseous tendrils filling the void left behind by those Ministerium agents and employees downed in the onslaught.

Knew beyond a shadow of a doubt now that what was coming next was nothing they wanted to stick around for. Because he himself was what would have come next after the toxic fumes did their work.

Purifiers...

And bearing goods that he had let loose countless times before.

Lucy coughed, wincing and blinking away tears beginning to flood her eyes. Sasha and Father Jim followed her lead. Jin had taken off his glasses and was wiping his eyes as well before heaving desperate breaths.

He'd built an immunity to it from years serving the Republic, even though his blood-stained helmet was equipped with the ventilation necessary to keep him safe. But some residual Elimino gas still got into his system anyway.

The sounds of his friends coming under its control snapped him back into action.

"Time to move," he said, rushing for the Archives door. He slapped his hand against the security keypad, waiting for it to work its green-light magic.

It didn't turn.

A cold, dark plate of glass mocked him from behind his hand.

Ford clenched his jaw and slapped it again, waiting a beat for activation.

No way, no how.

He huffed and slammed his fist into the thing. "What the hot Hades is going on?"

"The Enforcers must have deactivated the security measures during the assault," Jin said grimly, stepping to his side for a look.

"Well, can you fix it, maybe bypass it using all of your technowizardry?"

He shrugged. "I can try."

Ford stepped toward him and fixed him with insisting eyes. "There is no try in this rodeo, partner. It's do or die. So pick and choose wisely, homefry."

Jin swallowed hard and nodded before pushing his fallen glasses back up the bridge of his nose and crouching low to inspect the keypad.

"You'll need this." Ford handed him a knife from his boot, its blade polished and sharpened to perfection.

He took it and got to work, wedging the blade between the wall and the underside of the cover. Working it side to side, he popped it off. It fell forward but caught on a connector wire.

A tiny digital display still alighted with power was blinking a warning Ford had no clue what it meant. What was important was that Jin seemed to. He handed Ford his knife back and started pecking away, entering this and that to try and bring the thing back to life.

The seconds ticked by in slow-mo frustration as the Elimino miasma began spreading across the floor with a terrifyingly thicker consistency.

Sending Father Jim into a violent cough. Recovering, he said, "Jin, my boy..." before lapsing back into the hacking cough. It overtook the man before he heaved a breath and finished his thought: "If you could speed up the delivery, that would be smashing."

Jin wiped his head beading with perspiration.

Ford leaned over him. He whispered, "Come on you blasted contraption..."

"Almost there," Jin said as he continued pecking on the tiny screen. "Just a few more—"

A faint click sounded behind the wall before the door released open.

He leaned back and held up his hands, as if moving would frighten their success away. Then he grinned widely at Ford.

Ford closed his eyes and sighed.

Praise the—

A bluish-white glob smacked into the wall above his head, tendrils of electric charge cascading across the surface.

Shucky ducky.

Neutralizer.

"Inside!" Ford shouted. He wasted no time in swinging his own weapon around and letting it rip, sending a *one-two-three-four* reply.

Lucy ushered the other three men through the doors while Ford held off the next round of Republic Enforcers advancing toward them.

There they were, in all of their terrifying, menacing glory.

Not Enforcers. Purifiers.

Five of them arrayed across the hallway into a V, faces masked with shiny chrome visors against crimson uniforms of polycarbonate. Ensuring that what little reply Ford offered them would do the job.

Except he knew better. Knew where the weaknesses were, because he trained the Purifiers to guard against them.

Catching one in his sights, he aimed straight for the neck-line where he knew a flaw in the design would put the Purifier six feet under.

Triggering *one-two-three* rounds of his own bluish-white blobs, he sent the Purifier staggering backward with sudden smacking force, and then down to the floor in a crumpling, dead heap.

Ford grinned. Score another for the Ministerium.

His success was short lived.

Four more Purifiers ready to answer the call of duty. And they did, opening up on Ford's position.

But not before he ducked inside to safety, slamming the door with force and hoping to the good Lord above the thing held tight.

A beat later, a tugging against the door confirmed he was right.

They were safe.

For now.

CHAPTER 8

THE VAST SPACE was a far cry from the chaos that had ensued on the other side of the just-closed doors, the void humming lowly with cool, sanitized air blowing from the HVAC system controlling the humidity and temperature of the entire subterranean headquarters.

The Archives was the crown jewel of Ichthus, bearing all of its precious manuscripts and documents and codices of the Church's past. Ichthus transferred many of the most important of these assets from the Vatican's collection to the vaults beneath for safekeeping, preserving them with incredible foresight before the Reckoning, and even before the climate change Armageddon swallowed the former Papal state into a watery grave.

The real magic, however, was the vast digital collection summoned by the AI-assistant Qoheleth, a nod to the wise man who authored the Book of Ecclesiastes from the Hebrew Scriptures. It offered the Ministerium instant access to a billion-book digital archive from the storehouses of the Church's knowledge and across the expanse of history. And apparently it also served as a panic room should the Ministerium be invaded by the barbarian hordes.

Like today. And by Republic Enforcers of all things.

The size of a gymnasium, the floor was paved with large square black and white tiles and lined down the center with solid squat columns supporting a vaulted ceiling that arched two or three stories high. Lining the columns were frescos of saints. Splashed across the ceiling were more frescos of celestial beings and brightly colored patterns of greens and reds and blues. Many of the walls continued the theme, portraying scenes from the Old Testament and the Gospels. A few other walls displayed spine-out books neatly arrayed on darkly stained wood shelves, which were really digital copies of the original source material. Gilded tables sat in between the columns, mounted by glowing green banker's lamps for research.

The space was serene and studious, sacred even, betraying the sense of urgency bearing down upon it just outside the reinforced steel doors Ford had just shut with a defensive slam. It smelled like a thunderstorm, with the hint of an old library filled with must and paper accented by tendrils of spicy smoke from a fire still crackling away at one end, completely oblivious to the mayhem banging at its gates. Literally.

A threatening thud followed by scraping and several rounds of *chew-chew-chews* searching for a way through made everyone startle with gasping fear. Blessedly, the door held steady.

Ford spun around with weapon raised, aiming for dead-center door, huffing from the thrill of the fight as much as from the fright of the fight.

Sasha aimed for the grouping of chairs and couches anchored in front of the fire, flopping down with exhaustion. Lucy and Jin leaned against the tables, catching their breaths. Father Jim hoisted the Shroud on one of the tables and took a seat.

All of them counting their blessings for their escape from no uncertain doom just beyond the doors and a respite from the Solterran onslaught.

However long it lasted.

As the seconds ticked by, their coughing eased and they were able to recover their breaths, and the irritation from their eyes cleared up. Father Jim explained the Ministerium had the foresight to build out a panic room sealed off from the rest of the facilities should the unfortunate conditions warrant it—even wiring it off separate generators and routing the ventilation off separate HVAC units.

Pretty good foresight. Especially given the toxic Elimino fumes congregating outside the reinforced door taking a beating from the Purifiers and Enforcers giving it hell.

He just hoped it held.

"That's fine and dandy," Ford said. "And don't think I don't appreciate the foresight of the Ministerium to carve out a panic room should the personnel require it. Because clearly we did. But Jin, you better have done something to that security doodad out there to keep 'em locked out for good. Or our little escape is going to be over right quick."

"Not to worry," Jin said, pushing his glasses up again and joining Ford's aim. "There was a manual override embedded in the code that required an encrypted passcode known only to a few Ministerium techies. You can thank your lucky moons I was one of those few Ministerium techies."

Ford eyed the man, who was grinning widely. "Encrypted code? Aren't those things, like, super long?"

"Super-duper, actually. Thirty-two characters, to be precise."

"Glad you're on our team, then."

And glad it was all quiet on the Western Front. For now. But he knew the fact the thudding and scraping and *chew-*

chew-chewing died to nothing meant nothing. Just biding time until they formed a plan to enter.

Because he knew the Republic would bust through that door and haul their butts to a reprogramming camp. One way or another.

"Now what?" asked Lucy, padding to Ford's side with weapon at the ready.

"Now we get the heck out of Dodge. Padre," he said, turning to Father Jim still sitting at a table, "where's that escape route you mentioned."

"Hold on just a minute," the cardinal said, raising a hand. "Sasha, my boy, what do you suppose is happening to our intrepid time travelers back in Smyrna—given the disruption to the phasement signal you indicated back in your laboratory?"

Sasha took a stabilizing breath and glanced at Ford. "I am not being sure. But I am having to imagine the pair have gotten a very rude awakening to their time travel devices being offline."

"Meaning, they're stuck," Ford said.

"That is being correct. Not until we can bring the time-travel algorithm back on line and—"

"Yes, I understand," Father Jim interrupted, "but I wonder if you would be able to use the Archives's technical resources to tap back into the trunk of the Ministerium's network and start retransmitting the necessary code to bring Alexander and Rebekah back home. Do you think that could work?"

A faint knocking again at the door startled the five, spinning their heads toward the exit and reminding them of the dangers still lurking.

Sasha shrugged. "I have to be imagining that could work."

"And you also have to be imagining," Ford said, "that you could work your magic at some Ministerium safe house outside of Dodge, correct?"

"John Mark," Father Jim said with no small amount of irritation, "there is no telling when or where we will have the next opportunity to bring our agents back. The enemy is at the gate—"

"And we've got moments until he's hot on our tails!"

Father Jim opened his mouth to respond, then closed it in a huff as Sasha walked up to one of the tables with his laptop, ignoring them both and snaking a cable from the workstation device to a connection at the center of the pillar.

The Ukrainski professor wasted no time, clacking away as Ford paced in silent irritation.

Which was soon broken by mechanical screeching that broke through the door with penetrating alarm.

"What the hey-ho day is that?" Lucy said, raising her weapon toward the door and gripping it with purpose.

Ford echoed her stance, raising his Neutralizer and aiming dead-center door again. "Sounds crazier than a one-legged mule, whatever it is."

"They're trying to break through," Jin said, voice breathless and shaky.

"Padre...we've got a narrow window here."

The cardinal was on his feet and at Sasha's side as the man continued clacking away, another menacing, mechanical screech followed by a grinding assault at the door.

Signaling the Purifiers on the other side meant serious business. The same business Ford himself would have meant if the Unfits he had been chasing had outfoxed him.

How ironic, and not at all a good feeling. To be hunted by the Republic—and as an Unfit, no less. The good Lord above certainly has a sense of humor. He just wished he'd get a different joke book.

Ford also prayed whatever Sasha was doing did the trick.

And fast.

SMYRNA. AD 107.

Alexander and Rebekah sat in stunned silence in the soft earth, their heads hung with dumbfounded defeat and backs resting against an olive tree overladen with its fruit, its squat, stout, aged trunk twisting with tubular irregularity.

Waves gently lapped against the shore in the near distance in sync with a modest breeze winding through the grove, the leaves above whispering their confusion at the pair below and master still lying prone and unmoving a few meters away—though how much longer was anyone's guess.

Their devices sat next to them, impotent with disfunction and completely indifferent to their lot in life. But for the blinking red indicator light and the repudiating 'Nyet', their blank, black screens stared back at the pair with mocking accusation, as if waging an 'I told you so' finger at the hubris of traveling through time without consequence.

This was the ultimate fallout to their risky adventure. Stuck in time with neither the recourse nor resources to survive.

Everything within Alexander wanted to melt under the weight of the moment, anxiety coursing through him like an anesthetic—numbing him, paralyzing him.

But he couldn't give in. Wouldn't give in. He had to keep it together.

"Stuck in time," Rebekah said. "Who could ever have conceived of such a thing."

Alexander chuckled and shook his head. "Perhaps the estate of *Doctor Who?*"

Rebekah turned to him, face lighting up with surprising excitement. "You know of *Doctor Who?*"

"Of course! What else is DiviNet good for than watching pirated copies of old-school television?"

She smiled and clutched her chest. "I do believe I've found a kindred spirit, Alexander Zarruq."

"But now which version? The pre-1990s, the relaunch in 2005, or the re-relaunch in 2063?"

"Oh, definitely the first relaunch in 2005, but only until 2018. It got way too political for me. And then the 2063 re-relaunch was just a precursor to Solterra's agenda, if you ask me."

Brows raised with confusion, Alexander shifted toward her. "Too political? Isn't the whole thing one bloody political theater?"

Rebekah scoffed. "No way! It's an exploration of the human condition and our hopes and dreams for the future."

"Agree. But—"

"And don't forget the shades of Christianity embedded in the series," Rebekah went on with interruption. "Not that it's an apologetical defense of the faith, or anything. But the ideas of resurrection and personal identity are bandied about."

"Sounds like we've got a real fangirl on our hands!"

She chuckled. "You could say that. Those episodes are about the only thing that kept me sane when...."

Rebekah's face fell as she trailed off. Then she leaned back and stared out into the canopy of diamonds strewn across the clear dark sky, bringing a hand to her ear and playing with it, as if reliving a sour memory.

Alexander frowned, wondering what she was thinking. He wanted to ask her about it, desiring to plumb the depths of her story. Oddly, even desiring to offer to hold it with her, with understanding, with protection. But he knew that was nonsense anyway. The last thing she needed was protection—

she was clearly more than a capable woman who could hold her own.

And the last person she needed was him of all people, someone who could barely get his own stuff together let alone help someone along through their own baggage.

But still. She had grabbed ahold of his heart in a way no one had in a very long time. Probably just puppy love, but he felt a connection to her like no other woman he had met. She was smart and capable and sure of herself, and she loved Jesus. And those eyes, all twinkly and full of life, along with that bright and wide smile—all of it sent his heart soaring.

He ran a hand through his thick hair matted now with dust and sweat from their journey in the past, his mind a jumble of thoughts that was compounded by their seemingly irredeemable lot.

Stuck, in the past. And with no way out but for the grace of God and Sasha's technical know-how.

"Alexander," Rebekah whispered with interruption, placing a hand on his leg.

He startled at her touch, his heart jolting forward with elation.

"It's alright. I'm sure Sasha will figure something out. I only wish—"

"No, Alex—" she said with exclamation, bolting to her feet and pointing to the ground. "Look!"

His breath seized in his chest, expecting their drunken friend to have been aroused only to find something far different flashing at him.

A green Cyrillic word. 'GO!'

Alexander closed his eyes and sighed, leaning his head back against the gnarled tree.

Thank you, Lord...

Then he brightened and bolted to his feet himself, smiling

wide and offering a muffled repeat of his thanksgiving: "Thank you, Lord!"

Rebekah threw her arms around him and squealed with her own measure of relief. Then she started dancing, her hips wiggling and arms swaying in the air with an extroverted version of thanksgiving.

"I will extol the Lord at all times," she said, quoting Psalm 34 from the Hebrew Scriptures. "His praise will always be on my lips. I will glory in the Lord; let the afflicted hear and rejoice." She continued dancing, giggling with glee.

Alexander felt just as joyful, although he found it difficult to bust a move, given his shy, introverted nature. But he did join in with her quoting of Psalm 34: "Glorify the Lord with me; let us exalt his name together."

She replied: "I sought the Lord, and he answered me; he delivered me from all my fears. Those who look to him are radiant; their faces are never covered with shame."

Now it became a sort of game, a back-and-forth mutual reveling in the goodness of the Lord that almost sounded like a rap battle.

"This poor man called, and the Lord heard him," Alexander replied, his heart warmed by both quoting the Word of God and sharing the moment with Rebekah, "he saved him out of all his troubles. The angel of the Lord encamps around those who fear him, and he delivers them."

"Taste and see that the Lord is good," Rebekah went on, twirling and lifting up her hands in worship even as she lifted up her voice in quoting the Psalm. "Blessed is the one who takes refuge in him. Fear the Lord, you his holy people, for those who fear him lack nothing."

Alexander went to reply just as their drunken friend began to stir at their feet, moaning and mumbling something under his breath.

Jolting the pair from their ecstatic worship and quieting them with fear.

They held their breath, looking at each other with wide eyes before scurrying behind the olive tree.

The man's eyes were still closed, but he was definitely coming to. How long until he was back to his feet and ready for a fight was anyone's guess.

No reason to wait to find out.

Alexander motioned toward the two belts still lying in the earth underneath the tree. "Best get to it," he whispered. "The last thing we need is our drunken friend to awaken while we're still here."

"Or watch us jump phases back to the future," Rebekah added.

"Wouldn't that be a tale to tell? *'Honey, you'll never believe what I just witnessed!'* They'd lock him up in the looney bin, for sure!"

She giggled, and the man stirred and grunted again.

Spurring the two into action.

They each hustled to their belts and promptly strapped them around their waists.

Alexander checked Rebekah's belt, tightening it and smiling with relief at the continued flashing *'Go'* on its face. She checked his as well, then nodded.

"Shall we?" Rebekah said.

Alexander nodded, grabbing her hand and leading her out several paces into the grove toward the crashing waves, ensuring there'd be nothing in the way when they jumped phases back to the future.

Then he grabbed her hand, punched the flashing button, and closed his eyes.

Hoping to the good Lord that he didn't have to jump phases back in time again anytime soon.

CHAPTER 9

NICAEA, ARABIA-PERSIA. AD 2123.

TIME TICKED by like a taunting bully. The only soundtrack for the Ministerium's recovery was the dull HVAC hum and their heavy, recuperating breaths, offering a confusing respite with nary a word from Solterra.

It was quiet, too quiet for Ford's liking. Maddeningly so. Completely unlike the Legion and its Enforcers, which went in guns blazing. Standard operating procedure.

Which was why Ford was halfway through an over-ripe apple he found perched on a side table.

What did it mean? Had they given up the chase? Given up on the Ministerium altogether? Were they biding their time—waiting, assessing, planning for a renewed assault that would make them wish they had kicked the can and hopped aboard the glory train bound for Saint Pete's pearly gates?

The questions kept coming with every chew, relentless and unknown. He was on his way to ripping through the core in short order, seeds, stem, and all. Anything to keep his mind off from whatever the heck was happening—

Sparks exploded through a hole at a corner along one side of the entrance door with wicked intent, startling the Ministerium crew and sending Ford into a choking fit.

He doubled over as the furious, fiery arc blazed into a July Fourth celebration worthy of America's days of yore right there in the Archives. Did the man's heart a touch of good to witness a Hallmark card display of patriotism from his Noramericanan childhood celebrations past on full display.

But just a little. Because it wouldn't be long until the Republic had cut clear through the wall and around the door like a hot Hades knife slicing through butter.

And then they'd be screwed.

He heaved a breath after recovering from his fit and hustled over to the Ukrainski professor still hunched over his laptop and working that keyboard like it was nobody's business.

"Sasha..." Ford said, voice faltering on a shaky breath before recovering. "Talk to me, doc. What's your status on bringing our kiddos back to the future?"

Ignoring him, Sasha's fingers continued racing across the keyboard, a line of sweat now beading across his forehead.

"How much longer do we have?" Father Jim said to Ford, not hiding his own shaky breath one bit.

He glanced behind then spun around and took a step toward the door with not a small amount of surprise and trepidation.

The Purifiers were making quick work of the Ministerium architecture, reducing it to molten steel and concrete charred to a crisp.

Ford put his hands on his head and huffed a worried breath.

Like a hot Hades knife through butter is right. Not good...

He turned back to the crew. "Not long. Which means it would sure do us some good if—"

"It worked!" Sasha announced with a chuckle bordering on surprise.

The man looked up from the workstation laptop bearing an elated, accomplished grin.

Ford raced to his side, hopeful yet not counting their chicks just yet until they were sure as the rising sun they were ready for hatching.

"So it's done? It worked?"

"Yes, it is being done. Look." The Ukrainski professor pointed to the screen showing the signal locked onto the targeted time travel devices from the hidden node on DiviNet and through the wormhole. It was transmitting a clear sci-fi-inspired signal across phases of time—the two Ministerium agents' lifeline back home.

Alexander and Rebekah were jumping phases now.

Which meant them future folks could get out of Dodge before the Republic struck back with force. Pronto.

And not a moment too soon.

The arcing July Fourth blaze had crested the door's zenith now and was making its way toward the other side.

Drawing ten wide eyes for a look-see before sending ten legs activating for escape.

Ford raked a hand across his close-cropped hair.

Shucky ducky...

"Padre..." Ford said. "I do believe it's officially time to put your brilliant plan of escape into action."

"I do believe you are right, John Mark."

The cardinal stood and motioned toward the back of the room.

Sasha snapped his laptop closed. Lucy and Jin left their posts at the door and joined the other three.

The group hustled across the polished black and white tiles, another streaming set of sparks, its spout having seemingly grown in size, spurring them onward.

"Qoheleth," the cardinal called out, addressing the

Archives AI assistant, "commence emergency protocol *Megiddo*."

"Megiddo?" Ford questioned.

Father Jim nodded. "The prophesied end-times battle location in the Book of Revelation."

"How apocalyptically apropos."

"Indeed."

The AI assistant announced, "Megiddo will commence upon receipt of the passcode."

Ford scrunched up his face with worry. "We've got to provide a passcode to open the hatch in the midst of saving our backsides? Why all the theatrics, and who designed this thing, anyhow?"

Father Jim frowned. "I'll have you know I did."

"Sorry..."

"And the reason for the theatrics is because the protocol offers far more than merely an escape hatch. It launches an entire destructive sequence on the entirety of the Ministerium complex that rivals the end-times destruction."

"Again, how apocalyptically apropos."

The sparking stream officially reached the door's other side now, rounding the top of the door and coming down for a landing that would end in their apprehension or death.

If they were lucky, the latter.

Because Ford would be damned if those Purifiers caught his backside and dragged him and his friends to some reprogramming camp.

No way, no how. Been there, done that. With the beer koozie to prove it. Not to mention the scars and disabled implant chip still lodged at the base of his skull.

"Better hop to it, Padre, before they bake our asses—err, I mean..."

"No worries, John Mark. Under the circumstances, perhaps a Legion tongue is warranted."

Father Jim started rattling off a series of numbers that made Ford's head spin.

45310. 45323. 4558. 45623. 4510910. 451013.

"My land!" Ford said. "You're as intellectually spry as Jin here."

"By the grace of our Lord and the power of the Holy Spirit," Father Jim replied. "But really, it's quite a simple one for those in the know."

Lucy chuckled knowingly, as did Jin.

Ford gave them an irritated look. "Apparently I'm neither in the know nor in on the joke."

Lucy said, "Oh, come on, Johnny Mark. The Roman's Road?"

Ford said nothing, staring at her blankly.

"That's right," Jin said. "The chapters and verses from the Book of Romans, forty-fifth book of the Bible, showing the way of salvation."

"Clever. If I'd had it my way I'da—"

One of the digital panels arrayed with book titles interrupted Ford's reply, swinging open on unused hinges with a gust of stale air smelling of mold and concrete. A darkened void opened beyond, coming to life with LEDs throwing spartan light through a long corridor for escape.

And not a moment too soon.

The sparking stream ceased.

Ford turned back to assess the shift.

Just as a *BOOOM!* from well-placed charges obliterated the only barrier between what was most likely the last remaining Ministerium personnel in the Republic and their Solterran pursuers.

The vast space behind them instantly bloomed with a fiery,

furious cloud of destructive debris that charged toward the escaping quartet with menacing intent.

Everyone crouched and gave a startled cry before lunging toward the door with activation.

Lucy and Jin helped Father Jim bear the Shroud through the opening door into their only lifeline while Ford and Sasha made up the rear.

"Qoheleth," Ford boomed, "shut the door and keep the Devil in the night!"

"As you wish," the AI assistant echoed back.

"*Go, go, go!*" Ford commanded the other four as the door began closing.

Jin agreed, ushering Father Jim bearing the relic and Sasha bearing his laptop down the corridor.

Lucy turned back, weapon ready to back up her partner.

Ford was having none of it. "Get them out of here!" he said, waving his hands at her with irritation.

She protested, "But you can't—"

"That's an order, sassafras!"

Just as crimson and charcoal bodies emerged through the blooming smoke and barreled toward their escape route.

Making Ford instantly regret his decision.

But she relented and joined the other three.

Leaving Ford with the terrifying sight of the elite Legion soldiers with their oversized bodies covered in attachments, wires and tubes and pneumatic hubs, their faces masked with those black reflective visors.

Augers, the most menacing of Enforcers aside from Purifiers whose mind and body were augmented by somatic and neural enhancements for the ultimate fighting machine.

And with weapons extended and ready to be put to good use.

But Ford was as ready as they were.

He swung his Neutralizer around and let loose a barrage of charges, slipping round after round of bluish-white blobs into the void past the now half-closed door. He heard them smacking with contact into two of the five relentlessly pursuing Republic soldiers.

Two Purifiers.

He couldn't help but stand in mocking salute and let out a howling, exuberant *"Yee-haw!"* at the sight.

The soldiers dropped hard, the electrical tendrils still doing what they did best: neutralizing their subject. In this case, given the setting Ford used, into oblivion.

But three more kept charging forward, Augers in all of their augmented Enforcer glory, their own weapons raised now and sending a proper, forceful Republic rejoinder mercilessly barreling toward the exit.

Most smacked into the fast closing door, but a few shots slipped through. Nearly catching Ford along the way.

He slammed against the wall and began backing up, even as the others kept moving farther into the corridor in escape.

He needed to see this through, needed to make sure the door closed with one fantastic flourish before he left his post.

The gap to the outside world narrowed with blessed assurance.

Almost there. Just...

Four. Three. Two—

Eight fingers connected to two hands connected to one Enforcer reached around the inside of the door and halted the door's final advance.

Gears inside the wall screeched with thwarted advance as the augmented Legion soldier held tight, even wrenching it open several centimeters with a shudder.

Now a foot appeared in the gap, ensuring the door would not close as planned.

Ford's chest tightened at the sight, his head filled with dizzying fear. The Grip was fighting hard to paralyze him.

Over my dead body...

Another shudder ran through the door still struggling to close against the Auger's grip.

Ford slipped a knife from his boot and cried out with a Berserker's bloodlust, then lunged for the soldier.

Just as the barrel of a Neutralizer punched through the gap and sent *one-two-three* rounds sailing inside the space.

They whistled past Ford's face. So close he could feel their heat and smell their electric charge.

Close enough that one singed a burning streak across his cheek, adding burnt flesh to the mix of sensations and a lancing pain.

That'll leave a mark...

He paid it no mind.

Instead, he slammed his foot into the Neutralizer, wrenching it from the Auger's grip and sending it skittering across the Archives floor beyond.

Then he grabbed the hilt of his knife with both hands and raised it above his head, coming down hard and raking the blade across the eight fingers.

Slicing every single one in half.

The fleshy nubs still clothed in charcoal fibers bounced to the floor like sausages, blood streaming down into an arcing pool below from the stubs pulling back with a shrieking cry.

Ford smirked. "Sissy...."

The door agreed, jumping back to life and slamming into the Auger's foot now wedged with immobility and being progressively crushed.

But the boot held, forged with synthetic fibers said to be as strong as titanium.

But not strong enough to withstand a Neutralizer blast held at point-blank range.

Ford shoved the weapon into the fleshy roadblock and fired at will.

Blowing the foot to pieces and sending fleshy chunks of charred flesh inside the corridor still sparking with bluish-white static charge.

Just as the door to the escape route slammed shut with finalizing closure.

Ford held his breath, eyes bugging out with the thrill and fright of the battle, his face slick with sweat and caked with dirt, his body taut with activation waiting, intuiting, discerning his next move to keep his people safe from harm.

But nothing else came.

No more Augers, no more sounds, no more fight.

No more nothing.

Ford finally heaved a stabilizing breath, then another. He wanted to slump to the floor and nap the year away. But the echoing footfalls several meters up ahead snapped him back to the moment.

They were safe. For now.

But the truth of what had just happened slammed into Ford as he ran after the others.

War with Solterra Republic. And joined by Nous, the Church's archenemy stretching back to its birth.

Which meant for Ichthus—for the people of God, the Bride of Christ, the Church—it was about to get real.

CHAPTER 10

IZMIR, ARABIA-PERSIA. AD 2123.

THE SUN WAS BLINDING and beating down upon Alexander with unrelenting mercy, the heat heavy and assaulting and suffocating. A far cry from the past phase of the exact same spot he and Rebekah had left behind moments ago—or what felt like moments ago. He wasn't a climate change alarmist, especially in the radical political sense that seemed to grip much of the previous century, but there was no mistaking the truth of Saint Paul's words: *'the whole creation has been groaning as in the pains of childbirth right up to the present time.'* Whether past time or future time, didn't matter.

He was also standing chest-deep in seawater, waves crashing into the shore ahead and a powerful tow grasping for his ankles underneath. He would have preferred landing on solid sand. But it didn't matter.

He was home. Had made it safely back to the future after jumping phases in all of its blinding luminescent, static-charge scented, vacuum-pressured hum glory.

The shoreline was a good thirty or forty meters ahead, the beach house where they had begun their journey right where they had left it. And not a soul to be found.

Alexander heaved a breath as he came down off the high of time travel and glanced to his right, then his left looking for—

A wave slammed into his back with the force of a thousand sledgehammers, cresting over his head like a blanket of titanium chains and dragging him down beneath the turquoise surface.

Water tasting of salted fish flooded his mouth and throat, threatening to overtake his lungs and drag him down to death. He flailed his arms as the wave tossed him like a rag doll. At first toward the shoreline, but then back out to sea with a menacing sucking force that was quickly sapping his reserve energy.

Alexander reached the surface and flailed about, struggling to recover any sort of breath, struggling to get some sort of bearing on his circumstances—it was all too much with the continued onslaught of crashing sea water and undertow. Soon, his vision dimmed to darkness, and a sinking unconsciousness began to overtake him, dragging him toward the underworld and filling him with cold dread.

He would have drifted farther out to sea and succumbed to Poseidon's clutches for good had it not been for a set of arms grabbing him by the shoulders and pulling him to the surface.

He was out cold: his heart not beating, his lungs not heaving air.

A hand tilted his head back in the sand and wrenched open his mouth edged by lips quickly turning a bluish-purple.

Lips pressed against his mouth and filled it with warm air. Then strong hands, one on top of the other, pushed with purpose against the center of his chest several times before repeating the whole process again.

Just when all seemed lost, and Alexander's very soul seemed as if it had sunk deep beneath the surface into a permanent unconscious void, a stream of sea water arced up and out of his mouth onto his chest.

He snapped open his eyes with a frenzied search for life and heaved a frantic breath for air as more water came up, leading to a coughing fit that ran his throat raw.

After several more breaths trying to regain a foothold back in the land of the living, he found Rebekah leaning over him with panicked eyes.

"I thought I lost you for good," she said, heaving desperate, worried breaths herself.

"You almost did," Alexander moaned.

He sat and coughed again. He closed his eyes and squeezed his hands tight around the hot sand, as if holding on to the future world for dear life—not wanting to leave it for the past, not wanting to leave life itself. Though he was certainly eternally prepared, if it ever came to that.

Then the truth of what had happened came crashing into him: Rebekah had saved his life. Yanked him right out from the sea's clutches, dragged him up onto the shore, probably gave him mouth-to-mouth resuscitation as well. Which was both a blessing and a curse—certainly didn't want the first such encounter to be under the throes of death.

But still. His mind threw the truth of it all on repeat: She had saved his life.

Alexander eased to his knees, every fiber of his being protesting the gesture. He turned toward Rebekah and threw his arms around her with gratitude.

"Thank you," he said breathlessly, emotion rising in his chest. "Thank you..."

She smiled and patted his back. "You're more than welcome, Alex. More than welcome. I suppose one thing from my training as a child soldier was redeemable."

He chuckled. "I'd say!"

The two held each other, dripping underneath the unrelenting high-noon sun as much with sweat from the heat of the day as sea water still clinging to their clothing. Grateful to be alive, grateful to be sitting in the sand of Izmir rather than Smyrna.

Finally, Alexander pulled back, wiping his eyes brimming with emotion from the journey, from being on the brink of death. He nodded and offered another grateful smile, then began reddening at the show of affection—and even more at the reality of her life-saving maneuver. He hoped one day they'd return to such affection under far different circumstances.

He sighed and glanced around, the sound of powerful waves crashing upon the shore a reminder of the fate he had just escaped. He wondered if it was worth it, returning back in time, to experience the past, to retrieve the past and record—

His face fell and eyes widened with alarm.

The neural sensory receptor!

Alexander threw his hands to his head with a startled gasp.

His heart sank to the sand, dragging his bowels with it, at what he found.

Nothing.

An absolutely empty head, the device having completely detached itself.

"It's gone..." he mumbled to himself with an almost schizophrenic disbelief.

He spun around on his knees and searched the sand, hands trembling now and anxiety rising to an unrelenting throb in his head at the loss.

Perhaps it fell off during Rebekah's mouth-to-mouth maneuver.

Nothing but sand and 22nd century crap—cigarette butts and broken bottle shards, even a used condom. He stood and continued the search on foot.

"What's gone?" Rebekah asked as he continued his madcap hunt, eyes wild and feet shuffling about, arms taut and angled for redress.

He ignored her, continuing his frantic pursuit, tossing sand about and shuffling in the sand.

She scrunched up her face and put her hands on her hips before running to his side and putting an arm on his back.

He jolted away as if thrust with a live wire in his spine.

Rebekah put her hands up and took a step back. "Oy, Alex! Where's the four-alarm—"

"The—the—the device," he stammered. "It's gone..."

"What...what are you talking about?"

"*The neural sensory receptor!*" he shouted.

He swallowed hard and heaved a breath, huffing it out with frustration—both at the situation and his response.

Her face fell. "Oh, no..."

Alexander turned around toward the sea, raking a hand through hair that had gone nappy from the past and present. "I'm sorry. I shouldn't have exploded at you like that."

"I understand."

"But all of our work in the past...it's all for naught!"

He strode out to the shoreline now, praying like he'd never prayed before. That the Lord would extend his mercies by carrying the device back on a wave of providential provision and opening their eyes to its location.

'Hear my prayer, Lord; listen to my cry for mercy,' he murmured from Psalm 86 as he searched the ground beneath the azure waves. *'When I am in distress, I call to you, because you answer me.'*

He waded farther in, already feeling the familiar tug that had launched the whole blasted problem in the first place, searching the floor beneath and continuing his prayer: *'Among the gods there is none like you, Lord; no deeds can compare with yours....For you are great and do marvelous deeds; you alone are God.'*

But there was nothing. No answer, no bloody neural sensory receptor cap.

Alexander was nearly waist-deep in the water, wading farther out and spinning around to try and glimpse it in the sea, at its bottom—anywhere it might have gone in the return and subsequent crash.

But the truth of it began to crash within, even as waves crashed against his chest with furious intervention.

It was lost at sea.

He had lost it to the sea when he couldn't keep his sorry excuse for an Order Master upright after they'd made the jump. And why the heck did he allow them to jump back into the sea in the first place? Oh, right, because he had the bright idea to hide their belts in the most obvious place imaginable so some drunkard could find them and dangle them in their faces before being cold-cocked by an ultramodern She-Ra, all the while they had not a bloomin' clue where they should jump back to because he didn't mark their point of entry.

His body began convulsing under the weight of the moment now, and throat constricting with dread under the emotion of it all. Then his eyes began flooding, and he thought he would double over right then and there, finally succumbing to the clutches of Poseidon—this time with abandon for having given up the will to keep going in this useless fight to keep the faith alive.

Somehow, his legs carried him back to shore, and his body kept him from toppling over. Perhaps it was Rebekah still standing and waiting for him, shoulders slumped and arms at her side, calling out to him to take care, her own eyes puffy with the same emotion and bearing a look that told him that it would be alright.

If only.

Each step was like bearing the leaden weight of a magnacraft. Yet he persisted, trudging back to shore and burning up now from the wicked sun and exhausting pursuit.

Please, Lord...Could you just throw us—

And then he saw it. The closer he reached the white sand, the clearer it became.

Black and flat and shimmering a faint reflection through a tangled web of seaweed at the edge of the shoreline.

A wave crashed into it, threatening to take it back down into the abyss. But it held firm.

For now.

Alexander's face grew wide with hope and he let out a yelping scream, wild arms pointing toward the object and startling Rebekah with his theatrics.

He lunged forward through the water, carrying his legs high with a sort of ecstatic dance to hoist himself out from the tow still snatching at his ankles underneath the water. He made quick work of it, reaching the wet sand and sinking deep as the waves carried it along.

Then he tripped over his feet and landed face-first, the sand's hot powder getting up his nose and in his mouth.

Alexander gave a cry and spat with irritation, but he pressed forward, every muscle screaming for relief. But every ounce of his being not willing to let their lifeline to the Church's past get swept away.

And he succeeded.

Flopping hard over the tangled mess of sea life and technowizardy, Alexander scooped up the pile and held it close to his chest. Relief flooded him even as another wave crashed into him, spraying his face with fishy salt water and nearly sending him into another choking fit.

Rebekah was at his side now, helping him back to the shore into dryer ground.

Reaching it, he brought out the package and untangled the mess, picking out the weeds and a dead, half-eaten fish but confirming—oh, blessedly confirming!—they'd retrieved the neural device.

No, the *Lord* did, answering his prayer and providing for his people a lifeline to their faith.

Crawling farther ashore, Alexander flopped to his back, grinning widely and hugging the black cap to his chest. A drunken giggle escaped with the joy and relief he felt at the cap's recovery, almost the same elation when he and Ford were presented with the Holy Shroud, as if the cap were a sacred object.

Which it was, given the memory of Ignatius's words from the past.

Rebekah slumped to the sand at his side now. She squeezed his shoulder and smiled.

He nodded and eased himself up, grabbing the neural cap in one hand and holding it up as a trophy.

Able to take deep breaths, now that he and their prized possession were safe, Alexander heaved the humid air tinged with aloe and fish and fried food and curiously exhaust—which was odd, since most combustible engines had been banned by the Republic post-Reckoning. He glanced up the beach, then back toward the sea. He spotted a fishing boat gleaming in the distance, a trail of seawater arcing out its back from hoovering up what lived within.

His mind instantly jumped to that fateful day when the Solterra Tracker drone had buzzed around his parish church, right before he went home and saw the news of Panligo's formation and Sasha's discoveries, which was right before Zakaria told him Tara Rodriguez had stolen herself into his study bearing the message from Father Jim asking him to come to Nicaea for the conclave, which is when everything went to Hades.

And now look at things...

Zakaria was dead, along with his parish. Tara had been a double agent all along, working for Panligo and the Republic and apparently Nous, some ancient nemesis of Ichthus stretching back to the Church's founding. He himself survived jumping phases back to the past—not once but three times, retrieving the audio and visual inspiration of the Church's once-for-all faith. And then he was crowned Master of an ancient religious order that had petered out to a remnant, the Order of Thaddeus. All so that the Remnant of Christianity itself, Ichthus, could survive under siege from multiple fronts, both inside and outside the Church.

He just hoped it worked, that what he and Rebekah and Ford before her had brought back from their visits to the past wasn't for naught. Because he didn't know how much more he could take. They needed to start putting the fruits of their labor to work. And pronto.

Alexander sighed and stood, then reached out his hand. "Come on. We should get back to the beach shack and check in with Father Jim. I'm sure they're worried sick about us."

Rebekah smiled and took it to stand. "I'm sure they are. I just hope everything is alright from their end. Because our misadventure from the past doesn't bode well for the future."

He said nothing, trudging through the stinging hot sand in silence, hands behind his back and a worm of worry souring his stomach with anxious dread, giving him a dreadful headache that made him thirst for one of his narcowafers.

Lord Jesus Christ, Son of God, by your grace and mercy may our friends with the Ministerium be safe...

CHAPTER 11
NICAEA, ARABIA-PERSIA.

THE CORRIDOR underneath the ancient city of Nicaea seemed to stretch on for ages, the only soundtrack for their journey the shuffle of feet and an occasional cough. Importantly, no banging from behind or echoes of July Fourth or blasts from no Neutralizer.

Ford thanked the good Lord above for that!

Just one long, boring tunnel of drab concrete, walls close and ceiling closer, all seeming to press in against them with suffocating indifference. Dim LED lighting was enough to get by. But throwing up shadows across the walls and floor that conjured devilish images was a cruel way to go about escaping the clutches of the incarnation of the Devil himself.

Went on and on like that with no end in sight. On the plus side, it was clean. So at least they had that going for them. And rat free. That Ford knew of.

The thought made his skin crawl with a shiver that ratcheted up his spine and spread across his limbs. He knew why. Felt embarrassed by it, too, given his past.

Back during Civil War II in the Americas, a depression hit all of Noramericana that would have given John Steinbeck a run for his novel-writing money. Put *Grapes of Wrath* to shame, it did. While Pops was off fighting for God knew what, family was so poor they didn't have a pot to piss in, much less food to eat. Sure, they had peanuts just waitin' to be harvested. But the continent didn't have much of an appetite for their crop, and man cannot live by peanuts alone.

Except the rats. Big, fat four-legged abominations straight out of one of Dante's circles of hell. They'd stripped their fields clean like a locust cloud. Which bankrupted the household and left it high and dry.

The Ford clan themselves pert near starved to death had Mama neither the wits nor the shots of Daniel Boone, that fabled folk-hero pioneer who settled much of his homeland. Seeing those devilish fiends that'd stripped them of their livelihood and dignity gave her an idea: looked to be the perfect meal for breakfast (sausage links), lunch (stew), and dinner (more stew and kabobs and steaks).

Perfect payback as far as teenage Ford was concerned. And the rumors were right: tasted like chicken. The brown, gristly meat, not the white stuff. But they'd survived. Gave him nightmares for months. Not only because they were big and hairy and screeched something fierce in the darkness. But also because of the damage their kinfolks did to their farm and the fill he'd had off their carcasses. He'd be quite content to never see another living rat-soul as long as he lived.

The hordes of Enforcers and Purifiers and Augers barreling toward them, Neutralizers locked and loaded, was enough. Add rats to the mix and he was liable for the Grip to have his way good, launching him into a full-on PTSD meltdown.

So, again, no rats. At least they had that going for them.

Father Jim cried out several paces ahead, snapping Ford back to the moment.

He raced to his side as Lucy righted him from taking a tumble.

"I'm fine, Ms. Jane," the cardinal said, voice laced with irritation. "No need to make a fuss. Just some bumps and bruises, that is all."

"Sir, you're bleedin'," she said, bringing a hand up to his forehead dripping with blood again, his wound from earlier having reopened.

"I've survived worse."

Padre hobbled forward. Jin came up to his side and wrapped an arm around his shoulder to help him forward.

"How much longer you figure we got, Padre?" Ford asked, glancing behind them with no chance of sighting the door and little worry they were being followed. Could never be too careful, though. Not with Purifiers on their tails.

"Haven't a clue. I do know that the Ministerium architects had in mind an escape that would lead survivors well out of range of any danger. And there were rumors of ample provisions for the continued journey at the end of the road. But, again, haven't a clue of those either."

"Sounds like the Ministerium thought of everything."

"Indeed."

"Guys, I think I am seeing something!" Sasha exclaimed. "Look!"

Through the dim distance, a door appeared. Narrow, itty-bitty thing of the same reinforced steel as back at HQ—or what was left of it.

Hope rippled through the group with excited shouts of thanksgiving.

Ford rushed forward and confirmed it. They'd made it. And best of all, the door was properly secured on the *other* side. Which meant no crazy doodads to offer codes and handprints or to tear apart and jury-rig with desperation.

He glanced behind, offering a grin and a nod to the crew. Then went to open the door—

But hesitated.

He took a breath and wiggled his fingers, anticipation pulling him forward but caution repelling him from inaction.

"John Mark, I'm not getting any older here," Father Jim complained. "And last I remember, the Republic had climbed the ramparts and overtaken the bloody castle!"

Ford frowned. "I know, it's just..."

"It is just being what?" asked Sasha.

He turned to him and the others. "That it's this point in the plot when either the goons come blasting their way from behind or some monster is waiting for us on the other side. Skittish, is all."

Lucy rolled her eyes and huffed.

Ford furrowed his brow at her as she shoved forward toward the door.

Then she twisted the handle and shoved through.

He gave a startled yelp, but there was no going back.

And there was nothing to worry about.

Greeting them was a single room, about half the size of the Archives with a low ceiling made of the same dull, drab concrete lit by a string of LEDs around the perimeter. A single sapphire display was anchored to one wall, with a desk underneath and a workstation on top connected to the wall with a series of snaking cables. On the opposite side, the wall was arrayed with rifles standing on edge in a neat row with boxes of ammo on shelves underneath. Next to those were more shelves with dried food and cases of water. Another door anchored the opposite side with a big, fat question mark blaring back as to where it led.

But importantly: no rats.

Ford whistled. "Now this here is legit provisions that would make any doomsday prepper nod with approval."

"The Ministerium is a resourceful bunch when it needs to

be," Father Jim said as the others quickly filed inside. Carefully setting the Shroud on the desk, he turned around and closed the door. It sealed with an audible *shi-chu* and a grinding of locks inside the wall.

Ford spun around, eyes wide with panic. He raced over to the door and yanked on it.

Didn't budge a millimeter.

Suddenly, a deep, guttural rumbling sounded from the other side of the door, the ground beneath them shaking for several seconds.

"What the..." Ford said.

"More from the Republic?" asked Lucy.

"The destructive measures I spoke of earlier, I'd wager," Father Jim said.

Then it was over, as quickly as it had begun.

"I guess that seals the deal, don't it," Ford mumbled.

"Literally," Lucy said.

"A final security measure," Father Jim explained, "to keep the Barbarians from reaching the last of the Ministerium officers fleeing for their lives."

"Which I guess makes us the last of the Ministerium officers, then," Ford said. "And it also means we're stuck."

Father Jim glanced at him, face falling with the truth of it all.

"What is this place being?" asked Sasha.

The cardinal said, "The room of last resort. With provisions to get us through to the next leg of our adventure."

"Which is being where, exactly?"

"And what the hot Hades is beyond this here other door," Ford said, walking up to it and eyeing it suspiciously.

Father Jim shook his head. "Haven't a clue."

Ford pressed his ear against it, hearing what sounded like the faint sound of crashing waves.

He stepped back, brow furrowed. "What the..."

Only one way to find out...

He grabbed the handle and yanked it open, revealing another corridor wholly unlike the other.

Dull, drab concrete was replaced by brilliant azure and turquoise, light from above undulating inside through clear, curved plates of glass. Twenty meters out sat another steel airlock door.

And something beyond it he never expected to find in a million years.

"A yellow submarine?" he exclaimed with dumbfounded disbelief.

Father Jim shrugged. "As I said, John Mark. Provisions."

"I feel a song coming on."

"Should be large enough to accommodate our escape, blending in with the other personal submergence vehicles that have taken over the seas the past few decades under the auspices of Solterra Earth Oceanic Organization."

Ford went to respond when his mobile device purred and vibrated for attention inside his pocket.

He took it out. Then smiled when he saw who was calling.

Alexander Zarruq.

His smile turned into a wide, relieved grin when he spotted his old time-travel buddy on the face of his mobile device.

About time, homefry...

He spun his mobile device around and flashed it to his companions. "Looks like our boy and girl made it back to the future, safe and sound."

Elation erupted from the other four. Jin high-fived Sasha, Lucy hugged Father Jim.

Ford answered the call on speaker, bringing an image of Alexander to the surface.

"Glad to see you made it back to the future, homefry!" he

said with a chuckle, surprised at a sudden rise of emotion at seeing the man.

Was never one to get sentimental, especially with people. Sort of the lone ranger type. But with Alexander, and Lucy and Father Jim and Sasha and Jin, it was different. They had become true friends over the past several weeks. And actually more than that: family.

"Glad to be back," Alexander said, sounding exhausted and exasperated, in a way Ford hadn't remembered hearing from him before. Although, he understood why, given what they had been through. Not sure he'd have fared all that better after getting stuck in a holding pattern back in the past—and almost permanently.

Father Jim leaned in. "And Rebekah is there with you, safe and sound?"

Alexander nodded and gestured off screen. Rebekah popped into view and waved. "Hello, Father Jim. Hey there, John Mark."

"So you are making it back alright?" Sasha said, coming around Father Jim's side for his own look-see. "All of your parts are still being in place and all?"

The two on the other line chuckled.

"We came back in one piece," Alexander offered. "Barely..." He turned to Rebekah and offered a weak grin. "Nearly drowned, had it not been for Rebekah here, among other things."

"What?" Father Jim exclaimed.

"The travelogue can wait. What we want to know is, what the blazes happened?"

Ford glanced at Father Jim, who nodded for him to share the sordid tale.

He did, leaving no stone unturned in the details

surrounding the assault by the Republic; the invasion by Enforcers, Purifiers, and Augers; their harrowing escape.

Sasha added the technical bits about how he figured the signal from DiviNet through the wormhole created by the time travel belts was interrupted when they had to bail. Thought it was an interesting point of scientific discovery he hadn't factored in before, and one he'd have to follow up on.

"That certainly explains things from our end," Alexander said. "As you can imagine, it gave us quite a fright, the thought of being stuck back in the past and all."

"Yeah, I am being sorry about that," Sasha said, rubbing the back of his neck. "There was being a part of me that was thinking that maybe it could happen on the off chance the signal was disrupted. But I was never planning that something like this was going to be happening."

"Now what about your own adventure?" Father Jim interjected. "Did you find Ignatius? Was he able to offer a word of encouragement?"

Alexander nodded. "We did. And he did. Looks like it recorded just fine, too."

"Brilliant! There's certainly a silver lining in all of these dark, foreboding clouds after all. Other than the mishap with the time travel devices, I trust everything else went smoothly."

The two on the face of the device could be seen glancing at one another knowingly.

"For the most part," Alexander said simply. "We had to improvise, but we made it. That's all that matters. And with the goods recorded by the neural sensory receptor. Safe and sound." Again, that knowing look.

"*Otlichnyy!*" Sasha said. "I am eager to be getting my hands upon the device again and seeing what you were being able to bring back to us."

"Speaking of which. Where are you? And where's our rendezvous point if the Ministerium has been shuttered?"

Ford shook his head. "Good question. As of now, we're a klick underground and on the edge of the continent staring down the barrel of the Great Sea. But, hey, at least we've got a nifty submarine out of the deal."

"A submarine?"

"Apparently the Ministerium's got resources. At least, it had resources. Anyway, you got any insight into next steps, Padre?"

Father Jim pulled out a chair from behind the desk and slumped into it, rubbing his head and sighing. "Haven't a clue. I dare say we should make our way into the submergence vehicle docked on the other side of that door, but I'm sure none of us know how to operate it."

Ford smirked. "Yeah, let's hope our Ministerium benefactors provided an operating manual. Or the five of us are gonna get close right quick with these quarters."

"Indeed. Prudence would dictate secreting away under the Mediterranean's coverage to regroup with our surviving brethren and sistren. However, we're flying completely blind here. We haven't a clue what is transpiring up above. The entire world could be on fire for all we know, set ablaze by the Republic. The whore of Babylon could be swallowing the Church whole and we wouldn't know it!"

The man shuddered and shook his head, emotion brimming at his eyes now, the events clearly catching up to him.

"Perhaps this will be helping us understand." Sasha turned on the sapphire display anchored to the wall above the desk.

The broadcaster flickered to life. Making them instantly regret the decision; ignorance really was bliss.

Max Bacchus, in all of his chipper glory, the stage name for the face of OneWorld News a throwback to the Roman god of entertainment, was chatting away, face drawn and serious.

Part carnival barker, part ringmaster, the man attracted the attention of the masses around the world to breaking news throughout the Republic while moderating that news. Since Solterra operated the only source of news—'For Humanity!' of course—he was more a propaganda maestro than anything resembling a news anchor.

The man played the part well, with his bleach-white teeth and perfectly coiffed hair dyed various shades of purple or blue or red, with those outrageously stylish getups he wore while holding his hallmark ivory walking cane tipped in gold and capped with an onyx knob.

And there he was, hair airbrushed a macabre bloody crimson, eyelids accented a similar shade, and wearing a black coat sequenced with complementary bloody crimson accenting.

Continuing to babble away with that face drawn into an emotive, dramatic pose, he clutched his chest then leaned forward and shook his finger at the screen.

Without even the sound on, they all knew what the man was reporting on.

And it was not good. The chyron said it all.

Radical Ichthusan Terrorists Defeated in Daytime Raid For Humanity!

Ford's mouth went dry, his bowels went weak. "The worm has turned, folks."

CHAPTER 12

"Turn it up, would ya?" Ford commanded, setting his phone on the desk to give Alexander and Rebekah a listen and moving closer to the broadcaster, his heart sinking with dread. Sasha obliged.

"...fought valiantly to uncover a nest of terrorists bent on the Republic's destruction!" Max reported. "That is right. I am afraid to report the Legion had identified a cell of religious radicals bent on defying the blessed wisdom and bountiful hand of the Regis, our Patron."

The man paused, closing his eyes and sucking in a stabilizing breath. More for dramatic effect than anything. And then he let loose: "*Unfits*, they were!"

The word exploded with dreadful meaning in the center of the room, even as it ricocheted across DiviNet from the mouth of official Solterra propaganda.

Ford sucked in a frightful breath at that freighted word.

The Ministerium, the governing body of Ichthus, last remnant of Christianity—the Church of Jesus Christ itself!—had just been declared to be terrorists, religious radicals.

Unfits...

Max bowed his head and took a deep breath. "Yes, it is true.

Some may have known these religious radicals as Ichthus, as *Christians*. Some might be your neighbors even, your children's playmates or co-workers. Unfortunately, there is a radical, rabid, reactionary nature to them that simply can no longer be tolerated."

Lucy smirked. "Can the man get any more alliterative?"

"This is no laughing matter, sassafras..." Ford said lowly, eyes transfixed on the Republic's crimson-haired mouthpiece.

She reddened and folded her arms, saying nothing as the man on the broadcaster continued.

"Purely in the interest of the Republic's peace, prosperity, and progress, our valiant Enforcers, in broad daylight for all to see—"

"That's a bunch of bullpucky!" Ford exclaimed. "It was the dead of night, moron!"

"—came to execute a duly authorized warrant for the arrest of said radicals, with the intent to try and convict under the auspices of the full-weight of Solterran law. Yet, the leaders of this radical group resisted."

"Resisted my ass! You—"

"John Mark, please..." Father Jim tsked.

Ford held his breath and nodded, heat creeping up the back of his neck at both his outburst and the blatant mischaracterization of what had happened back at Ministerium HQ. Well, former headquarters.

His stomach clenched with the realization, and he crossed himself for the dead who had given their lives for the sake of the Church's survival.

Max continued, "Even after all the merciful extensions and accommodations our valiant Enforcers offered, yet they resisted. To the point of slaughtering our beloved commander without mercy, on top of our brave boys simply seeking to keep the peace, prosperity, and progress of our beloved Republic."

"What's he gettin' on about?" asked Lucy.

Ford shook his head. "Who knows. I sure ain't responsible for slaughtering no Republic commander without mercy. Believe me, I'da known about it. And so would they."

"More propaganda, I would imagine," Father Jim said.

He turned to him and nodded.

Max sat up straight, smoothing his hair at the sides with both hands and fussing with the top before smoothing the lapels of his jacket.

"Which is why our benevolent Patron," the propaganda maestro said, "the Regis of our beloved Republic, is right now meeting with his cabinet officials in Capitolium before later addressing the full Senate with plans for addressing this rising menace across Solterra."

He leaned forward, twisting his head slightly but eyeing the audience beyond, one end of his mouth curling upward slightly, as if he were letting Solterra in on a secret.

"Now, I cannot get into specifics," he went on, leaning back and shaking a finger. "But mark my words, this menace will be dealt with—'For Humanity!'"

He saluted the camera before it dimmed to white, a powder-blue logo of the Pangea supercontinent spinning within olive branches.

The room stood and sat in stunned silence at the turn. Whatever it was.

"What just happened?" Lucy said, turning first to Ford before glancing to Father Jim.

"I dare say," the cardinal said, intercepting Ford's own reply, "that the Republic has thrown down the gauntlet."

"To the Ministerium?"

"No..." Ford said, face drained of color and stomach twisting with dread at what he knew was coming.

She furrowed her brow. "Then what?"

He waited a beat, taking in a stabilizing breath to see if Father Jim would answer. He didn't. Which either meant he wasn't quite sure himself or he didn't want to give voice to the truth of the matter.

So Ford did it for him.

He pressed a hand to the back of his neck, surprised at how warm it was. And now that he thought about it, he did feel achy.

Whatever. Focus, John Mark.

He rubbed it and sighed, then got on with it: "The gauntlet, so to speak, has been thrown down to Ichthus. The Church."

"The Church?" exclaimed Alexander from the face of the phone from over at the desk.

Ford forgot the other two were still on the line. He walked to it and picked it up. "That's right, partner. The Church."

"That seems extreme."

"It is."

"How can we be certain?" Lucy said.

Ford replied, "Because of the word our resident propagandist used, that Max Bacchus character."

"Terrorist?"

He shook his head.

"Religious radical?" Sasha added.

"Not that one either," Ford said. "Unfit."

"So we're the detritus of the Republic," Alexander said "What of it?"

Ford threw his head back and chuckled. "Detritus of the Republic. I like that. But that's far from what an Unfit is."

"I suppose you would know, being that you were a Purifier."

It was Rebekah. He'd forgotten she was on the other end as well.

His face fell, the truth of his past rushing to the fore,

memories of his duties as the Canceller in Chief flashing in rapid succession. The disabled, the too-old, certain religious sects like the Israelites—even the Resistance with Ichthus itself.

He clenched his jaw and cleared his throat. "As I was saying, getting declared an Unfit means you're *persona non grata.*"

"Meaning, what exactly?" asked Lucy.

"It means you've been given a death sentence with neither recourse nor relief," Father Jim said lowly, having slumped back into his chair.

Ford nodded. "The cardinal is right. According to Solterra's mouthpiece, we're dead to the Republic. The Ministerium, Ichthus—"

"The Church...."

"Which means what, for the rest of Ichthus beyond this holding room?" asked Lucy. "Not just the Ministerium, but the Remnant that's still out there resisting Panligo and the Republic?"

Father Jim said nothing, his face falling further and whitening with misting eyes.

"Like I said, the worm has turned," Ford offered, "Time will tell, but if what Max Bacchus said is true, that the official policy of the Republic is declaring Ichthus, the Church, individual believers Unfits...well, then, there's a whole world of hurt coming their way."

"*Our* way," Father Jim corrected. "Because this turn of events is our fight now."

The revelation sat in the center of the room like the exploded Queller ordinances that leveled the Ministerium building itself above. Silence permeated the space as its fallout, indecision and confusion and shock at the blow Ichthus had been dealt.

This was the Church's new reality. Ichthus had been declared an enemy of the Republic.

Finally, Alexander spoke up: "Then what do we do about it? Where do we go from here—literally, as we're still holed up in a beach shack that's seen better centuries?"

Ford shifted and rubbed his chin. "Good question, partner. But our lot in life ain't much better. We're holed up in a shack all our own under kilo-tons of rock with a mile-long concrete walk-of-doom on one end and a little submarine on the other without a whole lot in between."

"All I am knowing," Sasha said, shaking his head, "is that I was not at all signing up to this nonsense when I agreed to be helping you travel back in time!"

He huffed and hung his head, then mumbled something under his breath in a foreign tongue that sounded like a string of cuss words.

Ford chuckled. "None of us did, partner. Yet, here we are."

"Again, what are we going to do about it?" said Alexander from the other end of the phone.

"Fight, damn it." It was Father Jim this time, letting his tongue get the better of him by violating his own non-Legion-potty-mouth policy.

He neither apologized (which Ford found amusing but couldn't care less) nor elaborated (which Ford found concerning). How the heck were they, the last remaining Ministerium members, going to take on Solterra? How the heck was the rest of Ichthus across the Republic going to take on the world-wide governing body?

"With what, spit and toothpicks?" Lucy said.

The cardinal raised his head and frowned.

She shifted but held his glare. "No offense, Father Jim, but how is it that we can have any hope of giving any sort of practical resistance to the Republic? We're—" She paused to take count of the room, adding: "—seven strong. With a rack of weapons, sure, but that ain't gonna cut it. Sorry."

"Ahh, but that is where you're wrong!" Father Jim said, popping up to his feet with newfound life. "*'This is the word of the Lord to Zerubbabel,'* the prophet Zechariah said in the Holy Scriptures, *'Not by might nor by power, but by my Spirit, says the Lord Almighty.'*"

Ford snorted and shook his head with a laugh. Then instantly regretted it.

The cardinal fixed him with a glare that would melt the paint off a magnacraft in an instant. "Something you want to add, John Mark?"

He cleared his throat. "Sorry, sir. No sir—well, yes, there is. That's a nice Hallmark card little ditty you got there—"

Father Jim gasped. "Hallmark card little dit...That's the Word of God you're talking about, John Mark!"

Ford hung his head. "Duly noted and, don't get me wrong, respected. But I've got practical considerations like Lucy. Spit and toothpicks sounds about right when it comes to confrontin' Solterra."

"And yet, what does our Lord remind us? Not only does he say, *'Blessed are you when people insult you, persecute you and falsely say all kinds of evil against you because of me. Rejoice and be glad, because great is your reward in heaven, for in the same way they persecuted the prophets who were before you.'* That is exhortation enough from Matthew's Gospel!"

Father Jim took his seat again, as if gearing up for the home-stretch of his sermonette. Ford was worried what he was about to bring.

"But don't forget what Jesus also said, as the Apostle Luke wrote in his own Gospel: *'When you are brought before synagogues, rulers and authorities, do not worry about how you will defend yourselves or what you will say, for the Holy Spirit will teach you at that time what you should say.'"*

"Yeah, but this ain't no synagogue!" Ford said. "This is Solterra Republic. And let me tell you what: You ain't wanna be labeled no Unfit. Because that there is a sure ticket for a reprogramming camp!"

"My point is," Father Jim clarified, "that none of us should be surprised by this. After all, this is how it will be in the last days before the coming reign of Christ. Let us just remember Christ's other words Luke recorded: *'I tell you, whoever publicly acknowledges me before others, the Son of Man will also acknowledge before the angels of God. But whoever disowns me before others will be disowned before the angels of God.'"*

"Sort of like what the Apostle John told me," Alexander piped in from the mobile device. "What he said when this whole blasted thing started weeks ago."

"And what was that, Alex?"

"That the one who perseveres, who is victorious through it all, will receive the crown of life. Seems like we're about to get a hot and heavy dose of the sort of persecution Jesus was envisioning."

"Indeed," Father Jim said gravely.

The room went quiet again, the true gravity of the shift settling in.

"Alright," Ford piped in, "but the original question remains, the one Alexander asked: What do we do about it? You said 'Fight damn it!' Your words, not mine, Padre."

"I said that, really?" Father Jim exclaimed. "Echoing your Legion's mouth?"

He frowned, but let it go. "At any rate, my point is that you say we should fight, press on and continue the mission to preserve, fight for, protect, *et cetera, et cetera.*"

"Indeed!"

"Fine, but how?"

"By doing what we've been doing, and what we've left unfinished. Because mark my words, brothers and sisters in the faith, the work of the gospel continues until the return of Christ. Regardless of whether we're so-called Unfits or bound by chains or being torn asunder, limb from limb!"

A shiver ratcheted up Ford's spine. For he knew it was far worse than that if the Republic got hold of ya.

"It's like Saint Paul said in his letter to the Philippians," Rebekah said, now chiming in from the mobile device. "*Now I want you to know, brothers and sisters, that what has happened to me has actually served to advance the gospel. As a result, it has become clear throughout the whole palace guard and to everyone else that I am in chains for Christ. And because of my chains, most of the brothers and sisters have become confident in the Lord and dare all the more to proclaim the gospel without fear.*' His chains, his persecution was actually the mode through which the Lord advanced the gospel, shared his story of rescue and recreation with the world."

"Yes, that is exactly right!" Father Jim exclaimed. "And spoken like a true preacher, Sister Rebekah!"

Ford rolled his eyes, becoming impatient with inactivity. "Again, granted. But what are we going to do, Padre?"

The cardinal motioned toward the rolled-up burial linen still resting unassumingly on the desk. "First, we are going to locate the Order of Thaddeus remnant Brother Theophilus so kindly directed us to. That was the next order of Ministerium business before the Solterra Legion surreptitiously interrupted us. The Order has always existed for such a time as this. And actually, precisely for such a time as this. To preserve, protect, steward, and fight for the once-for-all faith entrusted to the Church—from threats within and without."

"Using the yellow submarine?"

"What else?"

Ford raked a hand across his close-cropped hair, not liking the idea one bit diving under the black lagoon of the Mediterranean without nary a plan for next steps and contingencies and all of the other things one pieces together before a mission.

Let go and let God, I guess.

Boy, did he hate that magnacraft bumper sticker.

He glanced at Lucy and nodded. "Alright, chief. We'll saddle up. But you mentioned a first. What's the second?"

Father Jim opened his mouth to answer but hesitated. Taking a breath, he turned toward the phone and said, "For that we'll need the help of Alex and Rebekah."

The room turned toward the mobile device. The device remained silent.

Until a voice, low and restrained, broke through.

"I dare hope you are not asking what I think you are asking of us, Padre..." Alexander said.

Father Jim replied, "Now, Alex. You know good and well what we are up—"

Then the mobile exploded with interrupting, unrestrained opposition.

"You have got to be kidding, Padre!" Alexander exclaimed. "We barely jumped our asses across past phases back to the future, nearly getting outed by some drunkard after he found our time travel belts and had a run in with the bloke—And now you want us to go back to the past?"

The boy's anger surprised Ford. T'was to be expected, he reckoned, given all they'd been through. He'd probably be more apoplectic if Padre asked him to jump phases with him.

Rebekah said something to Alex on the other end of the device that seemed to calm things. Back in the panic room, things were a wee bit uncomfortable.

Then she came on the line. "What is it you're asking of us, Father Jim?"

He closed his eyes and sighed. "Don't mistake my asking for your help as indifference to or an unawareness of your situation, you two. I am fully aware, and if there were any other way—"

"Padre," Alexander interrupted, "where are you sending us?"

Father Jim sighed again, then got to it: "I dare say we are looking down the barrel of a wave of persecution that will end in a level of martyrdom the Church has not seen in generations. Even with all of the opposition from the progressive Solterran culture and other nation-states and secularism from decades past, this latest maneuver by the Republic will change that."

"No doubt," Ford said. "So who we gonna call to lend a helping hand."

"Well, the first absolutely verifiable eyewitness account of early Christian martyrdom was the death of Polycarp, the bishop of Smyrna."

"Wait, we've just come from there," Alexander said.

"Indeed. Polycarp's martyrdom followed Ignatius's by nearly half a century, around AD 155 at the age of eighty-six. Like Ignatius, he was a disciple of John the Apostle, who probably personally appointed him bishop of the Roman province."

Ford asked, "So why this early Church father? Why Polycarp?"

"An account of his martyrdom, aptly titled *The Epistle Concerning the Martyrdom of Polycarp*, primarily depicts him as a sort of kindly, saintly old man. However, he was also a fierce guardian of orthodoxy. Told the heretic Marcion that he was '*the firstborn of Satan*' to his face, he did, for denying that the Old Testament is Scripture."

"Fascinating..." Alexander said, sounding as if he was warming to the cardinal's time travel plan.

"Sounds like quite the character," Ford said.

Father Jim replied, "If you think that's fascinating, Polycarp's death is a captivating account of his uncompromising adherence to the historic Christian faith. The church at Smyrna wrote about this account to a neighboring church as an encouragement during times of intense apostasy and persecution by antichrists in their day."

"Sounds right up our alley."

"Which is why I believe the future Church would benefit from this account of his witness and faithfulness to Christ. As much as it pains me to send you two back. And it does, believe me."

"I understand, Padre," Alexander said. "So what is that account, of his martyrdom? What are we getting ourselves into?"

"His martyr's story," Father Jim explained, "begins amid a violent persecution of the Smyrnean church. Polycarp's friends begged him to leave the region, but he refused. Instead of fleeing, he remained stubbornly, faithfully fixed inside a country house not far from the city and praying for the Church. Soon, the Empire came for the bishop after torturing a houseboy to learn of the man's whereabouts. When they arrived, the old man came downstairs and ordered that his captors be given food and drink. All he asked in return was for an hour of prayer to prepare for his prophesied demise. He ended up praying out loud for two hours and all were struck with awe and regret. Finally, the bishop was placed on top of a donkey and marched into the city, where he was persuaded to renounce his faith. 'Come now,' some men pleaded, 'where is the harm in just saying Caesar is Lord, and offering the incense, and so forth, when it will save your life?'"

"What is that about?" asked Alexander.

"The imperial cult of emperor worship. Was a central component of life in the Empire, and one that became grounds for the imperial pogrom of Christian persecution when believers refused to worship Caesar as Lord, instead insisting that Jesus is Lord and worshiping only him as such."

Shifting in his chair and drawing closer to the mobile device, Father Jim continued, "At any rate, their pleas for him to worship the Emperor fell on deaf ears, and eventually Polycarp was led into the town arena. There, a deafening cry for his blood arose. He was brought before the governor, who also urged Polycarp to recant. But Polycarp would not relent."

"Ballsy," Ford said. "Have to give the man that. And sounds just what the doc ordered."

Father Jim furrowed his brow. "Yes, well, I agree with you there. That he and his story is just what the Church needs during these perilous times."

The room fell silent again. More importantly, so did the mobile device. Half expected Alex to hang up and close up shop, go dark and go home. Or what was left of it. Wouldn't blame him.

But Alexander did what Ford knew the man would do. What he was made to do.

"Alright, Padre. We'll go. And that's only because Rebekah reminded me of another passage of Scripture that seems appropriate for our journey. Yours and ours."

Father Jim sighed, as if he were literally holding his breath until Alexander gave the green-light, thumbs-up signal he was a go.

He said, "And what's that, my boy?"

"From the Book of Acts, chapter 20, when Paul is leaving Ephesus for Jerusalem, and the Holy Spirit compelled him to go even though he didn't know what would happen to him there. The only thing he knew for sure was that in every city the Holy Spirit warned him that he was facing prison and hardships. Yet his answer was this: '*I consider my life worth nothing to me; my only aim is to finish the race and complete the task the Lord Jesus has given me—the task of testifying to the good news of God's grace.*'"

Alexander paused, perhaps collecting his thoughts, perhaps collecting himself after those weighty words.

Wouldn't have put it that way himself, but Ford got what he was driving at. Gave him a heart check himself after feeling leery about jumping headlong down the rabbit hole in the yellow submarine docked a few meters away.

"So we go," Rebekah added this time, "Alexander and I, we both go compelled by the Holy Spirit to inspire our fellow brothers and sisters in the faith, to further the gospel of our Lord."

Father Jim wiped his eyes and nose on his sleeve and gave a sniff of emotion. "Thank you, my children. Thank you for your faithfulness, your sacrifice."

"You just better be able to get us there and back, Sasha," Alexander said.

"I am already being on it, *bratishka*," Sasha replied, workstation laptop open and shuffling over to the one sitting on the desk.

He set it down and Father Jim stood for the man to sit and work his magic. The prof craned his head around the existing device and grinned when he found what he was looking for.

Yanking a cable from the other computer, he plugged it into his laptop. "There we go. Now we are accessing the same network trunk as before inside the now-demolished Ministerium."

He clacked away. Then he stopped, his face falling and his hand moving to his mouth.

"Uh, oh..."

Ford frowned. "You've really got to stop doing that, doc. What now? No way for our boy and girl to jump phases?"

"*Nyet.* It is not being that." He turned to Ford, then to Father Jim.

"Apparently, we were not the only ones who were being hit by Enforcers."

CHAPTER 13

ALEXANDRIA, KEMETIA.

A WICKED WIND whipped across the maw still sizzling with the smoldering remains of the den belonging to those religious radicals who threatened all that Solterra held dear—all that *humanity* held dear—sending sparks sailing high into the dusking sky and smoke swirling with discontent until a revelry of flaming tendrils reached back up from dormancy and activated with menacing intent.

Just as the man whom that bloody fool from the Ministerium called Colonel Sanders wanted it.

The man smiled at the characterization, being likened to the founder of that Noramericana chicken franchise littering the Republic, peddling its genetically modified, factory grown chicken-like food fare. Thought it an appropriate, if not pedestrian, comparison, given his white goatee and accompanying white mustache curled at both ends. His bronzed face probably looked like a white man tanned to Noramericanan perfection, rather than the olive complexion of his Tripolitanian ancestors.

But no matter. The rapscallion was probably smoldering in his own ruins underneath the soil that had forged his former faith, the Ministerium having finally met its match and force fed its just deserts where it all began in the soil of Nicaea.

The man stood tall as the chaos swirled around him, the hovering magnacraft and aircraft, lights blaring blue and white, still zooming in to contain the blaze from engulfing the surrounding town of ultramodern sophistication. After all, the Republic couldn't afford to lose nightclubs and high-rise apartments and tech start-ups to the Purge, as it had been dubbed at the Capitolium by those in the know.

A large Destroyer, those tank-like vehicles recommissioned by the Republic after the Reckoning to bring about Pax Solterra —a peace by might and power if need be—sat perched at the edge of the quaint cathedral's remains nestled in the heart of one of the former power centers of the early Church. A carcass looking more like the exposed ribcage of a mastodon picked clean by some prehistoric buzzard than a former place of worship still bearing witness to the faith gasping its last breath in devotion to that dead man-god playacting as humanity's savior and lord.

Which was just as he wanted it.

About time the two-thousand-year-old blight on humanity went the way of the dinosaurs, finally giving up its last dying wheeze after clinging to life the past few decades.

He crunched forward across the still-smoldering ruins of a cathedral that had been decimated in the Republic's campaign to root out the menace he himself had once been part of.

Ichthus. The Church.

The Ministerium, in fact, reaching the upper echelons of ecclesial power.

He pressed a hand against his nose as he took in the sight, shielding his senses from the fetid stench of burnt flesh rising from the burned-out husk of stone and steel stretching back hundreds of years to Christianity's glory days. When it still carried breath in its lungs, when it still dominated the continent, the world even, bearing a privileged place across Europa and the Americas, even across parts of Muscovia and Vostokana and down into the former nations that made up Alkebulana.

Not anymore.

Now, it was a shadow of its former self, an emaciated body bloating at the stomach, its ribcage jutting out like a poor, malnourished child hunched over in a starved death kneel before a vulture waiting to pick it clean of all that remained.

He was the vulture, Ichthus was the child, and soon its remains would be scattered to the four winds of Solterra, serving as a lesson to those who defied the Republic and clung to regressive superstitions, rejecting the ideologies of the Patron that led to the world's peace, prosperity, and progress.

An over-sized Enforcer magnacraft hovered past. He glimpsed through narrow windows arrayed on its charcoal side a collection of faces, men and women and even children, all bloodied and bruised searching for an out to their petrification.

The man chuckled to himself at the sight of those who had once been his brothers and sisters in the faith being carted away like the cattle that roamed the hillsides of his former home.

But then a twinge of sorrow needled him, regret even. For the scene playing out before him—with its apocalyptic blacks and grays; crimsons and burnt oranges, the decimated churches now strewn across the Republic in the Purge to rid Solterra of Christian Unfits; the men and women and children who claimed the name of the dead man from Nazareth as their Lord, their Savior—all of it reminded him of a sermon series he had preached in that cathedral perched along that bluff next to the Mediterranean in Tripolitania.

It was from the Book of Revelation, the final book in the Christian Scriptures. He closed his eyes and recalled the passage that sat at the heart of his homily from memory, two separate sections from chapter twelve:

A great sign appeared in heaven: a woman clothed with the sun, with the moon under her feet and a crown of twelve stars on her head. She was pregnant and cried out in pain as she was about to give birth. Then another sign appeared in heaven: an enormous red dragon with seven heads and ten horns and seven crowns on its heads. Its tail swept a third of the stars out of the sky and flung them to the earth. The dragon stood in front of the woman who was about to give birth, so that it might devour her child the moment he was born. She gave birth to a son, a male child, who "will rule all the nations with an iron scepter." And her child was snatched up to God and to his throne. The woman fled into the wilderness to a place prepared for her by God, where she might be taken care of for 1,260 days.

When the dragon saw that he had been hurled to the earth, he pursued the woman who had given birth to the male child. The woman was given the two wings of a great eagle, so that she might fly to the place prepared for her in the wilderness, where she would be taken care of for a time, times and half a time, out of the serpent's reach. Then from his mouth the serpent spewed water like a river, to overtake the woman and sweep her away with the torrent. But the earth helped the woman by opening its mouth and swallowing the river that the dragon had spewed out of his mouth. Then

> *the dragon was enraged at the woman and*
> *went off to wage war against the rest of her*
> *offspring—those who keep God's*
> *commands and hold fast their testimony*
> *about Jesus.*

He chuckled and shook his head at the quaint imagery that had been part and parcel of Christian apocalyptic visions stretching back to its foundation.

A few verses in the middle of the chapter identified the great dragon as *'that ancient serpent called the Devil, or Satan, who leads the whole world astray.'* Back in his parish in Tripolitania those many decades ago, he had made the point that the Devil knew its days were numbered ever since the beginning of creation, when God cursed the serpent, the Devil, and announced even from the start of human misery the proto-gospel, the promised elixir, the fix to rescue and repair what our human ancestors destroyed during their rebellious uprising in the Garden of Eden against the Authority. There, in the Book of Genesis, God announced to the Devil that Eve's *'offspring'* would *'crush your head and you will strike his heel.'*

So when the moment finally came for the Blessed Virgin to give birth to the Child, the promised Messiah, the Son of God, Satan was waiting to devour the Christ from Mary's womb.

But he failed.

And ever since that failure, even when he thought he had succeeded at the cross by devouring the Son in death, only to be denied once again his victory through Christ's resurrection, the great dragon reverted to Plan B: he *'went off to wage war against the rest of her offspring—those who keep God's commands and hold fast their testimony about Jesus.'* That is, Ichthus, the Church, the world-wide communion of believers in Jesus Christ.

Again, how quaint, that Christians from the start had a persecution complex embedded within its religion.

But also, how interesting. Because the child's fairy tale seemed to be playing out all across Solterra. The devouring of *'those who keep God's commands and hold fast their testimony about Jesus'* was indeed coming to pass.

With him at the center of it all.

But then, in the midst of the smoke swirling heavenward with the fetid, charred stench of dead saints like an incense offering; the flames still sparking and flickering to life in the wind; the screams and agonizing cries of the injured, along with those grieving beside crushed loved ones and fellow parishioners—in the midst of it all, a haunting thought struck him:

Was he the dragon?

Was he the Devil incarnate?

The antichrist, even?

A chill washed over him even as a twinge of doubt about his chosen path ratcheted throughout his head and down his spine in a shiver that sent him reaching both arms across his chest in an embrace to stave off the chill.

The humming and whirring of air from above snapped him back to the moment. An aircraft descended suddenly before coming up and landing at a rest. Doors lifted on the side and out strode the two men he had been waiting for.

Apollos Nicolai and Dominic Weiss.

Right on time.

The man smoothed down his mustache before curling the ends with vain delight. Then he strode to meet the men who would carry out the plans he had carefully laid the past several months.

A shudder ran up the man's arm as he grasped the albino's hand, feeling as milky to the touch as it looked.

Not the marriage he would have imagined a decade ago when the two served together in the Ministerium. Couldn't stand the man, and not just because of his curious features. Far too arrogant and self-assured for his liking. Although, could he really deny the same for himself, given what he had done and where he had gone with his faith?

Yet there they were, now reaching in for an embrace as if lifelong friends, brothers even. The Universe certainly had a sense of humor. Who would have thought the two would turn out to be true kindred spirits, the kind that would dismantle Ichthus, limb by limb?

Then there was the matter of Apollos, the young man with broad shoulders and a mane of gold who had been something of an up-and-comer, rising fast through Oxford before his cushy appointment in Germania. Had certainly gotten an earful of the man's exploits that made him all the more eager to come to his aid, guiding him, nurturing him, grooming him to carry on his work. Where his own son wouldn't...

Apollos reached out his hand, fixing him with those penetrating and as equally self-assured eyes as Dominic's. Like mentor, like mentee.

The man took it, giving it a firm hold before pulling back and gesturing toward the ruins.

"This way, gentlemen," the man said. "I trust your journey gave you no trouble?"

"I was bearable enough," Dominic said. "Made all the more delightful with the news coming out of Iznik, from *Nicaea*."

Weiss spat the last word with a particular amount of disdainful vinegar. Couldn't blame him. After all, he himself had renounced Nicene Christianity years ago, right before he went into hiding, biding his time and waiting for the fullness of time to strike.

He flashed the cardinal a knowing grin. "Yes, I just received the final report an hour before your arrival. Total destruction."

"Which was not the plan, my friend."

My friend...

The man clenched his jaw, face reddening at being talked to with such egalitarian disrespect. As if Dominic was an equal in this string-pulling maneuver of his.

But then he let it go, taking a breath and relaxing his jaw until the heat rising up his neck and flushing his face released.

"Yes, well, apparently the Ministerium was rigged to explode with finalizing measures. Who knew?"

"We certainly didn't," Apollos answered. "And neither did our contacts within the Ministerium."

"Which means that James Ferraro did," Dominic said, "and probably that wretched Alexander protege of his as well."

The man's breath caught in his chest at the mention of their names. But for different reasons.

Apollos went on, "But surely you don't imagine James Ferraro, Master of the Ministerium, flipped the switch and went down with the ship in a blaze of glory, do you?"

As the trio continued walking toward a command vehicle ahead, Dominic and Apollos drilled him with questioning stares. Heat began rising again, his jaw clenched with irritation at their glare.

He was not answerable to them. There were only two. Lucius Severus, the Regis of the Republic himself, with direct access to the man to commence the Purge. And the Thirteen of Nous, of which he was Grand Master, having reconstituted the ancient enemy of Ichthus from the shadows of history to rise again to new life.

But again, he let it go. In the interest of their shared mission to rid the world of Ichthus.

And the person who would help them get the ball rolling was twisting with agonizing shouts on a makeshift rack just beyond the cathedral's charred carcass.

"We're looking into it," the man simply said. "Can't have gotten far, if they did escape. Which certainly is an *if* at the moment. But no matter. We have other more pressing matters at hand."

He led Apollos and Dominic toward the man writhing in pain, the visual on their approach confirming the reason: skin had been flayed from the prisoner's thighs and forearms, muscle and tendons visibly shown and blood pooling on the magnapavement beneath.

The man with the white goatee and curly mustache smirked. All his life, he had preached against violence and for mercy. After all, that was the way of his Lord, the one he had believed and served and witnessed to—before walking away.

Now look at him, sanctioning torture. At least it was for a good cause.

For the man represented the last barrier standing between the Church and utter annihilation.

The Order of Thaddeus Remnant.

"Well, well, well…" he cooed on his approach, Apollos and Dominic at his heels on either side, interested in the display while apparently not at all interested in getting their hands dirty.

Not him.

The man strode to the Purifier clothed in crimson, face masked by those ghastly helmets symbolizing all the secret, hidden potential of the Republic's terror. He snatched from him the flayer used to strip the apparent Order Remnant's husk. He leaned over the man wielding the device for his observation.

His eyes were closed, and he was surprisingly calm, serene

even. Not the sort of response he expected to having one's skin peeled off, layer by layer. Perhaps he was delirious, numb with shock.

The man with the goatee and mustache pulled back then slapped the Order Remnant across his face.

He cried out with acknowledgement, having been awakened from unconsciousness or simply reminded of his current lot in life, he wasn't sure. Nor did he care.

All that mattered was extracting from this pest the answers he wanted. The answers the Thirteen needed to finally put the Order of Thaddeus out of its misery.

For good.

"So the man lives, does he?" he said, removing from the inside of his cloak a vial of white powdery crystals.

A whimpering snivel was his only reply. This was the one Ichthus was leaning on to defend, preserve, protect its faith?

The man scoffed and shook his head then popped the top to his vial. "Do you know what this is?"

The Order agent eyed the man then trained his focus on the vial now hovering over one of his arms. He licked his lips, chapped white and cracking, a stark contrast to his ruddy, bronze skin. He struggled to swallow and made no other movement.

"Salt," the man simply said. "That's what's in this vial. And I shouldn't have to go into detail the amount of pain that you will experience should it get into your open wounds."

"What is it you want?" the agent questioned, voice strained and lilting with the memory of North Alkebulana, of home.

"Now he speaks. And with forthright directness. I like that in a man. Cut through the bull and get down to business." He chuckled and smiled at his two companions, who smiled back and nodded.

He drew back the vial, but kept it at the ready. "What I

want is simple. A list of names and locations of the Order of Thaddeus Remnant."

The Order agent swallowed again, face registering nothing. No hint of a response or direction.

The man crouched down to his ear and said lowly, "There's no use fighting it, no use withholding from me. I will not be denied. And besides, the Order is on life support. You know it, I know it. Especially since the head was chopped off earlier, with the death of the Master in Edessa, a clever hideout to be sure."

A sound began to well within the agent strapped to the rack. The man couldn't tell what it was exactly until his mouth widened and a giggle escaped followed by a guffaw that made his ears burn red with rage.

He stood upright again. "And what has you in stitches, agent?"

"You think that because one Order Master is dead the Order is on the brink of death?"

Another giggle followed by another guffaw.

The man shifted with irritation, a rage rising in him he needed to contain if he wanted any hope of making headway with his mission.

"The fact that Master Theo is dead only ensures the survival of the Order. For before he passed, he would have found another to take his place."

Dominic Weiss twisted up his face, stepping up to the man's side now. "What do you mean by that? That there is another?"

"And what of the others?" Apollos pressed. "The Order Remnant scattered about Solterra?"

The Order agent heaved a breath and swallowed again before moving his mouth as if he were going to finally share, succumbing to the torture.

"Never…" he said instead before lobbing a wad of spittle uselessly toward the men, its glob landing on his hip instead of anywhere close to the three men gathered around him.

Dominic and Apollos laughed at the effort.

The other man's face fell. "Oh, you will spill all." He took a step closer to the man, leaning down close to his ear again and drawing in a breath. "Believe me, you will."

And with that, he stood straight and let loose half the contents of the vial he had been holding over one of the man's exposed forearms, the salt quickly descending with a whisper and filling exposed tendons and muscles and nerve endings.

A horrifying cry arose into the dusk, like a squealing hyena from his homeland being ravaged by the cheetahs that once roamed the countryside before their extinction.

One way or another, Colonel Sanders would find that new Master and the others, exacting his pound of flesh.

CHAPTER 14

SMYRNA. AD 155.

Fourth time now jumping phases and Alexander had to admit: As much as he had pitched a fit to Father Jim for his return jump, especially after their run in with the drunkard from the past, coming up against the limits of future technology, and nearly being marooned in the past—in spite of his recent trip and all of the inconvenience and smells of the past, he was beginning to sort of love it.

Loved the full-on sensory experience, loved the high he got from jumping across phases. A far greater high than his narcowafers ever gave him—from the humming vibrations along every fiber of his being in the familiar long, undulating waves to the thunderstorm static-charge smell; from the blinding luminescence to the soundless void.

It all came rushing back again after Sasha calibrated the signal down in the bunker on the edge of the annihilated Ministerium headquarters on the edge of the Mediterranean Sea. He'd had major doubts about going back again, pitching that fit he was reliving through the jump out of fear and frustration and the exhaustion from it all.

But then Father Jim reminded him what he said the first time he'd jumped: *All things worth fighting for demand sacri-*

fice. Ford echoed the sentiment with his report about plenty of men and women dying in the Ministerium itself from the Solterran invasion. Men and women who sacrificed themselves for the Church.

But it was more than that: because there were also reports coming in from Ministerium field offices and churches to the secure network socket on the Ministerium's hidden node on DiviNet that put an exclamation point on the danger Ichthus faced. Reports of a purging by figures clad in crimson and bearing menacing Neutralizers, letting them rip through parishioners gathered for Mass without mercy and leveling entire cathedrals and smaller parish church buildings, even businesses and houses suspected of harboring resistant Christians.

Alexander thought Father Jim was going to have a stroke from the freighted weight of the turn of events. Lucy had stepped in to comfort Father Jim while he and Ford and Sasha and Jin made a plan of action. The always-entertaining Max Bacchus was calling it a Purge, which rang true to Ford from his days with the Legion as a Purifier and also sounded about right considering what was taking place around the Republic.

Solterra Republic was purging it of the latest round of Unfits. Purging the world of Ichthus, the Church of Jesus Christ. Which bore an eerie echo of the same sorts of persecuting, purging violence of Empire Rome in the first century.

Which was why Father Jim was desperate to send Alexander and Rebekah back to the past. To not only retrieve what the Church needed to survive the rising apostasy. But also to weather what amounted to a rising anti-Christianism. Perhaps the incarnation of the Antichrist himself, the Beast warned about in John the Seer's apocalyptic vision he had overheard on his first mission that amounted to the Book of Revelation.

It appeared apostasy was taking on a new form, transforming from merely a peddling of false doctrine to colluding with the forces of this age, bending the knee to another lord and patron, and denying the singular Lord and Savior in the process.

It was decided that Ford and Lucy would continue their search for the Order of Thaddeus Remnant, using the apparent map the two discovered on the back of the Shroud of Turin as a starting place for their search. Oddly, a few of the major centers of purging—Alexandria in former Egypt, now known as Kemet; Jerusalem, which was probably far more coincidental, since the Holy City hadn't been a major center of power for Ichthus in centuries; even parts of Tunisia, which struck mercilessly close to home for Alexander and came quite near the ancient city of Carthage, an ancient hub of the early Church—each of the three cities had appeared on the map on the underside of the Holy Shroud.

Which for Alexander, the freshly minted Order of Thaddeus Master, seemed way too coincidental. He hoped it didn't mean what he thought it meant. That pockets of the Order remnant had already been discovered by the Republic.

And purged.

Regardless, they would leave behind Father Jim, Sasha, and Jin in the bunker they figured was designed for continued operations if need be. Why else would it be stocked with supplies for the long haul, with cots and food and water, and the continuous connection to Ministerium network resources?

Ford thought it was a helluva risky move, a characterization to which Father Jim raised an irritated eyebrow, but what else could they do? They needed the resources the network connection offered for Alexander and Rebekah to jump phases back in time. It also gave them a small base of operations, however long it lasted. Because one thing was certain: Solterra would stop at nothing to hunt them down and shut them down. So they had to take extra care in the coming days—no, coming *hours* to hide any trace of their continued activity.

Otherwise, Alexander and Rebekah really would be stuck back in time, the Ministerium would truly be no more, and the last remaining bulwark against Solterran incursions against the Church would be dismantled at last. For good.

And the Church of Jesus Christ would be no more.

The familiar sensation jumping phases, warm and fluid—like being dunked into a simmering jacuzzi just as a live wire was thrust inside—continued washing over Alexander as they zoomed back through time. Still as delightful, still as maddening of an experience!

Every one of his molecules tingled as they jumped back to the first century with static discharge, like walking across carpet in wool socks. He hoped Rebekah was faring better this time around, considering she was experiencing what he was: every molecule of his being set on edge by the electromagnetic force field that had opened up a wormhole to the phase beyond.

All five senses were firing on all cylinders now, turned on by an ecstatic Nirvana.

As time flashed by in rapid succession, not in a blurry motion of multi-colored luminescence but rather a blinding smudge of all images combining into one panoramic experi-ence, he smiled at the smell that reminded him of a midsummer Tripolitanian storm. When the Mediterranean air was charged by spiderwebbey streaks of lightning, with an added sweet yet odd mixture of salt and spice in his mouth.

Again, all the bright nuclear-explosion light without the heat. Just a steady temperature that seemed perfectly tuned to his body. He squeezed his eyes as he vibrated and tingled from the present to the past, again fearing that he would go blind from time's movement.

And then the sound of it all. Which was zero, as if he were encased in a vacuum sealed off from reality. None of the bassy and trebley ranges of modern life. No hum or tuning-fork ting.

He again tried sensing Rebekah as they rode the waves of time's phases together, arm in arm this time, so as not to lose one another. But it was as it was before: He was all alone in a capsule of soundless, blinding, tingly, sweet-and-salty nirvana that smelled of electrified rain, jumping farther and farther along the phases of time.

Just when he thought he would burst from the sensory overload, all at once it stopped, as suddenly as it started.

No more tingling, no more warm fluidity, no more static scent of thunderstorms, no more blinding luminescence and soundless pressure.

In fact, there was nothing at all.

It was pitch black. With a faint, distant clomping of hooves and random cheers rising in the distance punctuated by familiar lapping waves. And a solidness underneath their feet, rough and uneven, yet distinctly different than the soft soil from four decades ago when they landed in an olive grove.

Except, they were in the same olive grove! Or, at least, supposed to be. Apparently, their drunkard friend had moved on to bigger and better things, selling his land to the local real estate developer, where a subdivision of two-room houses replaced a grove of olive trees.

There really was nothing new under the sun; the past really was prologue to so much of modern life.

He could feel Rebekah's arm still slung within his own, which meant they had made it. Back to the first century.

Again.

He snapped his eyes open and heaved a lungful of air, then another.

Right before he felt a hand cover his mouth, as if quieting him.

It was Rebekah. He could tell even before his eyes adjusted to the past phase, her hand smelling of the familiar lavender and vanilla.

But then they did adjust, and the reality of their situation came crashing into him.

They were standing in the middle of a room. Which was most certainly inside a home. Someone's home!

The idea had crossed his and Sasha's minds back at the start of this whole blasted time travel business. With visions of jumping back into the middle of walls or being impaled by trees.

Which is why they tried to ensure they made the jump outside and near familiar natural landmarks, like seas and beaches and hillsides, where they were likely to end up in the same underdeveloped settings in the past, like fields and seas. Preferably not the sea, but it was better than randomly zapping into some random house in Smyrna AD 155!

A cold panic flooded Alexander from head to bowels. He held his breath behind Rebekah's hand. Who began slowly withdrawing it and bringing a finger to her lips in a hush.

His eyes had completely adjusted to their surroundings now. Which wasn't much.

A window looked out into the dusking evening, a cool, salted breeze tinged with fish and then the familiar rotten waste of time wafting in, a burnt orange-red horizon giving way to that dark tapestry of diamonds they had glimpsed before everything went to Hades a few decades ago.

Nestled against one wall was what Alexander figured was a mattress. Looked like fabric of some sort stuffed with straw.

And blessedly empty!

Same for the rest of the room. For that matter, the entire

one-level modest home, the adjacent room beyond and open doorway a silent void.

Worst nightmare ever, but it looked like they lucked out.

Or rather, the Lord had provided a vacant dwelling for their jump.

He closed his eyes and sighed, letting his tensed-up limbs relax a bit.

Until he heard a menacing growl from just beyond the door. Low and guttural and feral, coming in from the darkened space in front of them beyond the window farther inside the house.

Didn't take long for him to spring into action. No use exchanging pleasantries with a—

Puppy?

A little furball, ears floppy and fur a fluffy beige and nose a black dot of wet cuteness came bounding inside the room, biffing it hard on the rough wood floor in his excitement but recovering quickly. The little guy bounded over to Alexander and offered a heart-warming yelp this time around.

Alexander stifled a laugh even as his fight-or-flight activated body relaxed again at the sight. He bent low and scratched the cute little thing behind the ears as he came up to him, mouth open in a panting smile and tiny pink tongue lolling as if asking for a handout.

He looked up at Rebekah and flashed her a relieved grin, who smiled curtly before her face fell with alarm.

Didn't get why. Also didn't get how the tiny little dude could have offered such a menacing warning to the two intruders.

Until a face appeared through the shadows beyond the door. Snout long and head held low, with menacing black eyes and ears pointed back on high alert, a mountain of fur standing on edge telling them all they needed to know.

They were intruding on mama dog's turf. And things were about to get real.

She bared her teeth now, all pointy and sharp and ready to tear the flesh off from anyone and anything that came near her pup and domain.

Like the two visitors from the future.

That deep, low, guttural growl that sounded like the mama clearly meant business returned.

And Alexander's heart jolted forward even as he froze with indecision, still scratching the pup who was completely oblivious to the grown up game playing out right then and there in the first-century home.

He released the puppy and held out his palms up in surrender. Then slowly stood, keeping his gaze fixed on the dog. Something he remembered reading on DiviNet some random night surfing back at his parish home about locking eyes to assert your authority.

The dog lashed out with vicious intent. Apparently, she hadn't read the same DiviNet post.

Which sent Alexander and Rebekah into action.

The idea came to him when he first saw the dog. Now was as good a time as any.

He twisted back toward the mattress grabbing one end and shouting for Rebekah to do the same.

Just as the dog inched closer into the doorway, snapping her jaw and barking wildly.

The two nodded at one another and lunged for the doorway, bearing the mattress and shoving it against the void.

Doing the trick, but sending the animal into a feral frenzy.

Now the pup was in on the action, yelping away and backing up against the wall.

"Poor thing," Rebekah said. "Probably wants his mama."

"Can't worry about that now. Let's go." He nodded toward the window and lowered his hands to hoist her inside and over.

She placed a hand on his shoulder and foot in his hands. Then pushed up and into the window and down to the other side.

The dog was going crazy now, growling and yapping away, the mattress itself jiggling as if she were giving it all she had to free her pup.

Couldn't blame her. Which is why, perched inside the windowsill, Alexander held on and leaned over, grabbing a side of the plug and yanking it free.

And free it came. Along with the mama dog sailing through the air for a rescue.

Jumping up to Alexander still perched inside the window with a furious lashing of teeth and knocking him backwards outside to the alleyway below.

"Arg..." he said, stifling a cry as he fell.

Thank the Lord he landed square on his back, and not his head.

"Oy! Are you alright?" Rebekah whispered, rushing to his side.

He winced and grabbed his forearm, pulling his hand away to find a laceration beading with blood. Arm hurt worse than his back, but he'd live. Maybe with rabies, another reason not to time travel. So he'd have to check on that when they jumped back to the future.

Alexander stood, cradling his arm.

"We've got to mend this," she said, checking it out in the moonlight as the dog kept at it just inside the window.

"No, what we've got to do is get the heck out of here before the owners of this house return and the entire town shows up."

He hobbled forward, Rebekah close behind, eyes searching

for some semblance of direction to make sense of where they were.

The outside walls from rows of dwellings pressed in against them, the scents of spices and fragrant rice and grilled meat still lingering and riding the breeze of salted, fishy air gusting off from the sea beyond. Winding their way through the maze of alleyways, they came to a familiar sight: the row of cypress trees where they had feigned being lovers for the drunkard relieving himself. Taller now and more numerous, but recognizable.

"Brings back such fond memories," Rebekah said, smiling as they hustled past and into more familiar parts of town, crowds lining the streets in revelrous bunches.

Alexander chuckled. "I'm not sure fond is the way to describe it."

"Oh, come now. Don't you want to offer an encore performance of star-crossed lovers caught in the throes of a nighttime kiss?"

He coughed and nearly stumbled at the surprisingly flirtatious forthrightness.

She giggled. "All in the name of the operation, of course."

He giggled as well. "Of course..."

My, my. What a tease!

"That's certainly a fancy new addition to the town!" He pointed to a rising stadium of several stories made out of red stone, looking like a mini Colosseum from pictures he had seen on DiviNet. A shudder ratcheted up his spine at the meaning of it: a venue for not only Roman games but Roman persecution.

"Let's just hope neither of us are destined to see the inside of that purgatory," Rebekah said.

"Agree."

They weaved past what looked like a corner bar, a large front-of-shop counter decorated in marble with flaming torches on either end. Pitchers of wine were mounted on top and smoky fumes billowed from behind, sending the aromas of cooking meat and vegetables and bread wafting past the gawking duo.

"Care for a drink at the local watering hole?" asked Alexander.

"With what money?"

He shrugged. "Figured you could talk your way into getting us a drink or something."

"I wish. So what are we looking for, anyway?"

Sighing as they continued on, he said, "I'm not sure. It's all just running together from the last time. And it does feel like the proverbial needle in a haystack."

"No white clapboard or stone building with rising steeple to lead the way to the Church?"

"Sorry, not in these parts. And not in this century."

"Perhaps we should pray about it," Rebekah suggested. "Ask for the Holy Spirit's guidance. The Lord seems to have led the way in the past. Or rather, the present. Or whatever we call this."

Alexander smiled. "Why didn't I think of that?"

They continued onward, praying silently along the way. That the Lord would guide them, provide for them, reveal himself in whatever way they needed—for the sake of Ichthus, the future Church and her—

"Wait a minute..." he said, stopping short in the center of a town square, a large fountain sputtering water a meter away.

He spun around, cocking his head and searching for the direction of the most beautiful, harmonious sound he had ever heard.

It was light and airy, yet had a backbone to it. A song clearly sung by a group of men and women, joining together in rapturous praise of something.

Or Someone...

His heart began racing with expectant hope. Who else would be lifting up their voices in song but those in praise of Christ, for his person and work?

And then he heard it. The opening lines of a Psalm he had himself sung with his former parishioners, the ones who had both died and lived through the terrifying persecution that had befallen his precious parish.

Alexander started after the sound without a word or warning to Rebekah, a siren song beckoning him to not only worship, but to discover a lost secret. The one he hoped would lead them to their mission's prize: the memory contained in the bishop of Smyrna, Polycarp.

He heard her call after him, but his heart was enraptured with the melody, the words of the opening stanza playing in his head even as those singing had moved on:

> *Whoever dwells in the shelter of the Most High*
> *will rest in the shadow of the Almighty.*
> *I will say of the Lord, "He is my refuge and my*
>   *fortress,*
> *my God, in whom I trust."*

A hand grabbed his arm from behind and spun him around.

"What the blazes do you think you are doing?" Rebekah said in a hushed rush, clearly not happy at him leaving her in his dust without word or warning.

"Sorry. But I heard it."

"Heard what?" she said with no small amount of exasperation.

There it was again. The song had resumed itself after a pause. Faint, but there.

Alexander grinned widely, sure of it now after hearing

more words: *'You will not fear the terror of night, nor the arrow that flies by day, nor the pestilence that stalks in the darkness, nor the plague that destroys at midday.'*

Psalm 91, a popular Hebrew poem sung as a worship ballad in the early Church.

It had to be them, it just had to be.

"Heard what, you ask?" he said before grinning widely with hope. "The Church of Jesus Christ, that's who. Come on!"

Without waiting, he started through narrow streets again on toward the sound.

'If you say, 'The Lord is my refuge,' and you make the Most High your dwelling, no harm will overtake you, no disaster will come near your tent.'

The siren-song kept pulling at him through the cramped, darkening corridors of Smyrna, beckoning him to taste and see the Lord's goodness.

'For he will command his angels concerning you to guard you in all your ways; they will lift you up in their hands, so that you will not strike your foot against a stone.'

Because the good Lord above surely knew he needed it. Needed to taste of the Lord once again, in all of his fullness and purity, unadulterated from staid, stuffy doctrine and useless, dishonest heresy alike. Returning to the essence of that goodness and love and mercy and grace.

"Because he loves me,' says the Lord, 'I will rescue him; I will protect him, for he acknowledges my name. He will call on me, and I will answer him...'"

They continued forward with cautious steps, trying to catch the song that seemed all at once surrounding them in the alleyways yet fleeting through the night.

And then it was gone.

No more singing, no more Psalm.

No more nothing.

Alexander stopped, throwing his hands on top of his head.

No...Can't be true! Where are you, Ichthus?

He was right there. Had them within his grasp. The Psalm and song. The Church herself, gathered within the Roman town in some small, cramped home with nothing but their voices and their memories of Scripture.

And then he spotted them. The elements before the people.

Through a darkened window, a single lit candle serving as a beacon of hope and illuminating several faces bowed in supplication.

And in the center of the gathered faithful sat a table, spread with nothing more than a loaf of bread, its yeasty crust now finding its way into the alleyway on a gentle breeze, and an earthenware pitcher. Its crimson content being poured into a simple, unassuming chalice.

Wine.

Blood...

Alexander smiled and raised his head heavenward.

Now that's what I'm talking about! Thank you, Lord Christ...

They had found the remnant, the Church.

And hopefully Polycarp himself.

CHAPTER 15

ANTAKYA, ARABIA-PERSIA. AD 2123.

THE YELLOW SUBMARINE was about as cramped quarters as
cramped quarters can get. Not only was the front half crammed
with two piloting seats and as much technowizardry as one
could get their sub-loving paws on. The rear held two beds and
one of those little kitchenettes with a microwave sink. Even had
a little porta-potty thingy, though he dared not venture down
that road. Very twenty-first century retro RV-like, when folks
still did that sort of thing.

But no matter. He was loving life and riding in style along
the way.

Ever since he was a boy he had dreamed of piloting a
contraption like this sleek sweet piece of Ministerium ingenuity. Or whoever made it. Probably Asiatica, knowing their technological prowess. The undersea world had been an obsession,
and he read old books and watched old shows that plumbed the
depths of the ocean blue. From Jules Verne to SeaQuest on that
now-defunct peacock television network. Anything he could
get his hands on to feed his obsession and tickle his fantasies
about one day driving his own sweet submergence ride.

Not that his pump was primed to take command of the

thing. He was nervous as a nun in a brothel. Or was that a saloon? Whatever it was from way back when—he was it.

Expressed his skepticism to the chief. In a way that didn't make him look like a scaredy cat sissy, mind you. But Father Jim persisted in insisting that he and Lucy go and track down the Order of Thaddeus Remnant while he and Jin and Sasha were holed up in the bunker at the edge of the obliterated Ministerium with nothing but a buck and a prayer to hold on to.

And that's what worried him. Because the metaphorical buck was nonexistent since the Reckoning, the blessed Republic having taken over all monetary schemes with their own Ponzi scheme *merca* credits. And then there was the prayer business, which seemed hard to come by as of late.

So if that's the hand Padre had been dealt, what did that mean for him and his co-pilot Lucy who was busy snoring in the back bunker, the two of 'em barreling toward no uncertain doom?

"*Boo!*"

"*Holybamoly!*" Ford cried out, bumping the navigation stick on the way to clutching his chest in a frightful fit. And sending the fish nose-diving toward Davy Jones's Locker.

Lucy snorted a cackling laugh that was all at once cute and annoying. Mostly because she managed to scare the everlivin' snot out of him. But also because it's something he himself would have done. So no use getting bent out of shape about it.

He grabbed hold of the controls and eased the submarine back into position. Then he threw on the autopilot and turned around toward the perp, pulling out his finger and putting on his most irritated face he could muster.

"You better watch it, little missy. I know where you live." Then he broke out into a grin and threw a wrapper at her from one of the MRE meals he had swiped before they'd shoved off on their mission.

She scrunched up her face and raised a brow. "I better watch it, huh? With that face of yours? Please! It's no wonder you survived however many years with the Legion. And as a Purifier of all things! Couldn't scare a bum into givin' up his change."

His face froze with a grin before falling with the embarrassment of his past.

She must have sensed the sudden shift. "Oh, no! I didn't mean—I mean, I shouldn't have said—"

"Don't worry your pretty little head about it," Ford interrupted, waving a dismissive hand before turning back around for the controls.

He took in a breath and swallowed. Hated everything about his past. His time with the Legion primarily. It was one of those things he could never escape. One he wished his new comrades didn't know about. Especially the one named Luciana Jane.

But then a verse from nowheresville popped into his mind. Must have been lodged in the back of his head from childhood, because he hadn't touched the Good Book in a while. Didn't feel he could after all the blood on his hands, even though Brother Benedict said otherwise.

Yet, there it was: *'if anyone is in Christ, the new creation has come: The old has gone, the new is here!'*

Yeah, alright Saint Paul. Whatever. Sure didn't feel new; sure didn't feel like his old life of murderous zealotry for the Republic had been tossed away like yesterday's trash that it was.

Then another verse bubbled up. *'Therefore, there is now no condemnation for those who are in Christ Jesus.'*

Alright. Got the picture.

But God wasn't done yet. Because the Second Person of the Trinity wanted in on the action.

'*If you hold to my teaching, you are really my disciples. Then you will know the truth, and the truth will set you free....Now a slave has no permanent place in the family, but a son belongs to it forever. So if the Son sets you free, you will be free indeed.*'

The one-two-three punch finally did it with those final words of Jesus, breaking through his thick skull to stay his self-flagellating hand.

Could hardly imagine the truth of those words the first time Brother Benedict explained it all to him, that he was a son—of God, no less. Absolutely did not compute. Mostly because his earthly one certainly never won no Pops of the Year medals of valor. And he'd never seemed to measure up to the man to begin with to be rightly called his son.

So to think God the Father in heaven looked on him like that...as a son? Again, didn't compute at the time and barely computed again with that darn teachin' of Jesus percolatin' in his brain.

But it did the trick, compensating for Lucy's careless comment she only meant in jest, yet twisted in his heart like a knife. The Evil One was quick to use his past against him to break him down. And it almost always worked. Nearly did then had it not been for the Spirit's divine counsel.

He said a quick prayer of thanksgiving to the good Lord above for his words, then wiped a bit of moisture from his eyes building from the confrontation with his past.

When a gasp came up from behind. "Johnny Mark...Did I make you cry?"

Laughing, he spit back, "No, you didn't make me cry! That's nonsense."

Folding her arms, she sat on the armrest of the chair next to him. "Because I didn't mean to offend."

"Something in my eyes. That's all."

"And I don't look atcha that way, as a—"

Ford grabbed her arm and grinned, trying to stuff his frustration with the moment away. "It's fine. You're fine. I'm fine. We're all fine! So let's just get on with it, shall we?"

She hesitated, then offered a smile.

An indicator light followed by a *purr* sounded.

Saved by the bell...

He said, "Would you look at that! Looks like we've arrived."

Lucy slid into the copilot's chair, the azure world outside sending sparkling rays against her milky-white complexion and perfectly coiffed blond hair. With those high cheekbones and button nose, light undulating across her face. And then of course there was—

"Ford?"

"Huh?" he mumbled dumbly, eyes wide as he snapped out from his observational trance.

"Can I help you with something?" she asked, forehead raised with inquiry and bearing a comical grin.

He quickly shook his head and returned to the task at hand: navigating their yellow submarine through the traffic and into port. And quite the port it was, with rows of airlocks receiving visiting personal submergence vehicles neatly arrayed one after the other, guided by automatons that looked oddly like grizzly bears, and lights blazing to aid the sun above in cutting through the darkened void of the ocean.

Not that it was anything more special than the others littered throughout the Republic after replacing airports. But it still felt like science fiction, with the whale-like deep submergence vehicle whooshing past and all the other little bitty car-like submarines zooming about, going this way and that from land to deep sea submergence stations commissioned by the Republic under the Solterra Earth Oceanic

Organization, and before that the United Earth Oceanic Assembly.

Planes had been abandoned for a century after the world's climate broke from too much CO_2 and the oil reserves finally depleted. At least, that was Solterra's official story, anyway. Ford never bought any of that propaganda mumbo jumbo. Discerning minds like his thought it was more about controlling how people moved about the Republic through carefully curated transportation access points than anything to do with power or pollution. Such was life under the watchful eye of Solterra—all *'For Humanity!'* of course.

The world had planned for such a development long before it arrived, having dived headlong into the seventy-one percent of Earth's surface yet uncolonized. As a wee lad, Ford had been something of a student of the world's deep-sea colonizing efforts. While most kiddos dreamed of space after the 21st century's second decade saw humanity finally establish its first lunar colony after the former Asiatica nation-state China beat his American people to the moon, Ford's heart was under the water.

And there he was. Commanding his own little yellow submarine.

Which, truth be told, wasn't all that special considering humans had been shuttling these contraptions around for the past century anyhow, once the world got its act together and colonized the undersea world in the 2030s. And while China's claim to fame was the moon, the former U.S. of A's was the first deep sea submergence station. Atlantis DS3.

Of course, the Asians followed up their lunar landing with their own DS3 version. Never one to let America get a leg up on the whole global hegemony business. But then a string of undersea conflicts nearly derailed the utopian dream of owning a plot of Davy Jones's Locker. Leading to the UEOA charter in

2045, the national and transnational peace and trade accord governing stations and outposts.

It also established the kinds of seaports anchored at the edge of what used to be ancient Antioch, now accepting the yellow submarine Ford was docking at a vacant airlock.

"You ready for this, sassafras?" Ford said as he powered down the personal submergence vehicle.

Lucy chambered a round in her trusty sidearm and shoved it in the front of her pants.

"I think so."

Ford stood and flashed her a grin. "Just don't go flashing that thing around or you're liable to get thrown into some reprogramming camp. And I'd rather not be standing next to you when that happens."

"I'll keep that in mind."

After the submergence vehicle finished running through its docking sequence, aided by the automaton outside, Ford took a breath and released the airlock, swinging the door inside and popping his head out for a look-see.

Looking left, he saw not a soul. Looking right, he glimpsed a few humanoids ambling down the metal gangway toward the exit, arm in arm, the distinctive sheen of their silicone skin shimmering under the white LED lights above.

Ford frowned, and a shiver ratcheted up his spine at the sight.

"Coast is clear," he said, "but for a few humanoid lovebirds up ahead."

He grabbed his own weapon and shoved it at his back underneath his coat. The two left, securing the door and praying the good Lord made their paths straight.

The pair of Ministerium agents held back some to give the humanoids their space, not wanting to attract any attention.

"Never in a million lifetimes will I get used to it," Lucy

said, nodding toward the pair ahead. "No matter how much the Republic wants to normalize such expressions."

"Agree," Ford said.

Sight was common enough now after the Reckoning extended the full rights and privileges of species who identified with being human to those automatons who were programmed in factories to playact as such. But why we wanted a world—no, *constructed* a world—that diminished our own personhood in favor of fake humanity was beyond him.

"Sight still makes my stomach turn," Ford mumbled. "Burlesque sacrilege, if you ask me. Thinking a robot can simply put on the costume of a human being and call it good—godly even. Like some sort of divine prerogative blessed by the impulses of the Universe itself."

"Careful what you say, Ford. The Patron might be listening. And you know what that means."

Sighing, he nodded. A trip to a reprogramming camp to realign his thinking with the beneficent wisdom of the Republic.

They mounted an escalator toward the surface, the humanoid pair ahead disappearing in the void quickly filling with the noise of ultramodern life.

Soon they were joining them, being dumped in the bowels of a city mirroring much of the Republic, a pastiche of pre- and post-Reckoning life with its sophisticated, angular high-rises of gleaming glass and titanium alloys in the midafternoon sunlight and quaint ancient ones of stone and wood and concrete. With its mixture of humans and posthuman automatons, all skittering about filling various roles to make the Republic run on schedule. With the hum of magnacrafts hovering above the magnapavement zooming across the city and beyond in an effort to stave off climate change and save the world, symbols of the peace and prosperity and progress the Republic had brought the world—whether through human ingenuity or brute force, it didn't matter.

From its structures and social arrangements to technological tools and redefinitions of humanity, all of it was done *'For Humanity!'* without questioning either means or motives. What did it matter when utopia was just a totalitarian tweak away?

"The cradle of Christianity, huh?" Ford said, hands on his hips and eyeing the hustle and bustle.

Lucy nodded, echoing his stance. "Sure is. The Church of Antioch stretches all the way back to the founding of Ichthus, when believers from Jerusalem were scattered from the persecution stemming from Stephen's sermon in the Book of Acts. From there it bloomed into a heavyweight power center of Christianity, even becoming known as an entire school of thought rivaling Alexandria, with particular views on interpreting the Bible and salvation and even the person of Christ. Birthed heretics and orthodox scholars alike."

Ford whistled, flashing a wry grin her way. "Look at you. All up on your Church history. A regular Eusebius in a skirt, aren't you?"

She giggled. "I don't know about that. But I should be, given I was a professor and all, as well as in ministry."

"A prof? You?"

She slugged him in the arm. "Don't act so surprised! There's more behind the blond locks and Valley girl persona."

"Oh, I don't doubt it. But as much as I'd love to hear more of that side of Luciana Jane, we've got work to do, prof."

"Right. The Order of Thaddeus remnant."

"Bingo. Except, where we begin in this mess of ultramodernity is the question. Too bad they're not throwing up smoke signals for us."

"Or, maybe they are..." Lucy pointed toward a trail of

smoke blooming in the distance between two high-rises angling into upside down ice cream cones of gleaming glass. "What are the odds that four-alarm-looking fire is the Republic, burnin' down the Church, or *a* church, or—"

"The Order..." he muttered.

She nodded, saying nothing.

"Then we'd best get to it and check it out."

They crossed the magnapavement intersection of crushing stop-and-go traffic, weaving through bumper-to-bumper magnacars and others on magnaboards hovering with irritation and looking for a way through the congestion.

The smoke was a signal fire now for Ford, pinging his lizard brain with high-alert concern for what could be the source. The closer they hustled along the city streets, the more he realized the peculiarity of it all.

No one seemed to be paying it any mind. In fact, it looked like pedestrian and magnacraft traffic were leaving the scene, avoiding it even. Which partly made sense, given the danger the fire and smoke posed. But no one even seemed curious, or panicked. Back home, his Noramericanan peeps would be rubberneckin' the entire thing to death.

Nope. Not here.

And no flashing blues and whites. No wailing sirens either racing to supplement Rescuers trying to control the blaze or letting the world know the benevolent Patron had everything under control.

Then they discovered why.

Cresting a hill, the smoking signal was the remnant of a blazing furnace that had reached its zenith hours ago. But that wasn't all of it.

Perched on the perimeter were a helluva lot of oversized charcoal Destroyers just waiting to put the hurt on anyone who moved.

And Enforcers, all black and prideful and in control like. Pacing the grounds out front of an ancient building of stone and steel reinforcements that had been reduced to rubble.

By the looks of it, it had been a massive cathedral, judging by the remaining spire still standing sandwiched between the ultramodern ice cream cones. It was a bony hand, shed of its skin and severed from its body, reaching toward Heaven for help.

We ain't the Almighty, brother, but we sure ain't turnin' away either...

The pair pulled up to the edge of a nightclub a block away. Ford withdrew a pair of ocular enhancers for a better look.

"Whatcha scein'?" asked Lucy.

He said nothing, adjusting his view and scanning the area.

A detachment of Enforcers marched along a street perpendicular to the destruction from stage left, joined by a handful of crimson-clad soldiers.

Ford's breath caught in his chest at the sight, and he shoved Lucy farther behind the nightclub's edge for protection.

"Purifiers..." he mumbled.

"Purifiers? Well that settles it."

Sure did. Because where there were Purifiers, there were Unfits.

Judging by the locals, no doubt they were here to either round up or cancel fellow brothers and sisters of Ichthus.

Then he saw it.

"Wait a minute..."

"Whatcha—"

Ford put out an arm as he homed in on a section of the rubble.

"There's a hole."

"A hole?" asked Lucy.

He nodded. "Leading beneath the grounds of the cathedral. The Purifiers turned into it, then disappeared into it."

But that wasn't all of it.

His heart sank to the ground and bowels went with it at the sight of the whack job bearing an interrogation package. Which meant beaucoup trouble.

"How much you wanna bet that there hole in the ground leads to the Order's former lair? One of the Remnants that was all X-marks-the-spot on the underside of the Holy Shroud?"

Three more purifiers slipped into the void, disappearing down beneath the rubble. Those Purifier whack jobs and that interrogation package made it a pretty good bet they'd found their target.

Which meant so did the Republic.

And someone down below was about to get the treatment he himself had doled out a time or twenty.

Nope. Not if he could help it.

CHAPTER 16

SMYRNA. AD 155.

Alexander hesitated before opening the door, drawing his hand back to knock but holding fast, the adrenaline-fueled chase giving way to common sense.

What am I doing?

None of this was like him. The clandestine sneaking around. The walking up to random strangers or doors. The swashbuckling and running headlong into no uncertain doom. His introversion precluded him from all of the above. And sanity should have intervened before he took off through the smelly, dusty back-alley streets of some backwoods town—and, really, before he strapped on that time travel belt and jumped phases again in the first place.

Yet there he was. Standing at the threshold of a random door, on a random street, at a random point in time's phases, hand clenched into a fist and hovering just above the rough planks that served as a door into a modest two-level home while who knew who was gathered on the other side.

Madness is what it was. How he ever agreed to it was beyond him.

Then in that moment, hand still hovering and brain swirling with second-guessing regret, Alexander remembered.

His parishioners. The ones who had given their lives in the face of persecuting violence. The others who had lived, whose faith had been shaken from it, and then even more people who were scattered amongst those who had survived and the greater Tripolitanian area on through Alkebulana to the greater Solterra Republic whose faith had frayed, to the point of confusion and bewilderment. The ones wondering if the ancient faith of Ichthus still mattered, if that old, old story of Jesus and his love still worked, still rescued people from a life of rebellion and ruin to put them back together than, both in this life, the here and now, and in the life to come at the resurrection when he returns in glory to make all things new.

So yes, madness. But also purpose. An *aim* and *task*.

'I consider my life worth nothing to me,' recalling again what Saint Paul had said in the Book of Acts. *'My only aim is to finish the race and complete the task the Lord Jesus has given me —the task of testifying to the good news of God's grace.'*

Alexander crossed himself. *May it be my life as well...*

He swallowed, then took a breath and glanced behind at Rebekah, whose forehead was creased with confusion but also urged him onward. He nodded and turned back toward the door.

Here we go...

He rapped his knuckles against the door, their sound echoing far louder than he would have liked.

Three times: *Thump, thump, thump.* Pause. Then two more: *Thump, thump.*

An ancient greeting of Ichthus announcing friendly visitors, using the sign of the Trinity—Father, Son, Spirit—and the two natures of Christ—humanity and divinity. It assured those within that a friend was nigh. Or so he hoped.

All sound ceased from the other side. Where there had been singing moments ago, replaced by someone talking and others joining in for discussion, it all paused to a breath-holding stand.

A clanging sound filled in the void. From behind and down the street.

A praetorian guard coming toward them, his steel gladius sword thwapping against his leggings with each step.

He swallowed again, his mouth suddenly running dry and head filling with dizzying anxiety.

Come on...

He repeated his entreaty: *Thump, thump, thump.* Pause. *Thump, thump.*

The guard was closer now, slowing his pace as he met Alexander's eyes.

Then the door opened, a stocky middle-aged man greeted them. Skin ruddy and bronzed, about as tall as Alexander but wider and more muscular. Salt-and-pepper hair shorn against his head and beard trimmed neatly, wearing a white long sleeve tunic with purple linen draped across his shoulders and around his waist. Clearly a man of means and probably the *pater familias*, the head of household.

"Hello, brother," Alexander spoke in a rush without giving the man a chance to speak. "We come as fellow persons of the Way, of Ichthus, having been crucified with Christ in heart and raised to new life in spirit. May we come in?"

Alexander fixed him with wide eyes, the sound of the guard's clang growing louder now and feeling as though it was about to bear down upon them with force.

The man frowned then nodded and ushered them inside, securing the door behind.

Six people were arrayed around the table he had glimpsed from the street farther inside the dwelling beyond the vestibule. Men and women, young and old, skin as dark as pitch like

Rebekah and skin on the lighter bronzy end like him and the man who greeted them.

Alexander knew it was rare to find such a community in the Roman Empire, where unlike society social codes and classes didn't tightly dictate every level of behavior. Yet that's what had become the norm with a group of people who had become known as the Way in the ancient world. Their members were neither Jew nor Greek, neither slave nor free, neither male nor female—just as the Apostle Paul had instructed them. The Church's social order offered a sharp contrast to the rest of the Roman world with stratified boundaries of social class and distinction.

The earthy scent of burning wood mingled with roasted lamb and freshly baked bread caused Alexander's stomach to rumble in protest as they stood waiting for the next move. He hadn't realized how hungry he was until that moment. Selfishly, he hoped they were offered some food.

All eyes glared at them, waiting for them to explain themselves. Alexander cleared his throat and gestured toward Rebekah. "We, my companion Rebekah and myself, Alexander—we thank you for welcoming us in the name of our Lord and Savior, Jesus Christ."

The others around the table nodded, some smiling with loving affection at welcoming two strangers into their worship, others with blank faces registering a mixture of apprehension and skepticism.

A woman stood and glided over to the man's side. The matron of the house, Alexander presumed, a tall woman with high cheekbones and long black hair braided and adorned with beads, wearing a silky blue dress. She smiled and opened her arms to him in a greeting.

"Welcome, my brother." She kissed him on both cheeks,

then stole a cautious glance through a window into the waning afternoon.

"I am Valaria," she said, then gestured to the other man. "This is Felix."

The patriarch of the home extended his hand. "Are you hungry, Alexander, is it? We just finished eating and had started our service. You're free to a leg or two of lamb and as much vegetables as your stomach can handle."

Alexander sighed and grinned with delight. "Yes. Thank you."

"That would be lovely," Rebekah echoed.

The man and his wife led them to a modest hall where the rest of the gathering was still seated, filled with plebs and patricians alike, all arrayed around a large table commanding the center of the space warmed by a crackling fire and that lamb and bread filling the home with dizzying delight.

Alexander took a seat next to an Egyptian man, by the looks of it, whose clothes were dirty and tinged with the sour scent of body odor. Rebekah sat on Alexander's other side, between him and a woman whose greying hair was swept up into a bun, wearing fine green-and-red dyed fabrics, clearly part of the other end of the social spectrum.

"Again, welcome to our gathering, but who are you?" asked Felix, gesturing toward the leftover food as Valaria handed them an earthenware plate.

Alexander nodded, reaching for a leg of lamb, while deciding how to approach the subject. He settled on honesty, figuring it was the best policy here. At least, that's what he hoped.

"We are with the Order of Thaddeus."

There was a collective gasp from those seated around the table. Which made him regret his honesty.

"The Order of Thaddeus, you say? But why?" Felix questioned. "Don't tarry for sake of food!"

"Let them eat, dear," Valaria corrected her husband.

Alexander tore a chunk off the leg with his teeth, chewed, and swallowed before continuing. He washed his bite down with sweetened milk and wiped his mouth on his sleeve. He realized the table was staring.

Glancing at Rebekah, who was eating in silence, he went on: "That's right, the Order. Sent to meet with bishop Polycarp. Is he here?"

He glanced around, making a show of it. He was trying to hold his head steady with confidence while reeling inside from the risk he was taking.

"He isn't," Felix said.

"Well, we need to see him."

The man leaned back with folded arms, fixing him with a stare. "Why? What's the urgency? And at whose order?"

"Whose order..." Alexander asked, searching for an answer, sweat building now at his brow. "Why, the Order Master."

Not a lie, per se, as he himself was *an* Order Master, sending Rebekah and himself on mission to do the very thing he was asking of Felix: retrieve Polycarp and his memory.

"But why would Titus do such a thing?" Valaria questioned. "Considering the persecuting violence engulfing us of late?"

"And given the men of ill repute," Felix went on, "Roman praetorians accompanied by legion soldiers, roaming Smyrna in search of the man."

Alexander shrugged. "All I know is, Titus asked for us to find him and glean from him a word for Ich—err, the Church during these dark times. Something we can pass along to those suffering under the errors of false teachers and the persecuting violence of the Empire, as you say."

"Well, a word he will certainly give you. And a thousand more!"

The table laughed knowingly. Alexander and Rebekah joined.

The table died down and Alexander wondered if he would get what he needed.

Valaria spoke up again: "He isn't here, but..." She trailed off, looking at Felix for confirmation.

Felix nodded, adding: "After praetorian guards stormed our gathering a few days ago, and as others persisted in seeking him out, he was moved to a house out in the countryside for safe-keeping. This was undertaken especially in light of those who gave their lives for our Lord."

"And others still who capitulated to the Empire," Valaria added.

The man nodded again then went silent, bowing his head and bringing a hand to his chin with contemplation. The table joined his silence, following his lead in bowing their heads as if in prayer.

"But don't forget Germanicus," the Egyptian next to Alexander said. "For although the devil did indeed invent many things against the brothers and sisters in the faith, thanks be to God he could not prevail over all!"

The others gathered offered a murmuring *'Amen'* in agreement, though for whom or what Alexander didn't know.

"I am sorry," Rebekah said. "But we are unaware of what you speak."

"The most noble Germanicus, a local elder of the Church of Smyrna," Felix explained, "strengthened the timidity of others by his own patient endurance through the Empire's persecuting violence. He fought the wild beasts with outstanding heroics in the stadium after he and others refused to swear by Caesar as lord and offer sacrifices to him in worship."

"Unlike others..." Valaria said.

Another murmur rippled around the table, the men and women shaking their heads, some folding their arms in disgust.

"And who would that be?" asked Alexander.

"Quintus," the Egyptian said, twisting his face in disgust and shaking his head.

"A Phrygian," Felix explained before literally spitting to the side at the mention of the man's name. "The man had recently arrived from Phrygia, and when he saw the wild beasts, after being rounded up with the rest of the brethren, he became afraid, giving into cowardice and persevering in the faith no more."

Again, more murmuring and head shaking from those gathered.

"Might as well have apostatized from the faith, publicly denying Christ as Lord and Savior."

"Which in effect he did by capitulating to the dogs of Rome," Valaria said.

"Fear and cowardice wasn't his only weakness," Felix continued the story. "For he forced himself and some others to come forward voluntarily for trial, where he was persuaded by the proconsul to swear by the Emperor and to offer a sacrifice in honor of the Empire."

"Not Germanicus," the Egyptian said proudly, grinning widely and emotion now rising to his eyes.

A woman to the man's right wrapped an arm around his shoulder in comfort. The man must have known the martyr at some personal level.

Valaria smiled. "Indeed. When the proconsul sought to persuade Germanicus to swear the same and offer the same sacrifice, instead our dear brother dragged the wild beast toward him, provoking it and desiring to escape all the more quickly from this unrighteous and impious world."

The Egyptian man wiped his eyes and added, "Upon witnessing this spectacle of martyrdom in the amphitheater, the whole multitude, marveling at the nobility displayed by the God-loving and God-fearing group of Christians, they all cried out: *'Away with the atheists! Let Bishop Polycarp be sought out and thrown to the lions!'"*

Felix folded his arms and chuckled. "But of course the most admirable Polycarp, when he first heard of this threat against him, that he was sought for by the mob, he was in no measure disturbed. Instead, he resolved to continue serving the city and the Church."

"However, cooler heads prevailed," Valaria said, flashing a knowing grin.

Felix reached for his wife's hand. "Indeed. He wanted to remain in town, but we persuaded him to leave. So he departed to our country house not far from the city. There, he has stayed with a few friends, engaged in nothing but praying for all the men and women under his care, night and day, and for all the churches throughout the world, according to his usual custom."

Alexander sat still, heart thumping with anticipation, realizing they had found their access point to their pot of Christian-insight gold. He chanced taking a stabilizing breath and easing it out his nostrils, so as not to garner attention

Then he said, "Would you be able to take us to him? Myself and my companion?"

Felix glanced at Valaria, grabbing a goblet of wine and taking a drink. He took a long pause before answering, then said, "When do you need to go?"

Alexander grinned. "How about this evening?"

CHAPTER 17

ANTAKYA, ARABIA-PERSIA. AD 2123.

"Johnny Mark, that's the nuttiest idea I think you've had yet since I've known you!" Lucy exclaimed in an alleyway sandwiched between a bakery and that nightclub they'd been staked out at.

"Tell me how you really feel about it..." Ford said, raking a hand over his close-cropped hair.

He rolled a glass bottle with a broken neck under his boot in the darkened alley filled with dueling scents from the bakery's freshly baked goodies and the nightclub smelling of cheap tobacco and booze and lots of tightly pressed bodies. An odd mix that oddly made his mouth salivate as his head swam with the plan—but for different reasons, given the differing pleasures they promised.

But she was right. It was nuttier than a bare-naked bear in a berry patch.

But what was the alternative? The way he saw it, they needed the Order remnant. There was a good chance they had been holed up all secret like under the central cathedral in what was once Antioch, the cradle of Christianity stretching all the way back to the beginning. The Republic sure was keen to get down below, sending Purifiers of all things. Which meant there were Unfits down there that needed the talents of Solterra's version of the Schutzstaffel, the Nazi's instruments of terror.

Getting down below wearing their street gear wouldn't cut it. And there was a good chance his face unmasked would be recognized, given he was a Defector and all. Which the lovely Luciana Jane had pointed out. That's why they needed a disguise. And he knew just how to do it.

"But going in as Enforcers? I mean, come on!" she exclaimed again.

"Keep your voice down, would ya?" Ford hissed. "And we're not going in as Enforcers, plural. It's me who's going in all clandestine like, and you're my prisoner."

"Even nuttier!"

"Again, the volume…"

Lucy opened her mouth to respond, then sighed. She raked a hand through her hair and started pacing, working it all out in her head while Ford prayed she'd get on board. Or had some better plan that didn't involve him taking out an Enforcer and stealing his clothing. Or the good Lord above gave him an ecstatic, revelatory insight into how the hot Hades they could get past the Legion's top guards and steal into the Order's purported regional headquarters.

Or both.

"Suppose I do agree to this cockamamie plan of yours," Lucy finally said, leaning against the nightclub wall scarred from decades of misuse. "How do you envision this working itself out?"

Ford went to answer when something heavy thudded behind him. Then a *chic-chic* echoed, sounding eerily like the Neutralizer he had spent years getting to know.

"This is a restricted area!" a voice bit at them with all of the guttural, mechanical familiarity of the Enforcers he had been evading for a year.

Lucy froze, her eyes wide with fright and mouth literally falling open with surprise.

So did Ford, legs anchored to the ground and back to the Republic's guardian.

I prayed for an ecstatic vision, Lord. Not the goods hand-delivered in some back alley in the armpit of the Republic!

As they say, the Lord works in mysterious ways. But no way in hot Hades was he going to turn around and hand-deliver himself to the Republic.

The Enforcer didn't get the memo.

"Who goes there? Identify yourselves," the soldier grunted.

Ford licked his lips and shifted on uncertain feet. Then he mouthed: *'How many?'*

Giving him just the answer he didn't want: She flashed him two fingers.

He closed his eyes and sighed.

Shucky ducky...

They had one shot at this. Maybe two. Definitely not three.

And definitely could go one of two ways.

Dead or alive.

"I said, identify yourselves!" the Enforcer bellowed, followed by another cocking sound of another Neutralizer.

"Al—alright. Hold on..."

Ford held his hands out and started backing up. One foot at a time.

Until he heard it.

"Halt! That's far enough. Now turn around and give me your finger."

Ford stopped short. Then he flashed Lucy a wry grin before dropping to one knee to retrieve the blade on the inside of his boot.

Hoping against hope that he was out of range of any reaction from the Enforcers behind him.

But, as most people within the Republic are well-versed, hope is hard to come by in Solterra.

A Neutralizer just behind his head let loose with a *one-two* blast.

Missing him by centimeters and burrowing in the pavement with bluish-white electric tendrils.

Felt the heat on that one. Definitely too close for comfort.

But he was ready. And so was Lucy.

He popped up and spun around, shoving the blade with purpose in the vulnerable spot just between the neckline and the helmet shielding the Enforcer's face.

All the while Lucy let loose three bullets over his shoulder toward the other threat.

One went wide, thudding uselessly into the nightclub wall.

The other ricocheted off the Enforcer's helmet, splintering pieces and sending them to the ground.

The final bullet should have been the proverbial nail in the coffin, aiming straight for the man's chest as Ford fell to the ground with his own prize.

But the Republic sure knew how to equip its military operatives. Stunned the man, and he faltered his steps, but didn't kill him.

Which was just enough of an open window Ford needed.

He swung around the Neutralizer from the Enforcer he'd just taken out and let it rip, sending electric globs sailing into the Legion guard and laying him flat on his back.

"Nice shot, sassafras," Ford said, removing the blade from the one Enforcer's neck and huffing a breath. "Definitely was some fancy shootin'!"

"Thanks," Lucy replied hustling over to the other Enforcer.

"Not too bad a shot yourself. Got 'em good. And pretty sweet gift of divine providence if you ask me."

Ford started removing the armored uniform off the one downed Enforcer. "How do you figure that?"

She bent down and started working the armored uniform off the other one. "Now I don't have to go into the hornets nest as your prisoner."

He cocked his head to consider this. "I like your thinking. Let's suit up so we can hightail it out of here before their buddies come a callin'."

Took them some doing, but soon they had stripped the Enforcers to their skivvies and suited up. Only problem was Lucy's helmet was damaged and the armored uniform was a tad bulky over her slighter frame, so that might turn some heads. Other than that, they looked like bona fide Solterran guards.

Now for the tricky part: uncovering just what the hot Hades those Purifiers were up to.

"Let's do this," Ford said, padding to the end of the alleyway and peering around the corner. Satisfied, he nodded at Lucy and took a step off the plank toward their date with destiny.

Felt exposed, and his heart was strumming a mean beat now, his head filling with dizzying worry. Prayed the Grip wouldn't get him on their approach.

He clenched his jaw and shook his head, then took a deep breath and sent up a prayer to the good Lord for protection and courage.

Time to get your head in the game, John Mark. No room for error.

The closer they got, the more he realized just how much the Republic had showed up in force. At least five or six more Destroyers were arrayed around the perimeter. Packs of

Enforcers were bunched and roaming, whether searching for signs of survivors or keeping the area cleared of intruders, he didn't know. Trackers were circling above as well, their whirl and hovering orbit making Ford sweat now.

But that wasn't the worst of it.

Large, jagged chunks of ancient stone smoldered and belched smoke with fingering flames still reaching for more victims and hissing in protest from water arcing into the cauldron from Rescuers anchored at the perimeter. From a distance it had looked almost cartoonish, as though a toddler had dumped out a bag of those plastic construction toys he had played with as a kid. Now it was gut wrenching, like after one of those hurricanes that ripped through coastal towns back home, leaving wicked devastation in its wake.

The Ministerium agents crunched across bits of crushed debris on their approach, kicking up clouds of fine dust left over from the pulverizing the ancient church had taken. An eerie, vacuous silence had been left behind in the aftermath of the Republic's persecuting campaign.

Ford's mouth tasted coppery from the adrenaline coursing through him now, his head hammering from the freighted moment.

Steady...

The one Destroyer they had spotted up the road was only a few yards away now, with an Enforcer perched up top and manning a massive gun with a barrel the size of a tree trunk. Another Enforcer, rivaling the Destroyer in size, was roaming around its base, weapon poised to dish some major hurt.

Ford glanced behind at Lucy, face masked and Neutralizer lazily slung around her chest.

Play it cool, John Mark. Play it cool....

And he did. Taking a breath, he strode past the pair of

advanced Legion guards and on toward the hole in the ground without nary a word from the blockheads.

He felt their eyes boring into them as they sauntered past, now at the front end of the massive idling magnacraft.

Just as Ford passed the Enforcer unit, Lucy gave a startled, low cry from behind.

He spun around, glimpsing her right boot caught on a chunk of debris and his partner tripping forward.

She fell hard to the ground, jamming her knee into the outsized rubble.

The Enforcers erupted in laughter, the one up top pointing and slinging a string of curses down to Lucy while the other doubled over.

Ford wanted to light 'em up then and there. But he held back.

Instead, he commanded, "Look alive, soldier! Pick your sorry excuse for an Enforcer back off the ground and get moving!"

Good for Lucy, she never cried out in pain, and the Enforcers were none the wiser on their little scheme.

Lucy hustled past, climbing the mound of rubble on toward the opening they had spotted.

Ford gave a grunting chuckle at the Enforcers. "Grunts. Can't live with 'em, can't live without 'em."

The two nodded, and Ford hustled after his partner.

"You alright?" he asked behind her, keeping his head down and voice low.

"Hurts like a mother," Lucy said, voice strained. "But I'll live."

"Good, because we ain't out of the henhouse yet. Not by a long shot."

Taking careful steps, they found a path that the Republic's hired hands had presumably cut through the rubble for easier access, leading right to the doorway down below. Crimson streaked several chunks of debris, and limbs could be seen poking up through the rubble. A cloth doll, lying atop the cathedral's remains, white stuffing spilling from a missing limb and streaked with blood, pretty well summarized the wickedness that had befallen Christ's community.

Lord have mercy, Christ have mercy, Lord have mercy...

Ford went to cross himself, then remembered what was what. Instead, he gripped his Neutralizer and plowed forward, vowing to get the bastards who had ripped apart Christ's flock.

If it was the last thing he did, by golly he'd tear 'em to shreds.

Another two Enforcers were guarding the entrance when they arrived, bigger and wider than the others they'd just passed.

"I got a bad feeling about this," Lucy mumbled.

"Feeling's mutual..."

A pair of Purifiers shoved past them on toward the opening. Giving Ford the blessed window to act.

"Come on," Ford whispered. "And act natural like."

Without waiting for a reply, he followed them, gripping his weapon and raising it higher at his chest, as if he were guarding the Republic's foremost security agents.

As they say, fake it till you make it.

He hoped they—whoever *they* were—were right.

Otherwise this would be a real short trip.

Holding his breath, the two Purifiers reached the entrance. Literally, a hole in the ground, rubble piled high and stairs leading down below the surface. Reminded him of the stairwell leading down into Master Theo's chamber in Edessa.

Paying no mind to the Enforcers standing guard, the Purifiers kept going.

And so did Ford, with Lucy hot on his heels.

Please, Jesus...Please, Jesus...Please—

And then they were descending. Down, down, down into a darkened void lit by a string of white LEDs looking like a mineshaft leading straight into hell itself.

Ford eased in a stabilizing breath as the four of them clomped one by one down narrow brick stairs hardened by time and heat. The cramped space, no larger than a prefabricated mobile home hallway, rang with their footfalls, the light casting eerie, claustrophobic shadows that threatened to give him vertigo.

It was growing cooler as they descended, now out of the beastly hot direct sunlight and carried ever downward, several stories by his estimation. Wet earth and mildew and ancient stone rode on an updraft of dry air, bringing relief to his high-alert body suffocating inside that blasted Enforcer armored uniform.

Brought a smile to his face too, because the scents reminded him of home and triggered memories of basement brawls and box-and-blanket forts with childhood friends in their modest farmhouse. When times were simpler, happier, less threatened.

A handprint, darkly crimson and smeared against the brickwork snapped him back to the moment.

There were more, echoing what he had seen above, as well as pools of darkened life-force spilled down the stairs, still wet and sticky and smelling of death. And then more streaking prints of people trying to escape or hobbling from harm's way.

Ford gripped his Neutralizer tighter again, his stomach clenching into a sickened knot.

Finally, a faint yellow signal of life beyond the stairs emerged before it grew into a warm, inviting glow and opened into a vast chamber.

Warm and inviting my hind quarters...

He wished he would never have descended or could just

turn back. The bloody handprints and spilled blood was hardly the worst of it.

A vast space the size of a gymnasium, built of beige mud bricks, was glowing from orange lanterns erected around the perimeter. At either end, fireplaces, throwbacks to bygone eras that echoed the ancient memories of the space in service of the Order of Thaddeus, lay dormant. Tables, mounted by sophisticated computer hardware were arrayed throughout the space, clearly a hub for the Order's activity, perhaps even clandestine.

And in the center, piled high, were bodies—perhaps three to four dozen, by the size of it. All bloodied and severed and flopping over without life. Reminded Ford of Mama's clothes pile waiting to be laundered. He wanted to retch but held steady.

A hand from behind gave him a gentle shove forward. It was Lucy, reminding him in some small way that appearances needed to be maintained.

He cleared his throat and strode forward, keeping his distance but ambling after the two Purifiers who kept going toward a hallway jutting off from the main hall.

Lucy followed after him who followed after them as they weaved through a series of corridors until arriving at another room. This one was guarded by a reinforced steel door and palm-reading keypad.

Ford grinned. Same make and model as the one he had disabled with ease back at the Ministerium weeks ago when duty called. Apparently, the Order of Thaddeus hadn't gotten the memo about their defectiveness.

One of the Purifiers removed a glove from his hand and pressed it against the device.

And apparently the Republic had made quick work of reprogramming it.

Duly noted.

Within seconds, a green indicator flashed approvingly, and the door unlocked.

The two pushed through. Ford went to continue, but was stopped.

"Wait here," the man said, with the same gruff, mechanized voice as the Enforcer from the alleyway. "Don't let anyone inside. Understood?"

Ford nodded, but caught a glimpse of what was inside over the soldier's shoulder.

A woman, hair jet black and skin a shade of olive, features angular and body toned, was standing upright against a wall just beyond the door in a cramped room, arms outstretched and secured by straps and without her shirt, chest bare before her captors.

Ford went to turn away from the immodesty of it all, when he saw it.

Something dark and oozing on her exposed chest, as if appearing through the fires of torture.

Literally.

The coppery scent of spilled blood and rising stench of burnt flesh filtered out from the room.

Branded on her chest was a familiar symbol. Two arcing lines intersecting at the ends, mirroring one another to form a fish.

The Ichthus.

The early Church had identified friend from foe using the symbol. Since the Reckoning, it had been adopted as a banner of pride to separate the remnant of Christianity from the rest of the world religions by adopting the culture's curse and reidentifying with its central figure and beliefs formed as an acrostic with its letters: *Jesus* (I) *the anointed Christ* (Ch), *Son* (U) *of God* (Th), *our Savior* (S).

It had also become a derogatory curse across the Republic

the past few decades as Christian brothers and sisters were forced to resurrect the symbol through the superheated fires of persecution.

And now it was being used like the old yellow Star of David badges used by Germanian Nazis from two centuries ago to brand Jews rounded up for mass extinction.

Except this symbol was branded on her chest, the arcing lines charred black into her skin and oozing blood.

Heat began rising up the back of Ford's neck even as rage coursed through his veins.

"Understood?" the Purifier growled again.

Ford swallowed and quickly nodded before the Purifier turned and strode through before shutting the door securely.

Oh, I understand. Perfectly.

Then he clenched his jaw with resolve.

Because no way in hot Hades would he let a sister in Christ be tortured at the hand of Solterra. And likely an Order remnant, no less.

Which meant they had to do something.

It was him and Lucy against the Republic.

Again.

THE HORIZON WAS INFLAMED NOW and sky high above the color of a bruised plum, the sun having set as the four, Alexander and Rebekah accompanied by Felix and Valaria, set out for the country home where bishop Polycarp was holed up.

It was a silent journey and darkening quick by the disappearing sun, the four of them mounted on horses stabled in the city. Alexander had never ridden a horse, and boy was his back side screaming the whole way. Feared every muscle was bruised beyond repair and every bone had been whacked out of joint. Not only did the past reek to high heaven, the animals themselves confirming that with every step, it also hurt.

Boy, did it hurt.

Felt like forever, but probably an hour later hills crowned with grapevines arrayed in neat rows came into view under the full-moon light. A nicely kept road of bricks led toward a modest one-level home, tendrils of spicy smoke rising from its center chased by the leftovers of some charred animal. Soon, they reached the farmhouse and dismounted, their horses neighing with relief and drawing two men outside.

"Lucas, Mateo," Felix said, securing his horse to a stone pillar.

"Master Felix?" one of the men said, young and stocky and sporting a shaved head. "What brings you this late hour?"

Finishing, he helped his wife dismount her own horse then set about securing it. "Two visitors, Lucas, dispatched by the Order of Thaddeus. Alexander and Rebekah."

Alexander had also dismounted and was helping Rebekah do the same.

"The Order?" the other man said, presumably Mateo. "But why? What business do they have disturbing Polycarp's place of refuge. They should know better, given the ongoing threats from the Empire."

"Forgive us," Alexander said, holding up a hand and walking toward the two men who might pose a problem. "We do not wish to compromise the bishop. But the Order is in need of advice and spiritual insights into this ongoing...threat, as you put it. Which our brothers and sisters are facing throughout the Repub—err, Empire, as you know."

Mateo, lean and tall like Felix with moppy brown hair, brought a hand to his scruffy face and scratched his chin, glancing at Lucas who was guarding the door with arms crossed. The two nodded at each other before stepping aside.

"Alright," he said, "but do not tarry. The threat has grown ever greater since he fled. And the bishop's latest vision does not bring us any comfort for a quick resolution to our plight."

Alexander offered a grin and nodded, thanking the man and wondering about this vision business. He would have to ask him about that before their time was up.

Opening the door, Lucas led the party inside after Felix secured the other two horses. The space looked similar to what the Ministerium pair had witnessed in past jumps through time: a large, unadorned room made of stone or plaster work, wood beams exposed and a fire crackling in a hearth before a wood table, two doors leading to other rooms in the dwelling.

The farmhouse felt as if it was barely used and lived in, probably serving as a holiday home and base of operations for their wine-making operation out front.

"Please, sit," Mateo said. "We will fetch the bishop."

Alexander took a seat at the table; Rebekah sat across from him.

Valaria took a ceramic pitcher of wine and poured them each an earthenware glass full. Felix brought over a loaf of bread, cold and crusty.

Alexander thanked them and promptly took a mouthful, the heavy, tannic wine filling his mouth with vanilla and cedar and boysenberry. He learned a third lesson: while the past smelled and hurt, its wine tasted far better!

"Here they are, Bishop Polycarp," Mateo said, gesturing toward the pair as a large man rushed inside the room, sporting a Buddha belly with a close-cropped white beard rising to encircle a balding head.

"The Order of Thaddeus?" Polycarp boomed, voice deep and buttery. "My pleasure, my pleasure!"

The two stood. Alexander went to extend his hand when he remembered that wasn't really a thing in the past. Instead, he opened his arms to mirror the man who was reaching in for an embrace. Rebekah was next, getting lost in the man's massive arms.

"Sit, sit!" he said, gesturing back to the table. Felix poured the bishop his own goblet of wine and retired with Valaria to one of the other rooms. Mateo and Lucas did not, leaning along a wall near the fire.

"I must say, I have greatly rejoiced with the Order in our Lord Jesus Christ, and all of the saints throughout the Empire, because ye have followed the example of true love as displayed by God."

Alexander smiled and nodded. "Thank you, bishop."

"I have been especially keen on how your members have offered assistance to those who were bound in chains, the fitting ornaments of saints, and which are indeed the crowns of the true elect of God and our Lord."

He nodded again, not having realized that aspect of the Order's work, helping the persecuted. Something he imagined would continue under his leadership in the coming months back in the future.

"Now, what is it that the Order of Thaddeus has sought from one such as I?"

Here we go...

Alexander took a breath, praying the neural sensory receptor was working without a hitch, especially after the tumble it took on future Smyrna's shore.

He said, "Put simply, we need your insight."

"Insight? Into what?"

"The rising apostasy plaguing the Church accompanied by rising persecution. The Order understands that you have been a bulwark against both, championing the pure roots of the Church's faith in Jesus Christ and perpetuated in the teachings of the apostles while also encouraging those suffering under the mighty weight of Rome. We desire to bring whatever you might share back with us to encourage the holy and Catholic Church sojourning in every place."

The man eased his large frame back, bringing a hand to his beard and stroking it. "I appreciate the sentiments, young man. I am at your mercy. What would you like me to share?"

Alexander chuckled. "Everything!"

"That certainly covers the full measure of it!" he said with his own full-bellied chuckle.

"What have you said to other churches seeking your advice, bishop?" asked Rebekah. "I understand you wrote a letter to the church of God that sojourns at Philippi."

Polycarp nodded. "That I did. And I supposed that is as good a place as any to begin." He leaned forward, taking a mouthful of wine before resting his elbows on the table. He went on, "What I shared with them I share with you: gird your loins and serve the Lord in fear and truth, forsaking the vain, empty talk and error of the Roman mob, and especially the whore of Rome itself!"

Pausing, he took another sip of wine before continuing. "Believe in him who raised up our Lord Jesus Christ from the dead, and gave him glory and a throne at his right hand, I wrote. For he who raised our Lord Jesus Christ up from the dead will raise up us also, if we do his will, and walk in his ways, loving what he loved and keeping ourselves from all unrighteousness, covetousness, love of money, evil speaking, false witness."

What convicting, challenging words—the heart of the teachings of the Christian faith! Which was exactly what the future Church needed to hear.

Rebekah shifted in her chair. "And how do we go about such walking?"

"It begins with those who would dare lead Christ's Church," Polycarp said without missing a beat. "These men and women should be blameless before the face of our Lord's righteousness, given that they are the servants of God and Christ, and not of men. They must not be slanderers, insincere, or lovers of money. Instead, let those who lead Christ's Body be self-controlled in all things, having compassion and working diligently for Christ's kingdom, walking according to the truth of the Lord, who was the servant of all."

Alexander smirked, thinking about those of the Ministerium, the leaders of the Church in the future, who had every characteristic *but* those Polycarp outlined.

Apollos Nicolai and Dominic Weiss, with all of their self-righteousness and slander and insincerity, denying the fundamental truths of the Lord. Even his old friend Josiah Abasi was far from blameless. Which gave Alexander pause.

Because if such a man could fall into apostasy, charting a course that walked a path veering so remarkably from the once-for-all faith, then who else was prone to fall? He himself certainly was, which sent a shiver ratcheting up his spine.

The Apostle Paul was right in his first exhortation to the Church of Corinth: '*So, if you think you are standing firm, be careful that you don't fall! No temptation has overtaken you except what is common to mankind.*'

Including the temptation to apostatize.

Thankfully, he goes on: '*And God is faithful; he will not let you be tempted beyond what you can bear. But when you are tempted, he will also provide a way out so that you can endure it.*'

Yes, a way out. But what was that way for the future Church facing such a supercharged temptation to jettison the once-for-all faith entrusted to God's holy people? Especially given the Republic's advances against free thought, free speech, free exercise of religious expression—and now the labeling of the Church as Unfit, as hostile to the agenda of Solterra's peace and prosperity and progress?

"Let them be compassionate and merciful to all," Polycarp went on, interrupting Alexander's thoughts. "Let those who would lead the Church of Christ bring back those who have wandered from the faith with all gentleness, visiting the sick. Their judgement should not be severe, knowing that we are all under a debt of sin. And let all believers serve our Lord Jesus Christ in fear and with all reverence, even as he himself has commanded us. Let us be zealous in the pursuit of that which is good, keeping ourselves from causes of offense, from false brethren, and from those who in hypocrisy bear the name of the Lord, and draw away vain men into grievous error."

One end of Alexander's mouth tugged upward, for there was his answer to his own question: men and women who rose to the challenge of leading Ichthus, and really all believers, holding fast to the once-for-all faith, remaining faithful to God's Word, and making disciples of Jesus Christ—baptizing them in the name of the Father, Son, and Holy Spirit, and teaching them to obey everything Jesus commanded, just as Christ himself had taught in the Gospel of Matthew.

Rebekah sighed and leaned back in her seat. "Sounds like a tall order."

Polycarp chuckled. "What do you mean, dear child?"

She glanced at Alexander, who nodded for her to continue.

"What I mean is, such false brethren, as you make mention, are all around us! What shall we do?"

"Have nothing to do with those who reject Jesus!" the man exclaimed, waving a dismissive hand. "Flee from the heretics who deny what the Church teaches about him. Instead, persevere in fasting and prayer."

"Explain that more, Bishop Polycarp," Alexander said.

"Consider what the Apostle John wrote in his first letter: *'For whosoever does not confess that Jesus Christ has come in the flesh, is an antichrist.'* And whosoever does not confess the testimony of the cross is of the devil. Whosoever perverts the sayings of Christ and what the Lord taught does so to suit his own sinful desires. These people say that there is neither a resurrection nor a judgment. The firstborn of Satan they are!"

This was getting good. Just what the pair had traveled back in time to collect.

Alexander smiled. "I understand, but what advice would you give the Church? After all, that is why we visited you from the Order, to seek advice from those who are enduring the tragedy of rising apostasy, as much as impending persecution."

Polycarp replied, "My advice is what I tell all believers I

have the privilege of teaching: Forsake the worthless speculation of the mob and cast aside their false doctrines, that which leads to apostasy. Instead, let us return to the Word of God which has been handed down to us from the beginning, the once-for-all faith entrusted to God's holy people, as Brother Jude Thaddeus himself said."

The man took a breath then a mouthful of wine. He settled back in his seat and folded his arms, looking like he was readying for a long-haul teaching session now. Which was fine for Alexander, considering their mission.

"Let us then continually persevere in our hope, and the earnest pursuit of our righteousness, which is Jesus Christ, '*who bore our sins in his own body on the tree,*' '*who did no sin, neither was guile found in his mouth,*' but endured all things for us, that we might live in him. Let us then be imitators of his patience; and if we suffer for his name's sake—whether at the hand of heretics, who would seek to transform the faith to tickle the ears of our cultured despisers, or the Empire, who would seek to make us reject Christ as Lord—regardless, let us glorify Jesus Christ."

"So practically," Rebekah interrupted, "how does this play itself out?"

"Two things: Obedience to the word of righteousness and the exercise of all patience. Consider the case of the blessed Ignatius, who was obedient to the end and patiently endured until his martyrdom in Rome, then also others throughout the Empire. The result? They receive their due place in the presence of the Lord, with whom also they suffered. For they loved not this present world, but him who died for us, and for our sake was raised again by God from the dead."

Rebekah nodded, glancing at Alexander. "Wise words, bishop. Wise words."

The man smiled and nodded before growing silent.

Sensing they were in danger of overstaying their welcome, and already having gotten plenty of worthwhile words to take back to the future Church, Alexander asked, "We should retire shortly, Bishop Polycarp, but I wonder if you have anything else you would like to mention."

"Yes, I should retire myself, as the hour is growing late. But I will say this: Pray for all the saints, and pray also for kings and princes, the Emperor and rulers of all sorts, especially for those that persecute and hate the Church of Jesus Christ, and for the enemies of the cross—that our fruit may be made manifest among the people and evident to all, so that we may be perfect in him."

"Fruit?" Rebekah asked, cocking her head.

"Yes, fruit. Through martyrdom," Polycarp said matter-of-factly.

The word settled in the room in a way that sucked the air out of it, causing Mateo and Lucas to stir from the sidelines, the crackling and popping of the fire the only sound now.

"I have written to various churches," he went on, "what relates to the martyrs. I only hope to put an end to the persecution, having, as it were, set a seal upon it by my own martyrdom."

"Bishop..." Lucas said with a huff.

"What? I do."

"You know how we feel about such talk."

"But it's true! For almost all of the events that have happened previously have taken place that the Lord might show us from above a martyrdom that is in accordance with the Gospel."

"You're speaking of yourself, Bishop Polycarp?" Rebekah said.

He nodded. "I am. For I am waiting to be delivered up, just as the Lord himself had waited, that my own willing participation in his death, taking up my cross, as it were, might exhort the Church of God that sojourns in Empire Rome to truly become his followers, imitators of Christ, not looking merely at what concerns ourselves but to the interests of our neighbors. For it is a true and well-founded love to not only wish one's self to be saved, but also all the brethren and sistren as well, the whole Empire!"

In theory, Alexander understood martyrdom as such, as a way to participate in Christ's own suffering and offer our neighbors a visual path for salvation, showing forth our true commitment to faith in Jesus, even unto death. But he had never truly considered it before. Perhaps he should, especially with the recent advancements of the Republic back home.

"All the martyrdoms, then," Polycarp went on, "were blessed and noble, which took place according to the will of God. And truly, who can fail to admire all the martyrs' nobleness of mind, and their patience, with that love towards their Lord which they displayed. Who, when they were so torn with scourges, that the frame of their bodies, even to the very inward veins and arteries, was laid open, still remained obedient and patiently endured, while even those who stood by pitied and bewailed them."

There were those words again: obedience and patience.

"Looking to the grace of Christ," he went on, "they despised all the torments of this world, redeeming themselves from eternal punishment by the suffering of a single hour. For this reason, the fire of their savage executioners appeared cool to them. For they kept before themselves an escape from that fire which is eternal and never shall be quenched, and looked forward with the eyes of their heart to those good things which are laid up for such as endure in Heaven. Things '*which no ear hath heard, nor eye has seen, neither have entered into the heart of man,*' but were revealed by the Lord to them, inasmuch as they were no longer men, but had already become angels.

"And, in like manner, those who were condemned to the wild beasts endured dreadful tortures, being stretched out upon beds full of spikes, and subjected to various other kinds of torments, in order that, if it were possible, the tyrant might, by their lingering tortures, lead them to a denial of Christ."

Then he paused, adding: "That is to be my lot as well..."

The bishop trailed off, staring out into the window and emerging night.

Lucas and Mateo shifted from the sides again, looking at one another and folding their arms in unison, as if deeply concerned for the truth of his words.

Alexander said, "What do you mean, that this is to be your own lot? Martyrdom, you mean?"

Polycarp took a breath and sighed, then fixed him with dead-serious eyes. "Several days ago, I departed to this country house of my dear friends, Valaria and Felix, with my companions, Mateo and Lucas. And doing nothing else, night and day, I have spent time praying for the sojourners of the Church of Smyrna, and for all the churches throughout the world. And while I was praying, a vision presented itself to me three days ago."

Alexander sat up straighter at the mention of the ecstatic vision Polycarp had made mention of at the beginning. "What was this vision, of which you spoke earlier?"

The bishop scooted to the edge of his seat and propped his elbows on the table. "Behold, I was sound asleep, exhausted from a full day fasting and praying, and the pillow under my head seemed to be on fire!"

"On fire?" Rebekah said.

"Yes, dear lady, on fire, I say. And in a flash of ecstatic

insight, I turned to Mateo and Lucas and said to them prophetically, 'I must be burnt alive!'"

"Bishop Polycarp," Mateo said with a sigh. "How many times must I tell you to hold your tongue from such nonsense!"

"The Church of Smyrna would crumble without your guiding hand," Lucas added, "the void being filled by every form of false doctrine. Surely the Lord Jesus Christ knows this. Why would he snatch your life?"

"And under such extreme circumstances?"

Polycarp went to respond when a sudden neighing cry sliced through the nighttime air. It was soon followed by a commotion outside the door. The clomping of hooves and the clanging of metal, and the firelight of a thousand torches.

Lucas immediately sprang toward the window overlooking the rolling hills of grapevines, and gasped. "They've come!"

"Who has come?" Rebekah said with a start.

"The Empire," Polycarp said with resignation, face set as flint. "Who else?"

CHAPTER 19

FEAR clenched hold of Alexander like a rabid dog, jaws locked around his head and shaking him with terrifying ferocity that wouldn't let go.

This is not happening. This is not supposed to be happening!

Their trips were meant as tourist jaunts. Nothing but fact-finding forays into the past to gather information and insight, maybe taking in the sights and sounds and personalities of the past phases of Ichthus's history, but then bringing it all back home. Safe and sound, no harm no foul.

Definitely not getting wrapped up in the imperial entanglements of said past personalities and phases!

Oh, what he wouldn't give for one of his synthetic ribbons of relief, with all of its soothing, satisfying, satiating power to quench the rising anxiety that threatened to consume him—petrifying him with immobility, darkening his thoughts, clouding his mind when what he needed most was his wits about him in this bloody—

A gentle hand rested on his shoulder, snapping him back to the moment.

"You alright?" Rebekah asked lowly as the rest of the room activated, with Valaria and Felix now running about.

Alexander blinked and swallowed hard, his throat like sandpaper from the dryness of dread. Taking a breath, he nodded.

They were now in the thick of it. And there was nothing they could do.

'Even though I walk through the darkest valley, I will fear no evil,' Alexander resolved, praying David's words from Psalm 23 with trust. *'For you are with me; your rod and your staff, they comfort me.'*

He took another breath and swallowed, the tension easing now and a peace stretching over him like a warm blanket.

Lord Jesus Christ, Son of God, please prove these words true this dark night...

"It is the same masked pursuers who terrorized Germanicus and the others," Lucas said at the window, "along with horsemen, a dispatch of praetorian guards, and—"

The man stopped short, recoiling from the window with wide eyes. "No...it can't be."

Mateo was at his side now, taking in the sight himself.

"What is the matter?" Alexander said, voice faltering at what was befalling them, but gaining a measure of stability that surprised him.

"Two youths that have been part of the community," Mateo said. "Both mounted on a horse. And looking battered and bloodied. They must have confessed under duress, the torturous means of the Empire drawing our location from them with pain."

"Betrayed by his own household..." Lucas growled. "Judases of our day."

"I wouldn't be too hard on them," Polycarp said. "What

man could stand under the weight of Empire Rome, let alone two youths?"

"Then it is time to go," Mateo said, leaving the window and shuffling out of the room with purpose.

"They are gathering their forces outside," Lucas said, the firelight glinting orange off his face in greater measure now. "There is still time before they break through the door."

"To the cellar," Felix commanded, "where an underground spring awaits us leading to escaping relief."

Mateo returned, a broadsword clinging to his hip and both hands bearing two more. He set one on the table in front of Alexander, its blade resounding with a clang, and handed the other to Lucas, who wielded it like it was his own arm.

Alexander eyed it with a mixture of trepidation and apprehension. What the heck was he supposed to do with this? Fight? A legion of Roman soldiers?

"Time to go, bishop," Mateo said, offering the man his hand. "We'll stay, the three of us men while you—"

"No," Polycarp said resolutely, folding his massive arms and holding his head high.

"But, bishop, you can't—"

"No! The will of God be done. I will not flee a second time. Should never have fled the first. Now is our hour of light."

Hour of light? What crazy talk, with the Empire bearing down upon them with persecuting intent.

But Alexander had to hand it to the man. A darkness, the blackest evil he could imagine given what he knew of the Empire's persecuting violence, was pressing in just outside the door. And yet, the man saw only light.

Instead of fleeing, Bishop Polycarp suddenly stood and moved to the doorway, the light as bright as day now from the assembled torches, and the neighing of horses and clanging of a legion of men resounding with ill intent.

Lucas went to intervene when the bishop silently put out one of his massive arms. With the other, he grasped the handle and opened the door. Then he strode forth and spoke with the men, approaching a soldier festooned with battle-hardened armor and a crimson sash, indicating a degree of rank.

Alexander's heart was strumming a mean beat as they waited inside, waiting for what came next, his head matching the tune with thunderous pressure.

The minutes ticked by. When he could stand it no longer he arose and made his way to the still-open door, straining to glean what he could from the conversation.

From what he could gather, the soldiers arrayed around the man seemed to marvel at his courage and his unwavering commitment to his faith.

One of them closest to the door mumbled to the man next to him, saying, "Was so much effort necessary to capture such a venerable man?"

Another was struck by his age and his calmness, surprised that the arrest of such an old man could be so urgent.

Alexander smirked and shook his head. Indeed, they were right.

Polycarp spun back toward the dwelling, ordering those of us inside to set something before the men to eat and drink, as much as they desired, whether bread or wine or meat and vegetables.

Then he turned back toward the man Alexander presumed was the captain of the guard and asked them to allow him an hour to pray without disturbance.

Surprisingly, he granted the bishop his leave.

Polycarp put his hands together and bowed. "Thank you, kind sir. Would you come this way?"

He led the group of eight or nine men toward the dwelling, Mateo and Lucas meeting them at the door, standing with folded arms rippling with taut muscles ready to take on the entire detachment of soldiers if necessary.

Alexander bolted to the window, his breath seizing in his chest at the risk of confrontation gaining a head of steam toward inevitability.

Not good...

And then it happened. Two of the praetorian guards, men the size of gorillas with rattling dull steel armor affixed to their chests, raced forward and shoved the men inside.

They stumbled back with a cry, thudding into the table anchoring the center, but quickly recovered, springing forward and striking back with blows.

A cold panic flooded Alexander's veins as he looked on, immobile and helpless to do anything but gawk and pray someone else doused the confrontation, and soon.

Swords from the rest of the group still outside were quickly drawn, and Polycarp was cast aside as the men raced in to assist their comrades, a logjam of eager bodies preventing them from gaining entrance.

"Mateo, Lucas!" the bishop shouted from outside, as fists swung inside with abandon. "Do not resist!"

Alexander feared the worst for his fellow brothers in the faith, but did nothing other than shield Rebekah and Valaria with his arms, who were huddled in one corner. Even Felix was standing on the sidelines, shouting for the mayhem to cease.

The bishop turned to the captain as the melee continued. "Restrain your men and I will bring this to a peaceful end," Polycarp pleaded.

The man nodded and called out for his men to fall back.

Surprisingly, they did as he commanded.

Bodies shuffled back outside and stood erect at attention. From the window, Alexander could see that both of the men who had started it all were bearing bloodied noses. He looked to Mateo and Lucas, who were wiping blood from their own faces, their eyes blackening and swelling now from the beating. But he took some small measure of satisfaction that the Empire had been bloodied, even for just a moment.

Polycarp stormed inside and had a few choice words for his companions, reminding them of Jesus' words: '*Do not resist an evil person. If anyone slaps you on the right cheek, turn to them the other cheek also....If anyone forces you to go one mile, go with them two miles. Give to the one who asks you, and do not turn away from the one who wants to borrow from you.*'

Alexander knew the latter reference was a particularly germane one, given it historically connected to Roman soldiers and their legal right to order citizens to carry their belongings. Which meant the follower of Christ was called to submit to the Empire, even when it seemed humiliating. Like that evening.

The men held their heads, blood dripping to the floor, and apologized. Then they hobbled outside and did the same to the soldiers they had bloodied. A humiliation, to be sure, but one that had probably spared their lives.

The captain brushed off the incident and led the detachment of guards inside. Soon, they were seated around the very table they had earlier gleaned so much insight from the good bishop.

Valaria and Felix and the other two men quickly began serving the soldiers. Polycarp retired to a room off the main, standing and praying, being full of the grace of God, so that his prayers could be faintly heard above the din of eating and drinking.

Alexander backed into a corner, taking Rebekah with him to give the rest all the room they needed, while trying to make sense of the mess they had found themselves in.

Again.

"What do we do, Alexander?" Rebekah whispered with a degree of calm he could only hope for.

He shook his head. "Haven't the bloodiest clue. Do you recall what happens to the man?"

"He is taken away and martyred," she said. "On the morrow."

Alexander held his breath then sighed, figuring as much.

And they were caught up in the middle of it all. Which meant they could very well receive the same fate.

Was he ready? Not only to die, but to do so under pain of torture before a crowd of bloodthirsty onlookers in a local amphitheater?

And for his faith?

They stood in the corner and said nothing more, waiting for the events to unfold and wondering how they would make it out alive.

Or perhaps they wouldn't. Perhaps this was their own lot, having cast themselves into the void of time's phases to retrieve the memory of the historic Christian faith, only to die a martyr's death.

Nearing the two-hour mark, the eating and drinking having finished as Polycarp continued praying in the room next door, Alexander heard the men grumbling about their assignment, even repenting that they had come forth against so godly and venerable an old man.

"This is taking too long," a man grumbled, the one with the armor and crimson sash.

"Perhaps I should retrieve him, Herod?" a young man next to him said, "Knowing how eager you are to bring him in to the stadium that Bishop Polycarp might fulfill his special lot, being made a partaker of that Christ figure whom he venerates."

Just as the captain went to reply, the praying ceased, the bishop having made mention of all who had at any time come in contact with him, both small and great, illustrious and obscure, as well as the whole Catholic Church throughout the world.

He came out from the room, and the whole table sat still.

Alexander was taken aback by the man's face, full of vim and vigor and almost glowing with a holy hue. Not what he would have expected from someone facing a martyr's death. And he dared to wonder whether he himself would have been as delightful, at peace—eager, even.

But then he recognized it. The man knew the time of his departure had arrived. And he was ready. More than that: He was willing. Willing to stand in the face of the rising apostasy and antichrist's of his own day and take a stand.

A stand for faith in Jesus Christ as singular Savior, despite what the apostatizing despisers were claiming; a stand for faith in him as singular Lord, despite what the imperial persecutors also claimed.

The captain now arose from his place at the table, and Polycarp strode forward.

Two more soldiers stood and seized the man, then promptly handled him through the door and out to an awaiting donkey, where they mounted him on top without fanfare.

Mateo and Lucas were also brought along, bound and thrust upon one of their own horses tied to a post out front. There was some debate about the other four, whether they should be similarly bound and brought to stand trial, given their association with the insurrectionist bishop and his two troublemaking companions.

A cold sweat overtook Alexander as they awaited their fate. Rebekah even drew close, slipping her hand in his for stability. He glanced down, her face more frightened than he had ever seen her.

He drew a small measure of strength from it, knowing that

she too was scared out of her wits. He wasn't alone in his fear of dying the death of a martyr at the hands of the Empire.

Valaria and Felix stood holding one another near the doorway to their country house, probably regretting their visit from two strangers. He himself was feeling no small measure of guilt for dragging them into history's turn of events. He wondered if this was how it played out in the past, before their arrival. Whether the couple had indeed paid a visit to the bishop holed up in their country home. Or whether they had made a bloody mess of things with the time-space continuum— or rather, the space-time continuum as Sasha would surely have corrected him.

He raked a hand through his hair as they stood waiting for their death sentence, praying to the good Lord above that he grant them a reprieve.

A soldier suddenly broke off from his conversation with the captain, the young man from the table earlier in the night.

"The gods must be shining down upon you this evening," he said. "You are free to go."

A sudden breath held with expectation exhaled with relief from Alexander. The soldier smirked at his weakness, but he didn't care. The only God who mattered had saved them from no uncertain doom.

Again.

"If I were you, I would recommend disassociating yourself from their lot," the soldier continued, nodding toward the three brothers in the faith slumped over on their steeds. "The Empire is taking a zero-tolerance stance toward the atheists who refuse to exchange worship of this Christ figure for worship of Caesar."

He spat on the ground and sauntered back to the group of soldiers, then mounted his horse. The rest followed suit, along with the captain, who grabbed hold of the donkey bearing the bishop and went to lead him.

"Wait!" Felix said, running toward the detachment.

Which immediately drew their swords of polished steel from their sheaths, the soldiers issuing rapid-fire orders and pushing him back.

He threw his hands into the air and backed up. "I only wish to know where you are taking Bishop Polycarp and his companions."

"Back to the city," the captain grunted. "What happens to them there is a matter for the Empire."

The man gave a grunting cry to his horse, which jolted forward down the path, dragging the donkey along with it.

Bearing Polycarp toward his historic ruin.

Which, in reality, was his personal victory.

CHAPTER 20
ANTAKYA, ARABIA-PERSIA. AD 2123.

"Are you sure about this?" Lucy asked, voice tinged with a slight tremble beneath that helmet of hers playacting the Republic's finest.

Ford sighed.

No, he wasn't. No way, no how. But what choice did they have? They had minutes before those Purifier whack jobs did God only knew what to that sister in Christ strapped like Christ to the wall.

And they were the only ones there to stop it.

He replied, "All I know is, we've got a few precious minutes before Thing One and Thing Two in there start flaying the skin off that poor woman. Who, by the way, is probably our lifeline to the Order of Thaddeus Remnant."

"Not if we get her killed. And us in the process."

True that.

But again, what choice did they have?

Lucy shook her head. "Never mind. If we're gonna do this thing, let's get to it."

Ford brightened a bit. "So you're game then?"

"Always game to kick a little Solterra ass."

"That's my girl."

"But you're sure you can bust through this thing?" she asked, eyeing the door.

"Positive."

"Looks pretty secure to me, and I'm not a fan of half-cocked impromptu rescue plans."

He scoffed. "And I ain't into executing half-cocked impromptu rescue plans. Step aside, sassafras."

Ford crouched before the door to take a second look at the security unit guarding it. "Just what I thought. Same crappy make and model of the ones I replaced back at the Ministerium —well, *former* Ministerium headquarters."

He stood and took a step back, aiming and readying to set things in motion that would rescue the Order agent hostage.

God willing and the creek don't rise, as Grandpappy Johnny Mark used to say, the man he stole his *nom de plume* from after fleeing the Legion.

"The Order must not have gotten the memo on the upgrade. Good for us." Taking in a stabilizing breath, he glanced to Lucy and added, "You ready?"

She nodded. "Let's roll." Then stood behind him with her own Neutralizer, ready and willing should it come to it.

Here we go...

Ford sent *one-two* quick bursts of bluish-white electrified balls into the unit. No use in overdoing it and making more ruckus than they needed.

The thing blew apart, its black casing melting in an instant and circuitry inside frying along with it, tendrils of smoke trailing upward in victory.

But the door didn't budge.

No turning gears inside the wall, no click of the lock, no swinging open of the door on cue.

No nothing.

Shucky ducky!

"Well, I'll be..." was all Ford managed to get out as he spun toward the corridor in case of trouble.

"What the heck happened?" Lucy asked with a hissing rush.

"How should I know? I'm just the head of ops."

"Now what?"

Before Ford could respond, the door opened from behind.

"What the blazes happened out here?" a gruff voice inquired.

He spun back around to find one of those Purifier whack jobs from earlier poking his head out of the interrogation room.

He grinned beneath his helmet.

The Lord works in mysterious ways...

Without pausing to contemplate the repercussions of his maneuver, Ford punched the man in the face.

Sending said Purifier whack job clutching his helmet and stumbling back into the room.

Before he could recover, Ford let loose *one-two-three* rounds from his Neutralizer.

Toasting the dude in an instant.

But not before the other Purifier whack job went for his weapon.

And another they didn't know about was rising from behind a table, helmet removed and chomping away on something that filled the room with the scent of heaven.

Smelled like pizza.

Ford backed up with weapon raised, like one of those old-school westerns to put the hurt on both men before they could mobilize.

But clicked empty.

Four more rounds of Neutralizer blasts spit out into the room, flashing past the surprised Order agent still exposed on the wall.

And sailing dead-center mass into the one Purifier before he could reach his weapon.

Ford spun to the side and skidded to the floor, surprised he wasn't writhing in a sea of bluish-white electrical charge.

Lucy was standing with feet planted apart, sending another *one-two-three* rounds to the other side.

Slamming into the other man's exposed head and snapping it backwards, nearly tearing it off from his torso. He slumped face first into his half-eaten slices.

But not before he got off a round that sliced the surface of Lucy's left shoulder.

Smacking into the wall behind her but not before singeing through her charcoal uniform and sending a shocking charge across her upper torso.

Lucy cried out and stumbled back against the wall, then slid to the floor.

"Luciana!" Ford exclaimed, scrambling over to her.

She moaned from the pain still bolting through her.

"Looks like just a minor static discharge," he reassured her as he checked her shoulder.

Smelled like a burnt T-bone steak, but it was only a flesh wound. Most of the damage was done to the uniform itself, its baggy bunchiness probably saving her.

"Looks like you'll live to fight another day, sassafras."

He stood and held out a hand. "And thanks for the backup, sister. I owe ya one."

Lucy smirked and took his hand. "Let's hope not."

Ford tossed his spent Neutralizer to the floor then turned toward the entrance. "Go take care of our asset while I grab the door."

As she limped to the woman who looked half conscious, he thanked the good Lord above she was safe and sound. Didn't know what he'd do if he lost her. Which was an odd, unexpected feeling.

Ford shook his head to get it back into the game.

The door was cracked only a few centimeters. Probably recoiled back when they stormed through. Hopefully, it was enough to keep most of the sound inside.

Before opening it for a look-see, he grabbed the Purifier's weapon then held his breath for a look.

Dead silent.

Too silent, for Ford's liking. Not a thing moved.

Although, they were a few stories underground and nobody seemed to be paying any mind to what was going on down here.

Still. He didn't like it.

But he'd take what he could get until they could make sense of it all.

He shut the door, the heavy reinforced steel locking with purpose.

"Who are you people?" the woman said, voice shaking and betraying fear.

Lucy had cut her from the straps holding her arms in crucifixion and retrieved the woman's shirt, a coral blouse streaked with crimson.

And Ford saw why.

Her nose was swollen, with crusted blood at her nostrils. Both eyes were blackening and there was blood crusted to one side of her head as well.

Clearly the Purifiers had had their way with her before turning to their final measures of torture. Which meant she wouldn't give up the information they were trying to torture out of her.

Ford hustled over, slinging the Neutralizer around his back. "Don't worry, ma'am, we're the good guys. That's who we are."

"We're with the Ministerium," Lucy explained. "What's left of it, anyway."

The woman's eyes widened. "What's left?"

He answered, "The same whack jobs who leveled your home leveled ours as well. The Ministerium headquarters are a goner."

The woman took a breath and a step back. "And above…"

"Same. Sorry. We were sent on an operation to retrieve the Remnant of the Order of Thaddeus."

She sighed and cast her eyes to the floor. A few beats later, she asked, "But how did you know where to find me?"

"Don't you mean us?" Ford said.

The woman shook her head. "There are no others. At least not in Antioch."

He took a breath. "Alright then, so you're it. Which means we better scram, and pronto. Because I'm guessing we don't have much time before the Solterra county mounties discover our little infiltration. Especially since whatever it is they tried extracting from you you didn't cough up. Good on you."

She pushed her dark hair behind her ears and averted her eyes to the floor again.

"My name's John Mark Ford, by the way," he said, then gestured to his comrade. "This is Luciana Jane."

"People call me Lucy."

"Kareema Salam," the woman said, offering a weak smile. "I am the regional director of operations for the Order. Or at least was. Before the Republic destroyed it all."

"Kareema Salam…" Ford said. "That Arabic? Muhammedan?"

A banging at the door drew their attention before she could respond.

Thud-thud-thud. Pause. *Thud-thud-thud.*

Sucking all air from the room and jolting the trio into action.

Ford cursed, then glanced at the ladies and blushed. "Sorry. Old habit."

Kareema padded over to the man whose head was a blackened, bloody mess behind the table. She grabbed his Neutralizer as another round of *thud-thud-thuds* intruded.

"Shucky ducky..." Ford said, taking in the room. "How the hot Hades are we gonna get out of this one?"

"How about the ventilation shaft?" Lucy asked.

He smirked. "Yeah, right. This ain't no bargain bin ebook thriller from DiviNet."

"She's right," Kareema said, craning her head toward the ceiling as she hustled to the back of the room.

"She is?"

A large grate as wide as two people sat near the ceiling at one end. It was painted over beige to match the room, which was why Ford missed it.

"Works for me," he said as Kareema and Lucy pulled over a table beneath the grate.

He hopped up and began working on the grate. Blessedly, it popped off with little effort.

"Through the looking glass we go, ladies."

He helped the Order agent up to the table, then interlocked his fingers together to hoist her up and inside.

She took a step and launched upward, her hands finding purchase inside the ventilation shaft and Ford doing the rest to shove her through.

One down, two—

The door exploded with fire and fury, filling the space with smoke and debris.

Shucky ducky!

"Lucy..."

Didn't have to tell her twice.

She did what Kareema did. Soon Ford was shoving her bottom through as well.

Just as a barrage of Neutralizer charges splattered in through the fog of war.

Ford jumped for the opening and grabbed onto two hands, which pulled him inside.

"Scram and all that jazz!" he hissed, to himself as much as his two companions.

Sending them skittering farther inside the ventilation void as a detachment of Enforcers piled into the room.

They kept going—without looking back, without speaking, without letting up—weaving through a maze of ductwork at least a century old, probably longer. Made sense, given the history of the cathedral now a heap of rubble up top, and Ford thanked the good Lord for it as they pulled away from danger without further incident.

"We're here," Kareema said abruptly, halting her advance and grabbing hold of steel grating anchored at the top.

Ford sighed with relief, his mind beginning to go muddy from claustrophobia.

"Does it look safe?" Lucy said. "Are we all clear?"

"Can't tell entirely. The sun has set, and I see piles of rubble from the downed cathedral scattered about, but no Enforcers or Purifiers. From what I can tell."

"Can you remove the grating?" asked Ford.

She twisted her face with effort and pushed with her shoulder, the grating giving with an echoey clang that sent Ford's heart racing with fear of being found.

Kareema held her position, the grate loose and balancing on her shoulder inside the opening.

They held their position a minute before she eased it up above.

Then she popped her head out and stood, climbing out and whispering for the pair to do the same.

The ductwork had put them in a garden on the edge of the lawn that once belonged to the Order, the cathedral a ruined mess strewn about and that bony hand of the remaining spire sandwiched between the ultramodern ice cream cone buildings still reaching heavenward.

"We better scram," Ford said lowly, "before our beloved Patron knows what's what. And I'm sure the new Order Master will be eager to get to know you more once he and Rebekah are back from Smyrna."

"Smyrna?" asked Kareema as they darted across the lawn under the cover of thick clouds.

"Long story."

"I heard about Master Theophilus's death. But who is this new Master you speak of?"

"Alexander Zarruq."

The woman stopped short and spun around, nearly colliding with Ford and Lucy, eyes going wide before brow dipping into a scowl.

"Za—Zarruq, you say?"

Ford tilted his head and furrowed his brow with confusion. "Yes...why? You a jilted lover of his, or something?"

Kareema grabbed Ford by both arms. "We must get word to the Ministerium Master. This changes everything."

CHAPTER 21

SMYRNA, AD 155.

THE NIGHT HAD STRETCHED into early morning by the time the four strangers who had been thrust into circumstances not of their choosing finally headed back toward Smyrna, the darkened blanket punctuated by those tiny echoes of starlights' memory slowly fading to the color of a bruised strawberry, the flaming sky beneath the horizon beginning to make itself known.

After Polycarp had been taken away, along with Mateo and Lucas, Valaria and Felix debated amongst themselves about next steps outside while Alexander and Rebekah awaited for word inside at the table where they had just been talking with the bishop hours before.

The two said nothing to one another. Too stunned by the turn of time to say much. Besides, what would they say anyway, much less do?

Finally, as the couple outside continued their deliberations, Alexander had voiced to Rebekah whether prudence dictated they return back to Smyrna on their own and seek the home where they had jumped phases. After all, this wasn't their fight. Literally, as they had jumped into the past not yet half a day ago.

Rebekah wasn't having any of it. She felt compelled to try and help the man—even though she felt that was a major no-no for the space-time continuum, yet according to Sasha they couldn't change the past anyway. She also thought they should capture more of the man's story to take back with them to the future. Considering all that threatened Ichthus from not only the rising apostasy, but the increased risk of a rising antichrist on par with the Apocalypse warned about in the Holy Scriptures.

The four finally decided to head back into town and seek the proconsul for the location of their beloved bishop's jail cell, hoping to find his companions as well. Perhaps they could persuade the man to make nice with the Empire. Or at least persuade the proconsul that the man was a threat to neither Rome nor Caesar.

So there they were, back on those bloody horses' backs, clippity-cloppiting down the road back toward Smyrna.

Along the way, Felix told stories of the bishop, how he had personally led him and Valaria to faith in Jesus Christ. How he had nurtured them in the faith and carefully answered their questions, even chastising him with a merciful mixture of grace and truth for his own struggles with doubt. How the man had stood up to the heretic Marcion for his blasphemous, apostatizing teachings against the Hebrew Scriptures, who claimed the God of the Old Testament differed from the God of the New Testament. How he stood for the true faith without apology.

Becoming choked with emotion now, he also mentioned that Polycarp's name meant *much fruit.* Alexander thought it an appropriate, if not providential name.

Not only for the way in which the good bishop stood for the once-for-all faith, bearing much fruit in his life by guarding orthodoxy in confronting such heretics as Marcion as well as doubts in the faithful. But also because of the fruit he would eventually bear in his faithful witness to Christ in death.

None of their companions would truly grasp this significance. All they saw was their beloved bishop and friend under the yoke of no uncertain doom.

The sun continued rising in all of its blazing brilliance, and Valaria mentioned that it was the day of the great Sabbath. Again, how providential.

As they clomped down the road back toward Smyrna, every muscle and bone crying out once again, not having recovered from their first horseback jaunt, Alexander recalled the words of the Apostle Paul from his letter to the Church of Philippi: *'I want to know Christ. Yes, to know the power of his resurrection and participation in his sufferings, becoming like him in his death, and so, somehow, attaining to the resurrection from the dead.'*

What better day to die than on the very day celebrating Christ's victory over death? What better way to share in these sufferings, as Paul made mention, than in suffering and dying for his name?

The horizon was on fire now, set ablaze by the rising sun beaming off from a smattering of clouds. Echoing the nature of Polycarp's death, burnt alive upon a pyre. It all again seemed providential.

They reached the town, and Felix led the party to the home of the proconsul himself, Philip the Asiarch. Apparently, the two of them went back ages. They exchanged words, and soon they had again mounted those bloody steeds, clippity-cloppiting back down the road toward the praetorian guardhouse.

Where they found Polycarp in a dark, dank cell fast asleep, his companions one cell over and wide awake.

The hallway leading toward the cell was musty and mildewy. It smelled of piss and ripe bodies, and almost no light shone inside, but for a few gaps near the ceiling. The darkness was suffocating with a humid, heavy hotness, compounded by the walls of misshapen, badly cut stone blackened by age and the evil that resided within.

Alexander thought he would retch. He stood sweating from the freighted anxiety of it all, standing next to Rebekah whilst Felix aroused the elder bishop from his slumber.

After finally waking the man and conferring with the head praetorian guard, the party was granted permission to speak with Polycarp in his cell, joined by Mateo and Lucas.

The wood door was locked tight with two Roman guards standing inside, swords strapped to their waists and muscles rippling underneath battle-hardened leather jerkins. They made Alexander nervous, but none of the others seemed alarmed.

"It does my heart good to see you," Polycarp said, embracing Felix and then Valaria. "But trouble yourselves not for me."

"Are you hurt?" asked Felix, looking the man over.

He shook his head. "Upon riding back to the city, I was treated with the utmost respect, being brought to the very cell in which you find me. I went willingly, without incident. Once here, I spent time praying for the Church of God who sojourns throughout the Roman Empire. For their safety, yes, but also that those who might find themselves in a similar predicament might join me in joining with Christ's example of suffering and death. Then I drifted to sleep."

Alexander considered this, praying the same for those of Ichthus, the Remnant of the Church, who sojourned back in the future.

Praying the same for Rebekah, for himself.

Before the bishop could continue, the door swung open with a thud.

"You have visitors," a guard announced.

Mateo, left eye swollen shut and blood caked to the side of his head, took a step toward the man. "Who?"

The Roman guard narrowed his eyes and took a step himself. "Back away, *atheist cannibal.*"

Alexander took a breath at the term, understanding the Roman society believed the stories about Christians eating real human flesh and blood in their Eucharistic ceremony, feasting on people instead of the bread and wine, symbols of redemption.

Mateo's face fell, and he bowed his head, stepping back to the wall.

A satisfied grin flashed across the guard's face. He said, "Irenarch Herod, who is accompanied by his father Nicetes."

"The captain of the praetorian guard from this evening?" Felix exclaimed. "And his father, the powerful proconsul?"

"That is correct. The pair have come along in their chariot to meet the man."

"What do they want? What business do they have with the bishop?" Lucas asked, bearing all of the same markings of his friend, but wisely remaining along the wall.

"What business? Whatever business they bloody well please! They've secured permission to take the man up into their chariot. Now stand up and get along!"

The guard strode toward Polycarp who stood and outstretched his hands in surrender. Two more guards appeared at the door, moving in to secure Mateo and Lucas, and then two more for good measure.

Alexander backed up, along with Rebekah. Felix and Valaria stood still, as the men bound Polycarp's hands with rope and led him out.

"Out!" one of the other guards commanded the four visitors.

Felix offered parting words of encouragement to Mateo and Lucas; Valaria embraced each of them and offered a kiss on their cheeks. Then the four were ushered out of the holding cell and back into the dawning Sabbath morning.

"This is madness!" Felix complained on the steps of the guardhouse.

Valaria put a calming hand on her husband's shoulder. "We must trust our Lord with his life now. Brother Polycarp is in his hands."

Alexander couldn't help but feel relief for having escaped both the praetorian guardhouse as well as the persecuting violence awaiting Polycarp.

But then he saw it, down the road several meters away perched under the protective boughs of a large oak tree standing guard outside the ancient police station.

A carriage.

And climbing into it from the road was Polycarp!

Ushering him inside, two praetorian guards closed the door to the ancient vehicle and posted themselves just outside, facing the road with backs to the carriage and walkway on the other side of the tree.

Alexander had an idea.

It was lunacy, and anxious jitters skittered about in his belly. But he couldn't help himself for thinking he needed to get close to the carriage. Enough to be able to hear the conversation the bishop was having. Even with the guards posted outside.

He and Rebekah had been sent to retrieve the man's memory, not only of the faith but of his faith experience. In all of its multidimensional glory. Which also meant whatever happened to him in his death as a martyr.

Including what was happening inside that carriage.

He took in a stabilizing breath to check himself. Then he sighed with resignation and glanced at Rebekah.

Now or never...

He put out a staying hand then darted along the street before he could change his mind, hearing a complaint from Felix, but paying it no mind.

He padded up quickly to the oak and pressed himself against its large trunk, praying its girth would shield him from the guards who were still milling about just beyond the carriage.

Breathing hard, he twisted his body just enough around to lean in for a hearing.

"What harm is there in saying, 'Caesar is Lord,' Bishop Polycarp?" a voice said from inside.

He instantly recognized him as the captain of the Roman police force, Herod.

"And in making necessary imperial sacrifices, incense and so forth," a second voice said, "and so ensuring your safety and the safety of the Church of Smyrna?"

He didn't recognize this one, but figured it was Herod's father.

Alexander recalled from Father Jim's explanation of Polycarp's story that both requests were anathema to the early Church. For to voice such a vow and make such ceremonial offerings would be to deny the truth of Christianity's central belief: that Jesus Christ and him alone is King of kings and Lord of lords; that every knee will bow and tongue confess that Jesus is Lord, not Caesar; and that to make such a cultural and imperial appeasement would be to offer up the worship due only Jesus' name to a pagan deity, for Caesar had styled himself as a god.

A long silence enveloped the inside of the carriage. He

imagined the man aghast at the suggestion, but he wondered what he would say, what would happen next.

With no answer, the men inside continued to urge him on, insisting on the confession and the sacrifice.

Finally, the good bishop spoke: "I shall not do as you advise me!"

And that was that. Case closed.

Alexander cursed himself for wanting more, the neural sensory receptor picking up all aural signals from his ears. But there was a simplicity about it that he respected. A simple *'No!'* to cultural power, and consequently a resounding *'Yes!'* to the gospel of Jesus Christ, was all that was needed.

Having no hope of persuading the man, Herod and his father began to speak bitter words.

Then the door to the carriage suddenly opened.

Alexander's heart lurched forward and his pulse joined it on a wave of fight-or-flight adrenaline. But it happened so fast without room to react.

Polycarp was cast from the carriage with a violent fury. The man tumbled out to the ground, crying out with pain, and another voice issued rapid-fire orders to the guards outside.

Alexander eased back around the oak's trunk as the carriage pulled away, the guards on the other side laughing without sympathy and commanding the man to stand.

"Get up, old man!" one guard commanded again, before kicking Polycarp in his backside.

Another cry arose from the man as he slid face first into the dirt.

Alexander held his breath as he stood just a few meters from the men.

Finally, the bishop managed to stand. "I've dislocated my leg, by the fall." Then he limped back toward the guardhouse, as if suffering nothing.

But the guards had other plans.

They followed after him, Alexander easing around the opposite way to avoid being seen.

When suddenly, a detachment of guards on mounted steeds rushed out from around the guardhouse and pulled up another few meters beyond.

"Time to meet your Maker, atheist cannibal," one of the guards grunted. "The stadium awaits."

He hoisted Polycarp upon one of the horses, and then they galloped away in a hurry, kicking up a furious storm of dust in their wake into the horizon blood-red from the sun's continued dawning rise.

Alexander stood panting as the cloud settled, thankful to have not been seen but wondering about next steps.

Felix, Valaria, and Rebekah came running toward him, giving him a fright as they rounded the trunk. Rebekah was the first to respond to his impulsive plan, slugging him on the arm.

"Oy!" Alexander cried out.

Felix did the same on his other one. "What on earth were you thinking? Do you have a death wish, running up to the carriage of the praetorian captain like that with guards standing near?"

Rolling his eyes, Alexander said, "I needed to hear what they were saying."

"Which was?" asked Rebekah.

"Which was, that he would not deny the name of Christ to ensure his safety. They've taken him to the stadium. I'm sorry, Felix."

Felix's face fell, draining of color. He looked off toward the horizon, where the detachment of guards had galloped off with the man. "I guess that settles it then."

Valaria started crying, leaning into her husband for comfort.

"Can I talk to you a minute?" Alexander asked Rebekah, guiding her away.

They walked down the road a few meters, the Roman couple holding each other now in their sorrow.

He said, "Forgive me for leaving you like that, but I had to make a decision."

"I understand. And I understand the mission called for it. I'll just be happy when we can put this whole bloody affair behind us and jump back to the future."

"Well...we may be holding off on that a bit further."

"Why? We've come for what Father Jim needed. His advice for the Church, just as before."

"Not all of it."

Rebekah scrunched up her brow with confusion and shook her head. Then it relaxed when it hit her.

"No..."

"Come on, Rebekah," Alexander said.

"No, no, no—"

"Experiencing the memory of his martyrdom will be as crucial for the future Church as the memory of his advice dealing with apostasy! I just know it."

She went to say something but took a breath instead. Then she put her hands on her hips and nodded.

Felix and Valaria walked over. The matron asked, "Is everything alright?"

"As good as it can be, considering..." Alexander offered.

She nodded.

"However, we wondered if we might impose on you for one final request."

"And what is that?" Felix asked, stepping close to his wife.

Alexander glanced at Rebekah. "We would like to bear witness to Polycarp's martyrdom. We understand how big of an ask this is, given the precarious nature of the threat against the

Church of Smyrna, and especially you two as leaders within the community. But as members of the Order of Thaddeus, we feel it is our duty. But we are unsure where to locate the stadium, and time isn't on our side."

The *pater familias* pursed his lips and narrowed his eyes, so that Alexander thought he was about to flat deny them their request.

Instead he said, "We will all go." He glanced at Valaria, who nodded. "The four of us."

Within the hour, they had made their way to the massive oval structure they had glimpsed the night before. It stood five stories tall, made of red cut stone and wood, flags flying the Roman eagle on top. Bloodthirsty cries of a crowd high on masochism greeted them on their arrival.

Vendors selling kabobs and bags of rotten vegetables— presumably the former for eating, the latter for throwing at the afternoon's entertaining spectacle—were out in force, yelling from rickety wooden carts canopied with tattered cloth of various shades of faded yellows and reds and blues.

Men and women alike huddled around them, some bartering and others exchanging Roman coins—as if buying hot dogs and popcorn at a Solterra rugby match or basketball game. Even children ran wild across the packed dirt that was the plaza to the entertainment venue.

Alexander wanted to retch at the sight of it all. Especially the children, being conditioned on barbaric violence at such a young age. Then again, was it any different from the DiviNet games that thrust young minds into virtual reality gore fests on par with the gladiators of second-century Rome?

Given their class, Felix and Valaria were able to usher the

pair of time travelers into upper-level seating. There, wine and cheese with various cured meats and fresh bread were arrayed on earthenware platters above the crowds below.

A group of young and old men laughed at a well-timed punchline down their row, whilst a grouping of similarly aged women fanned themselves farther up top at stone tables, sipping wine and popping grapes. As if what was about to transpire was as normal a social affair as a horse race.

"Makes me sick," Rebekah voiced, arms clenching her stomach and mouth turned downward with disgust.

Alexander nodded. "Agree. But I am happy we've come to bear witness. If not for our sake and the future Church's, then for Polycarp's."

"Perhaps he'll see us and take heart."

"Not likely," Felix said. "We're a good bit away. And besides, he will have enough to concentrate on down below, depending on what the Empire has in store."

"What do you mean?" asked Alexander.

The blast of trumpets cut through the din, startling Alexander and drawing his attention across the other side to a platform.

On top of it sat three chairs, and in them were two men and a woman. From what Alexander could tell, the proconsul of the region, the man Philip the Asiarch they had seen earlier to gain access to Polycarp, and his wife. On his other side was the captain who had apprehended the bishop.

The crowds began to quiet some. Until gates opened and in strode pairs of praetorian guardsmen.

They threw up a raucous greeting for the men, for they knew what came next.

Polycarp, the star of that afternoon's entertainment.

And there he was, striding in the middle of the grouping of

guards. Head held high, and walking with a hasty, almost eager gait.

A rush of conflicting emotion seized Alexander. For he was sorrowful for the man's impending death, but also overjoyed at the man's witness—and they were there to bear it. Not only for his own faith, but for the faith of the future Church.

Because Lord knew the Church's future was history without the witness of the past.

CHAPTER 22

POLYCARP CONTINUED STRIDING toward the center of the stadium, the crowd whipping into a frenzy at his appearance.

Alexander sat still, mesmerized by the man's composure. How does someone walk so calmly toward certain death, head held high with such courage, such resolve, such peace?

As the cacophony of voices arose into a rabid cheer for the main event to commence, the sun beating down now without mercy in a cloudless sky, and his clothes beginning to stick to him with sweat, he recalled a passage from the Book of Hebrews that put it all in perspective:

> Some faced jeers and flogging, and even chains
> and imprisonment. They were put to death
> by stoning; they were sawed in two; they
> were killed by the sword. They went about
> in sheepskins and goatskins, destitute, perse-
> cuted and mistreated—the world was not
> worthy of them.

Same for the man Polycarp, still striding with defiant witness before the Roman world in AD 155.

Philip the Asiarch, the proconsul, was conferring with his retinue and the crowd's tumult was so great now, that there was no possibility of being heard.

Except for the sudden intrusion of a voice.

Alexander heard it clear as a bell. So did the other three, who turned to one another with wide eyes until their mouths broke out into a grin and their eyes began streaming with the emotion of it all.

The voice was a voice from Heaven, saying, *"Be strong, and show thyself a man, O Polycarp!"*

It was clear no one else around them or in the crowds below heard what had been spoken to the man. The words were only meant for the beloved bishop and the witnessing Church, clearly those of the Holy Spirit speaking revelation truth meant for the man on his way to martyrdom, Alexander was sure of it.

The tumult became great and thunderous now, so that even the very stone benches they were sitting on were vibrating with a wicked hatred.

When Polycarp reached the center of the stadium, he was brought by a pair of guards forward toward the proconsul at the center across the way. Trumpets blasted again, quieting down the crowd.

A holy hush settled over the place, so that time itself felt stuck as eternity itself waited for the man to bear witness to his Savior, his Lord.

When the bishop reached the dais where Philip the Asiarch was seated, the governor asked the bishop whether he was Polycarp.

"I am he," the man boomed confidently so that all could hear, the Spirit clearly evident with a rippling reply of surprise from the mob by the man's strength and boldness.

On his confessing of his identity, the proconsul stood and began a curious maneuver.

He set about to persuade him to deny Christ.

"Have respect for thy old age," he said. "Simply swear by the genius and fortune of Caesar. Repent, dear man, and say, *'Away with the Atheists!'* and you shall go free!"

The crowd fell silent now, the menacing *caw-caw* of barking vultures circling above the only sound to be heard, their jet-black bodies silhouetted against the clear-blue sky an omen of his coming death.

Polycarp solemnly gazed with a stern countenance upon the multitude of the wicked, lawless heathens who were arrayed in the stadium. When he had taken in the full sight of the onlookers, he waved a hand towards them and agreed with Philip the Asiarch: "Away with the atheists!"

But his declaration meant not what the proconsul meant. For in the days of the Roman Empire, it was the Christians who were considered atheists, for they denied the gods of Rome in favor of the one true God of Christ.

Philip the Asiarch planted his hands on his hips, as if irritated with his reply. His urging continued: "Swear your pledge to Caesar, and I will set thee free; offer your reproach to Christ, revile him and liberty is yours!"

Polycarp fell silent, a silence that felt like an eternity, never dipping his head and never averting his gaze from his condemner.

Then he spoke: "Eighty and six years have I served him, acting as the servant of this Christ you yourself revile, and he never did me any injury, he has done me no wrong. Answer me this: How then can I blaspheme my King, the one who saved me?"

A thunderous, resounding mockery arose from the crowd. And so did the contents of those bags of rotten vegetables they had spotted outside the stadium. Vegetables of all sorts went sailing down below, a few even hitting Polycarp in the back of the head and back and face, their rotten bodies exploding over him with embarrassment and disrespect.

Still, he never recoiled, never guarded himself, never flinched.

The proconsul yet again pressed him: "Swear by the fortune and genius of Caesar!"

Polycarp answered, "Since you are vainly urgent that, as you sayest, I should swear by the fortune and genius of Caesar, and pretend not to know who and what I am, hear me declare with boldness this day, and do not forget my words: I am a Christian. And if you wish to learn what the doctrines of Christianity are, name a day and give me a hearing, and I shall teach you them in full measure!"

The proconsul chuckled, hands still on his hips and throwing his head back with a dramatic reply. Returning, mouth wide, he swept his arms around the stadium. "Persuade the people, then, dear bishop."

But Polycarp let loose a chuckle of his own, saying, "To thee I have thought it right to offer an account of my faith. To you perhaps I might have considered worthy of persuasion. For we who claim the name of Jesus Christ are taught to give all due honor and proper respect to rulers, which entails no injury upon ourselves to the powers and authorities which are ordained of God. But as for these, the rabble-rousers mobbing about in the stands, I do not deem them worthy of receiving any account from me and will not defend myself."

"You would do well to watch your tongue, dear bishop," Philip the Asiarch said. "I have wild beasts at my disposal. I will cast them to you at will, throwing you before their jaws unless you repent and change your mind."

"Call them then!" Polycarp answered without missing a

beat. "For we Christians are not accustomed to repent of what is good in order to adopt that which is evil. Instead, it is well for any man or woman to be changed from what is evil to what is righteous, of which my martyrdom will accomplish."

The proconsul threw his hands in the air and turned around. He planted his hands on his hips again before spinning back and saying to him, "I will cause you to be consumed by fire, then, seeing you despise the wild beasts. If you will not repent and claim the name of Caesar as lord, this shall be your fate, I promise you this."

Again, Polycarp laughed, a boisterous, belly laugh that echoed throughout the stadium. "You threaten me with fire, which burns for an hour until after a little while it is extinguished. But you, and all those whom you have brought as witness, are ignorant of the fire of the coming judgment and of the punishment reserved for the ungodly that burns for all eternity! Why do you tarry? Bring forth what you will."

Alexander marveled at the things he said, at his confidence and joy, that his countenance was full of grace in the face of death—whether by mauling or fire.

Even Philip the Asiarch, the proconsul, seemed astonished, throwing his hands up in the air again and shaking his head. He conferred with the other two with him then sent his herald out to proclaim in the midst of the stadium, not once or twice, but three times: *Polycarp has confessed that he is a Christian.*

This seemed to be a sort of siren call for the whole multitude of heathens living in Smyrna. For they cried out with uncontrollable fury, and in a loud voice, *This is the teacher of Asia, the father of the Christians, and the overthrower of our gods, he who has been teaching many not to sacrifice, or to worship the gods.*

Then the mob, rabid and frenzied with bloodlust, cried out

and besought Philip the Asiarch to let loose a lion upon Polycarp.

But the proconsul answered that it was not lawful for him to do so, seeing that he had brought to a close the animal hunts.

Suddenly, a request began rippling through the crowd, beginning below.

"Burn him alive!" voices began ringing out, until more joined in.

"Burn him! Burn him! Burn him!" the jackals taunted.

It was in that moment that Alexander remembered Polycarp's vision concerning his pillow, the one he had seen on fire while praying.

The crowd kept up its chant: *"Burn him! Burn him! Burn him!"*

The four believers looked at one another with a sickened dread as it continued crescendoing across the stadium and even to the upper levels of the sophisticated class.

Then all at once, Polycarp turned around. He raised his head heavenward, yet also seemed to have caught a glimpse of his companions from the evening. As if to the faithful that were with him in spirit and in presence, he spoke prophetically, with a voice that thundered like that of the Lord Almighty himself: "I must be burnt alive!"

The crowd quieted to a hush, as if it hadn't heard the man correctly. For who in their right mind would request such a thing?

A voice split through the silence: *"Burn him alive!"* Which activated the mob once more.

Philip the Asiarch strode forth with arms raised, stepping to the edge of the dais with eyes fixed on the great bishop. The crowd silenced, waiting for the man's verdict.

Which he gave: "Then let it be so!" the proconsul said.

"Light the pyre! And let's see whose god is greater—whether this man's object of worship will come to his rescue now."

A cheer arose from the crowd, frenzied and fanatical. Demonic, even.

Alexander sank lower, as did Rebekah, fearful they would be spotted and dragged into the arena to join him.

Immediately, the governor's orders were put into action, and apparently the entire stadium got in on the action.

With surprising swiftness, his pronouncement was carried into effect with greater speed than it was spoken, the multitudes immediately gathering together wood and sticks out of the shops and baths.

Felix and Valaria said not a word, their heads bowed and hands clasped inside one another in silent prayer. Alexander and Rebekah joined in the silence, praying but also fearful the mob would come for them next.

Soon, a mound of wood was gathered in the center of the stadium, prepared as a pyre for Polycarp's punishment of naming Christ as Lord.

Soldiers went to apprehend the good bishop, but he put out a hand. Then he began taking off his clothes, all on his own without any assistance or insistence. He removed his belt and then his sandals.

Once naked, but for a loincloth, immediately the guards surrounded him and began piling around him the wood and sticks which had been prepared for the pyre. They had also fashioned together a cross and were about to affix him to it with nails.

Polycarp insisted otherwise: "Leave me as I am. For he that giveth me strength to endure the fire, will also enable me, without your securing me by nails, to remain without moving in the pyre."

Clearly uncertain of the request, the guards looked to

Philip the Asiarch for guidance. The man nodded, but instructed them to bind him.

But Polycarp made it easy: he placed his hands behind himself, a willing participant for martyrdom.

Being bound like a distinguished ram taken out of a great flock for sacrifice, and prepared to be an acceptable burnt-offering unto God, the bishop looked up to heaven and offered a prayer with clarity and conviction:

"O Lord God Almighty, the Father of thy beloved and blessed Son Jesus Christ, by whom we have received the knowledge of thee, the God of angels and powers, and of every creature, and of the whole race of the righteous who live before thee, I give thee thanks that thou hast counted me worthy of this day and this hour, that I should have a part in the number of thy martyrs, in the cup of thy Christ, to the resurrection of eternal life, both of soul and body, through the incorruption given by the Holy Ghost. Amongst whom may I be accepted this day before thee as a fat and acceptable sacrifice, according as thou, the ever-truthful God, hast foreordained, hast revealed beforehand to me, and now hast fulfilled. Wherefore also I praise thee for all things, I bless thee, I glorify thee, along with the everlasting and heavenly Jesus Christ, Thy beloved Son, with whom, to thee, and the Holy Ghost, be glory both now and to all coming ages. Amen."

"Amen..." Alexander mumbled, joined by Rebekah, Felix, and Valaria.

Immediately, the guards set the pyre ablaze, the large wooden pieces and sticks gathered by the mob surrounding the bishop immediately taking fire.

A furious breeze riding in off from the Great Sea, salted and fishy, stoked the flames that much more, tendrils of spicy smoke being spun about and filling the stands with the stench of burning wood.

But something curious happened, miraculous even: The fire seemed to shape itself into the form of an arch, like the sail of a ship when filled with the wind. Instead of consuming Polycarp, it circled the body of the martyr!

"My God..." Valaria said, eyes wide with wonder.

"I agree, dear wife," Felix echoed.

"What is that smell?" asked Rebekah.

Alexander perceived such a sweet odor coming from the pyre, as if frankincense or some such precious spices had been smoking there.

"And look..." she said, pointing down toward the stadium center.

Polycarp appeared within the flames not like flesh which is burnt, but as bread that is baked, or as gold and silver glowing in a furnace!

Which the wicked men below began to perceive as well.

Philip the Asiarch motioned to the guards toward the fire, issuing a command to pierce Polycarp through with a dagger.

One of the meatheads sauntered over, drawing a blade from his waist and approaching the flapping flames. He shielded his eyes and face from the smoke and heat.

Then he jabbed for the bishop, striking him in the stomach.

He slashed at his neck, and on his doing this, there came forth a dove, and a great quantity of blood, so that the fire was extinguished.

Alexander held his breath at the sight, disbelieving his eyes and trying to avert them from the gore. Yet he couldn't. He wouldn't.

The man was bleeding out now, his soul having been taken up to heaven, his head lolling down and mouth open as if in a question. Yet the man knew more than any of the witnesses could know. For, as the Apostle Paul said in 1 Corinthians 13, *'now we see only a reflection as in a mirror; then we shall see face to face. Now I know in part; then I shall know fully, even as I am fully known.'*

Polycarp was seeing his Lord and Savior face to face. The man had fought the good fight. He had finished the race and kept the faith.

Felix and Valaria were stifling sobs next to him now, tears flowing freely as the truth of the matter sank deep into their bones, that their beloved bishop was gone.

For you, Bishop Polycarp, there is surely reserved the crown of righteousness. Well done, good and faithful servant. Run into the arms of your Savior; enter into the joy of your Lord...

Soon, the flames hissed to nothing, having been dowsed by the martyr's blood. The crowd soon broke up as well, becoming bored at the sight and their bloodlust satiated for another day.

"What of the body?" Rebekah said, sniffling and choking back her own emotion.

Before anyone could answer, the leftover pile of bundled wood and sticks were set ablaze.

Causing Felix to bolt to his feet. "What the..."

Within seconds, it became apparent.

One of the praetorian guards grabbed hold of Polycarp's body as the flaming pyre grew into a furnace blaze. He hoisted him up onto his shoulders and tossed the body in the midst of the fire.

Fingering flames hungry for fuel immediately began to consume it.

The four sat stunned, even as the renewed persecution elicited a riotous approval from the mob, some of whom had retaken their seats to watch the body burn, the fetid stench of burning flesh now filling the hot and humid arena.

The world was not worthy of them, indeed...

Waiting a few more minutes, Alexander finally said, "We best get going, brother Felix, sister Valaria."

Wiping his eyes, Felix nodded. "I imagine the Order of Thaddeus is worried sick over your exploits, wondering what has befallen you, especially once word reaches them about the events here in Smyrna."

Alexander smiled but said nothing.

Something like that...

They embraced, and Felix made them promise to carry Polycarp's story back to the Order and disseminate it amongst the sojourners of God's Church. Alexander promised they would.

The pair found their way to a private set of stairs that led from the upper-level seating down to the main entry way of the stadium. They stepped into the sea of bodies, as ripe as he remembered time travel the last time, and flowed with it out into the midafternoon neighborhood.

"I guess we can thank the Lord we know where we are this time around," Rebekah said, holding her head as they plodded forward.

Alexander replied, "That's one way of looking at it. Although we still have the pooch to deal with back inside."

"And its owners, I guess."

"And that."

They weaved past the familiar corner bar, with its large front-of-shop counter decorated in marble mounted with pitchers of wine, the aromas of cooking meat and vegetables and bread wafting past the duo.

"I'll tell you one thing," Alexander said, darting down another familiar alleyway he knew took them back to their jump point. "When we jump back to the future, I'm finding the biggest breakfast joint in town and filling myself with falafel, fava beans, and hummus with pita bread and tea until I can't stand it anymore!"

Rebekah hummed. "Add to that yogurt cheese, nabulsi cheese, and pita with pomegranate jam and I'm in!"

"It's a date then..."

She grinned and blushed, then said, "Looks like we're here."

Indeed they were, the dog from yesterday yammering away inside.

"I was thinking," Alexander said, "I believe we can just make the jump from here."

"Here?" Rebekah exclaimed, looking up and down the alleyway shielded from the sun from the high buildings crowding them. "But it is broad daylight!"

"I know, but once we start the launch sequence, we pretty much zap on out of here. And we're close enough to our original jump point that if we hug the outer wall, we should make it alright back to the future still inside the beach house."

She fixed him with wide eyes. "Should?"

Retrieving his belt from inside his tunic, he said, "Trust me, we'll be fine. Besides, there's no way we can climb back inside that house without being detected."

Rebekah folded her arms and huffed. Then she promptly retrieved her own belt and strapped it around her waist.

Alexander clipped his own belt into place, tightening it and smiling with relief at the continued flashing 'GO' on its face. He glanced at Rebekah's time travel device and confirmed the same all-clear indicator.

He sighed and grinned.

"Looks like we're a go," she said.

"Thank the Lord..."

She held out her hand and pressed herself against the wall, the dog suddenly jumping and snarling just above their heads.

They both jolted with fright, then giggled at the surprise.

Alexander stepped back to the wall and held out his hand. "Shall we?"

Rebekah nodded, grabbing it and standing next to him.

He stole a parting glance up and down the alley before closing his eyes and punching his button still flashing green. Rebekah followed suit.

Time to go home. And stay put for a while...

CHAPTER 23

IZMIR, ARABIA-PERSIA. AD 2123.

FAMILIAR UNDULATING, vibrating waves began to take hold of Alexander's body, shocking him and warming him all at once as he zoomed through the bright luminescence at speeds he could only imagine.

Every atom tingled with the familiar static charge, casting off the welcomed scent of time travel. He continued squeezing his eyes closed, concerned that if he opened them, his retinas would sizzle and head would explode.

But then something unexpected happened.

A pain lanced through his head, from side to side just behind his eyes, accompanied by a high-pitched ringing in his ears.

He nearly opened his eyes from the surprising agony of it, but he held them tightly closed, the ache a zapping misery that continued toward a climax he prayed to God would end in a quick denouement.

Then, as quickly as the warming vibrations and fluid tingles started, they all at once ceased. The feeling of levitation and weightlessness as he rode the waves of time's phases gave way to a heavy groundedness that felt solid under his feet, accompanied by the sound of lapping waves and squawking gulls in the muffled distance. The bright light also dimmed, but not completely.

And neither did the pain nor the ringing in his ears. Lessened, but a severe throbbing ache and pulsing sensation was like a supernova migraine—threatening to overtake him with topsy-turvy vertigo.

He cried out and snapped open his eyes, clutching the sides of his head as if it would help. His knees went instantly weak, and he thought he would retch from it all.

Falling to the floor on all fours, heaving desperate breaths and feeling some relief now in his head, he saw he was inside the beach house. One of its outer walls was tilting outward from disrepair to his right, a crack of the dusking light seeping past a rotten roof. Sure beat jumping back to the future in the sea.

Worry began working through his veins now with a cold dread. He had never experienced such a thing in his life, always having excellent health and being in top shape. But his head... the pain and the ringing.

He slumped back, sitting with legs outstretched and removing the neural sensory receptor still clinging to his head. He glanced at its face, green indicator lights confirming with blessed relief it was still in working order.

He set it on the floor and took in a stabilizing breath, then another, glancing around the sad looking shack.

And seeing no Rebekah!

He glanced frantically around, thinking his eyes hadn't yet adjusted, but she was missing.

His heart jolted forward from adrenaline at the shock, scrambling to his knees.

"*Rebekah!*" he called out, again thinking he had missed her.

His frantic voice was his only reply.

He sprang to his feet, then instantly regretted it, his vision dimming and his legs going wobbly. He steadied himself on the one wall, it giving some and the crack above opening now into a deepening fissure.

"No, no, no...Lord Jesus Christ, Son of God, please—"

"I'm out here!" a muffled cry sounded.

His breath seized in his chest even as hope seized his heart. *"Rebekah!"*

Taking long strides and ignoring his continued foggy head, he rushed out onto the darkening beach and called out her name again.

Rebekah sauntered through the sand around the corner, offering a wave and looking completely fine.

Alexander threw his head back and sighed with relief. Then he ran to meet her, throwing his arms around her neck.

"I thought I'd lost you..." he said, his legs feeling weak again.

"I thought I'd lost—"

He slumped to his knees and brought a hand to his head.

"Alexander, are you alright?"

"A migraine, I think."

"Here, sit down..." she eased him to the sand with one arm and held the other at his back. "You felt like this traveling back from the past?"

He nodded. "Part way, near the final leg of the jump."

"You don't think it came from time traveling, do you?"

"It's nothing, just a—"

"We better let Sasha know," Rebekah insisted. "This could be serious."

He laughed and waved a dismissive hand. "It's just a migraine, I swear. And besides, you didn't get a blinding headache, did you?"

She sat down in the sand next to him. "No, I guess you're right."

"And besides, I'm feeling better already. Must have caught a bug or something during the flight over."

She giggled. "Good one. On the positive side, at least I didn't end up in the beach house wall."

Alexander nodded. "I guess so."

"How about we better coordinate our time traveling the next go around, alright?"

"Or how about we never again jump through time to begin with."

"Oh, come on! Don't tell me you're already sick of time travel."

He smiled, considering her word *sick*. And wondering if there was some truth to it. *Worrying* there was some truth to it, that it might have made him sick with the ache continuing to pulse in the middle of his head.

Instead of replying, he stood. "We better check in with Father Jim. I'm sure he's been worrying his head off with how long we've been gone."

He held out his hand, and Rebekah took it. They began walking back to the beach house when they heard someone cry out.

"Ahoy, matey!"

Alexander spun around to find a large inflatable raft several meters offshore. And John Mark Ford standing with waving arms.

He twisted up his face in confusion and looked at Rebekah, who shook her head.

As the watercraft bobbed and dipped coming into shore, they could see three more heads: a woman he didn't recognize before glimpsing Sasha and Father Jim.

"What in the world?" he mumbled as he walked toward the crashing waves.

Soon the raft had motored up to the shoreline. "How the

heck did you find us?" Alexander shouted, his spirits soaring at the sight of his friends. "What's going on?"

Ford jumped out, his face creased with what he sensed was worry. Dread even.

"Help me drag this thing to shore and we'll tell you all about it," he said.

The two managed to bring it to rest in the sand. Soon a reunion was playing out with Father Jim and Sasha having disembarked, along with the mystery woman.

"Where is Lucy?" asked Rebekah.

"Back on the submarine with Jin," Ford said, motioning toward the water. "Volunteered to keep her afloat while we... well, retrieved you two."

Retrieved us?

Alexander's brow sank with confusion. They had driven themselves, so why the rendezvous? And why was he sounding so coy? He glanced around at the faces, noting how somber everyone looked, as if someone had died. Something crazy must have happened for them to go after them. Things weren't adding up.

"Happy you've made it back safely," Father Jim said, embracing Alexander.

"Us too," Alexander said, his mind still trying to make sense of it.

"How on earth did you find us?" Rebekah said.

"You can be thanking me for that one," Sasha said. "I was being able to use the coordinates from your jump back in time. And I am happy to be seeing you are returning in one piece."

"You and us both," Alexander said. "I don't understand, what about the Ministerium?"

"Abandoned," said Ford. "We returned for Padre and the doc and Jin once we found our way back to the yellow submarine. Boy, do I have a story to tell about that. Anyway, thankfully the Republic had better things to do. We took what we could, loaded up, and came for you both."

"But why? Why are you here? Did something happen?"

Ford's face fell, and he averted his eyes to the sand.

"Alex," Father Jim said, stepping forward. "We've received some...shall we say, intelligence you need to be aware of."

"What intelligence?" asked Alexander.

The man took a breath then paused.

"Just say it already. I'm beginning to think—"

"It's about your father."

Alexander's knees instantly weakened, and his head began swirling with dizziness. He took a startled step back and twisted his face up with confusion, the migraine springing back to life with unrelenting, nauseating pain from his quickening pulse.

"My—my...father?" he managed.

Ford went to say something when a woman stepped forward.

"Alexander," she said, "or perhaps I should say, Order Master."

"And who are you?" Alexander snapped, forgetting his manners as his mind raced with possibilities.

She smiled and bowed. "My name is Kareema Salam. I am one of the last remaining members of the Order of Thaddeus. Your colleagues rescued me from the clutches of Solterra Purifiers after the Republic destroyed our regional base of operations in Antakya, modern Antioch. We had been conducting reconnaissance for the Ichthus Resistance when they came."

Alexander's head was spinning, his mind not being able to concentrate on what the woman was babbling on about with word about his dead father.

"I'm sorry," he said, voice stern and irritated, "but what the bloody hell does any of this have to do with my father? He's dead, for Pete's sake!"

Kareema took a breath before speaking plainly: "No, he isn't."

It was as if someone had dropped one of those pre-Reckoning neutron bombs in the sand, its power radiating across the shore and consuming all life in a furious death grip yet leaving every one of those dilapidated beach houses intact.

"He...he isn't what?" he whispered, falling to his knees as the fallout from the revelation washed over him with cold, disbelieving dread.

"Sorry to break it to you, partner," Ford said softly. "But your daddy...well, he's alive. A recent OneWorld News broadcast announcement confirmed it, with the man babbling on something fierce."

"I—I—I don't understand," Alexander stammered, feeling faint. "He jumped from a bridge back home a year ago, taking his life. The authorities confirmed it all..."

Father Jim put a hand on his shoulder. "From what we can gather, he faked his death to get out from under the punishment and humiliation of the Ministerium after his apostatizing. On our way over, we confirmed that the authorities never recovered his body, only a few artifacts, isn't that right?"

"That's right..."

"Well, according to our new friend here, and I say this with all the care in the world for what you must be going through in this instance. At any rate, Kareema tells us the Order believed your father to be working with the Republic to destroy Ichthus. And then the man's ravings on OneWorld News confirmed the bloody truth of it."

The news of his faked death was crazy enough. But this? Working with Solterra Republic, to put the Church six feet under?

"In fact," the woman went on, "he's the Grand Master of Nous and chief architect behind Panligo."

Another detonation nearly as powerful as the one announcing his dead father's resurrection.

Alexander slumped backward in the sand, dizzy and vision blurring now. He found it difficult to breathe and his stomach was clenching as if he would dry heave from the freighted weight of the news.

Father Jim knelt next to him.

"I am sorry, Alex, to come bearing such news. I'm as shaken as you are by the whole bloody affair. But it makes sense now, how the Republic seemed to be taking such a targeted aim at us. Keeping one step ahead and finally culminating in the Edict of Cooperation. Then the destruction of the Ministerium and all of the other outposts we presume to be from the Order of Thaddeus itself. And that's not even touching on all of the other reports of persecuting violence springing up across the Republic. I'm afraid the Church of Jesus Christ has entered into a new phase, a final phase. Truly the last days of the apocalypse. With your father firmly at the helm."

Alexander ran a shaking hand through his hair then bolted to his feet.

This is not happening...

"I need to take a walk," he announced, bringing his hands to his head and heaving desperate breaths.

"Alright, I'll join you," Ford said. "To make sure you don't topple over into the sea."

He put out a hand and started forward. "No, I've got it."

"No trouble at—"

"I said, I've got it!" Alexander snapped in a rage, spinning around toward the man and throwing his hands into the air.

Ford recoiled and glanced at Father Jim for help.

"Sorry..." he said. "Just...I'm sorry."

Alexander spun around and started off, heading along the coast toward the horizon set ablaze with the fires of hell itself by the just-set sun, his throat constricting with emotion and eyes brimming with the same.

My father, alive?

Impossible! He had spent months trying to make sense of what had happened after it all went down a year ago, hounding the local police to search for his father when he could not bear to face the apparent truth of his suicide.

Then he recalled something Father Jim had said. Something about a OneWorld News report of the man?

He wiped his nose and reached into his pocket for his mobile. He pulled it out, an alert flashing from the Republic.

'*The Dawn of a New Spiritual Age Is Upon Us,*' it read, demanding he watch the alert before he could use the device.

So he did, bringing up a video featuring Solterra's propaganda carnival barker Max Bacchus. The man was wearing a brightly colored jacket in rainbow colors, his hair similarly colored and swept into a bouffant. He was grinning widely with sparkling eyes, wholly unlike the last time the man had broken in with breaking news on the demise of Ichthus.

Alexander continued ambling across the sand as the man yammered on about exactly what the headline had announced: a new spiritual age dawning across the Republic. Didn't go into specifics, but before long the video faded into a shot of the Senate chambers in the Capitolium.

Just as the Regis, Lucius Severus, was introducing a tall man with bronzed skin and wide shoulders, hair white with a goatee and mustache curled at both ends.

And bearing a striking resemblance to Alexander.

His father. Martin Zarruq, named after a long line of Zarruqs inspired by the famed Protestant Reformer, Martin Luther.

A drunken giggle escaped his mouth wide with delight at seeing his father, even as emotion began filling his eyes. He touched the face of the mobile device, caressing the image.

"Papa...it's you," he whispered. "It's really you."

The pain returned just behind his eyes, and his ears filled with a ringing. He winced, but the disbelief of what he was seeing drowned it all out.

A tremble began overtaking his body, and droplets of the tears running freely down his face landed on the face of the device, obscuring the picture of the man thought drowned in a desperate act to save face. His chest was heaving with racking sobs now at the sight of the man he had said goodbye to those many months ago without actually having found closure to his death. The man who had become the supreme leader of the Church's archnemesis stretching back to the first century. Who apparently had conspired with the Republic to destroy Ichthus, even architecting its dismantling by establishing the new alt-spiritual movement Panligo.

And now he was starting to address the Solterran leaders and the whole Republic from the dais at the heart of the beast that had just declared the Church of Jesus Christ to be Unfits.

Alexander wiped his eyes on his sleeve and turned up the volume to his mobile device.

"—dawn of a new spiritual age is upon us across the Republic! One the prophet Jesus of Nazareth himself had prophesied when he spoke of needing new wineskins to hold the new wine of a new dawning spiritual Republic."

He stopped along the shore to listen to his father, swallowing hard with dread at what he would hear.

"There is something within the Universe itself, something we find in all of the great spiritual traditions throughout Solterra just waiting to be tapped into. The sublime, the ground of our being that undergirds the entire Universe. It is the universal human ideal that has revealed itself in human existence through such people as the man from Nazareth. Jesus somehow grasped, in word and deed, the highest human ideal. And it is this spirit that he sought to impart to his followers through his earthly life, and we what ourselves can grasp through human gumption and ingenuity and progress."

The man paused to take a sip of water. He went on, "Now, Ichthus would have you believe that his death was important, but I am here to tell you differently. Jesus' *life* was far more significant than his death. His ideal life of love is what matters! His death is simply the culmination of that life, showing us what it looks like to live the universal human ideal embedded in the Universe itself. His loving life is what saves. His example is the hope of humanity!"

Alexander's heart was sinking the more his father spoke, his voice rising into the same fevered pitch he recalled growing up through countless sermons. There was something incredibly subversive to what he was saying. Of course there was some truth to it, too. Jesus' teachings about human dignity and justice and neighbor-love have been the bedrock of civilization stretching back centuries—things anyone should build their life upon. But his life doesn't save us. The Church has always taught his death does! So what was his father going on about?

"Jesus didn't come to start a new religion," the man went on, "but to announce a new way of life. He was the founder of a new countermovement to all other human regimes that others tapped into. We need a new system and a new story to repair and heal us, and he provided humanity the solution through his teachings on the Republic of Heaven and example of higher living that transcends this chaotic one."

The chamber erupted in thunderous applause at this line. Perhaps because of its mirroring Solterra Republic.

"The invitation into the Republic of Heaven is an invitation into the Age of the God-Man. The entire human experience has been one of constantly emerging from what we are into what we can become, this better version of ourselves tapping into the universal human ideal of love. Jesus understood this, as did others after him. And I aim, along with all of the others who have joined arms to form Panligo—we all aim to speed that process up of *becoming*."

Alexander scrunched up his face. *What is he talking about?*

"Unlike what Ichthus has insisted, the truth is that Jesus' death was a paradigm, like any of the ancient myths that have governed our collective unconscious for this salvation. We join with Jesus in dying—to our pride and agendas as a witness to the justice of the Republic of Heaven. His resurrection symbolizes the same, a rising to new, unencumbered life!"

Alexander's head was spinning with delirium at what his father was suggesting, completely contradicting historic Christianity. He knew the Bible itself taught the power of Jesus was in what he did on the cross by willingly offering himself as a sacrifice to pay the price of our sins in our place! Not Jesus' life, not his teachings and example of love, as his father was going on about. And his resurrection was not merely a *symbol*; his actual, bodily, physical resurrection is the heart of the faith—marking the end to sin's reign and the beginning of God's new reign. Because if Jesus is still dead, we're still screwed!

Something Polycarp had said rose to the surface:

> *And whosoever does not confess the testimony of*
> *the cross is of the devil. Whosoever perverts*
> *the sayings of Christ and what the Lord*
> *taught does so to suit his own sinful desires.*
> *These people say that there is neither a*
> *resurrection nor a judgment. The firstborn*
> *of Satan they are!*

Yet there was Martin Zarruq. The man who had taught Alexander all he knew about Jesus and faith in him. There he was throwing it all away. Denying the essence of Ichthus, of faith in Christ.

And for what?

"We do not need saving from our sins," the man went on. "We need saving from ourselves. We need a revolution to aid in the evolutionary progress of humanity, something to push the human race forward by revealing to us the universal ideal in a way that makes sense to our twenty-second century human condition. Placing man squarely at the center of our spirituality in the coming months—all *for Humanity!*" his father roared.

At this, the chamber rose to its feet and started shouting the familiar Republic refrain: *"For Humanity! For Humanity! For Humanity!"*

A tremor took hold of Alexander's hand at what he was hearing. He couldn't take it anymore.

His father had truly apostatized. Truly turned away from faith in Jesus Christ as singular Lord and Savior—faith in his life, death, and resurrection. And in favor of a pseudo-religion with humanity squarely at the center—and the Republic.

Alexander shoved the mobile back into his pocket, a million jumbled thoughts flooding him, and stood in the sand wishing that it would eat him whole.

Wishing it would drag him down into oblivion, erasing him from the nightmare that he'd been living for weeks now—ever since Father Jim had sent that damn post beckoning him to the conclave, leading to the destruction of his parish, nearly trapping him back in time, and doing who knows what to his brain.

And now to hear his father had been alive this whole time, faking his death and turning against Ichthus—turning against Christ himself in such a brazen way, bending the knee before the Republic, leading the pagan enemy of the Church, and forming the alternative spiritual movement co-opted by the Republic leading to untold destruction.

It was all too much.

He started off, picking up his pace until he was hustling across the shore as reality fueled him forward.

Soon he was running, arms pumping and legs rising like pistons on one of those old V-8 muscle cars Solterra had banned post-Reckoning. His head was thrown back and mouth open wide, lungs heaving desperate breaths as he padded across the sand without hearing his friends calling for him, tearing off toward the glistening town ahead offering freedom from his nightmare.

Having no idea where he was running to, but knowing entirely what he was running from.

Life. *His* life.

And no one would stop him.

a full-length novel in my thriller series for free! All you have to do is join the insider's group to be notified of specials and new releases by going to this link: www.jabouma.com/free

Building a relationship with my readers is one of my all-time favorite joys of writing! Once in a while I like to send out a newsletter with giveaways, free stories, pre-release content, updates on new books, and other bits on my stories.

Join my insider's group for updates, giveaways, and your free novel—a full-length action-adventure story in my *Order of Thaddeus* thriller series. Just tell me where to send it.

Follow this link to subscribe:
www.jabouma.com/free

Group X Cases **Supernatural Suspense Series**

Not of This World • Book 1

The Darkest Valley • Book 2

Against These Powers • Book 3

Luck Be the Ladies • Novelette

End Times Chronicles **Sci-Fi Apocalyptic Series**

Apostasy Rising / Season 1, Episode 1

Apostasy Rising / Season 1, Episode 2

Apostasy Rising / Season 1, Episode 3

Apostasy Rising / Season 1, Episode 4

Apocalypse Rising / Season 2, Episode 1

Apocalypse Rising / Season 2, Episode 2

Apocalypse Rising / Season 2, Episode 3

Apocalypse Rising / Season 2, Episode 4

Antichrist Rising / Season 3, Episode 1

Antichrist Rising / Season 3, Episode 2

Antichrist Rising / Season 3, Episode 3

Antichrist Rising / Season 3, Episode 4

Faith Reimagined **Spiritual Coming-of-Age Series**

A Reimagined Faith • Book 1

A Rediscovered Faith • Book 2

Mill Creek Junction **Short Story Series**

The New Normal • Collection 1

My Name's Johnny Pope • Collection 2

Joy to the Junction! • Collection 3

The Ties that Bind Us • Collection 4

A Matter of Justice • Collection 5

He Will Direct Your Paths • Collection 6

Find all of my latest book releases at: www.jabouma.com

J. A. Bouma believes nobody should have to read bad religious fiction—whether it's cheesy plots with pat answers or misrepresentations of the Christian faith and the Bible. So he tells compelling, propulsive stories that thrill as much as inspire, while offering a dose of insight along the way.

As a former congressional staffer and pastor, and award-nominated bestselling author of over forty religious fiction and nonfiction books, he blends a love for ideas and adventure, exploration and discovery, thrill and thought. With graduate degrees in Christian thought and the Bible, and armed with a voracious appetite for most mainstream genres, he tells stories you'll read with abandon and recommend with pride—exploring the tension of faith and doubt, spirituality and culture, belief and practice, and the gritty drama that is our collective pilgrim story.

When not putting fingers to keyboard, he loves vintage jazz vinyl, a glass of Malbec, and an epic read—preferably together. He lives in Grand Rapids with his wife, two kiddos, and rambunctious boxer-pug-terrier.

Connect at: www.jabouma.com • jeremy@jabouma.com

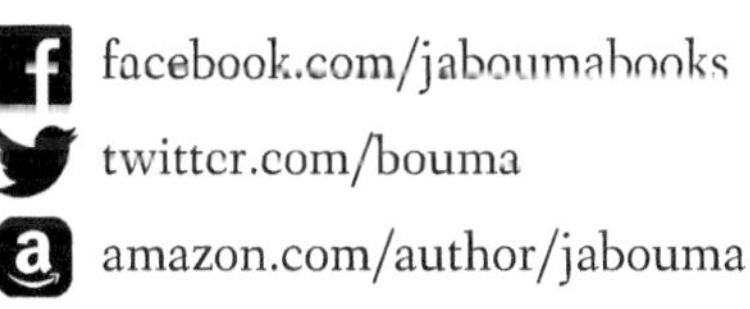